"I should leave. I—" He started signing as he spoke. "I do not wish to overwhelm you. We have plenty of time to explore this."

"Please. Stay."

"Why?"

She glanced away, too unnerved to answer, but he held on to her chin to hold her gaze. "Christina, why?"

"Because I would like you to stay." It was the best answer she could give at the moment. She had no knowledge of the specifics of what happened between a man and a woman in the bedroom but she knew enough to want this to continue. "Unless . . . unless you do not want to stay with—"

He pounced, grasping her shoulders, and his mouth took hers in a hard kiss. When they broke, he said, "I want to stay. I want to do every wicked and pleasurable thing under the sun to you."

Leaning back so he could see her face clearly, she said, "Then you had best begin."

By Joanna Shupe

The Four Hundred series
A NOTORIOUS VOW
A SCANDALOUS DEAL
A DARING ARRANGEMENT

The Knickerbocker Club series
MAGNATE
BARON
MOGUL
TYCOON

JOANNA SHUPE

A NOTORIOUS VOW

THE FOUR HUNDRED SERIES

AVONBOOKS

An Imprint of HarperCollinsPublishers

A NOTORIOUS VOW. Copyright © 2018 by Joanna Shupe. All rights reserved. Printed in the United States of America. No part of this book may be used or reproduced in any manner whatsoever without written permission except in the case of brief quotations embodied in critical articles and reviews. For information, address Harper-Collins Publishers, 195 Broadway, New York, NY 10007.

First Avon Books mass market printing: October 2018

Print Edition ISBN: 978-0-06-267894-2
Digital Edition ISBN: 978-0-06-267892-8

Cover design by Guido Caroti
Cover illustration by Kirk DouPonce, DogEared Design

Avon, Avon & logo, and Avon Books & logo are registered trademarks of HarperCollins Publishers in the United States of America and other countries.

HarperCollins is a registered trademark of HarperCollins Publishers in the United States of America and other countries.

FIRST EDITION

18 19 20 21 22   QGM   10 9 8 7 6 5 4 3 2 1

For Steve and Cindy,
the best in-laws a girl could ever ask for.
Much love and thanks.

Chapter One

"Character cannot be developed in ease and quiet. Only through experience of trial and suffering can the soul be strengthened, ambition inspired, and success achieved."

—HELEN KELLER

New York City
January 1890

Lady Christina Barclay was officially trespassing.

Yet as she stepped out of the mews and into the magnificent empty gardens behind this large Fifth Avenue home, she could not bring herself to care.

The home belonged to her cousin's reclusive neighbor, a man Christina knew very little about. Since arriving in New York three weeks ago from London, she had learned his parents had died some years ago and that he never left his house.

Her cousin Patricia hadn't ever clapped eyes on the man, not once in her eighteen years.

None of that mattered to Christina. She had no interest in the man's life or his problems, only the tranquil gardens behind his home. The space was full of winding paths, alabaster statues, and utter quiet. It had become her slice of solitude in a busy modern city filled with noise and smothering crowds every which way she turned. Not to mention the gazes that brimmed with judgment and scorn following her every movement. In this peaceful place, Christina could be alone, away from the rest of the world.

So yes, she was trespassing but for a noble cause. Namely, her sanity.

Early every morning she escaped her cousin's home to stroll about these gardens. Here, she could forget the scandal that had brought her family to America, as well as the pressure from her parents to marry a rich man, thereby solving all their financial troubles.

The future of the Barclays rests on your shoulders, her mother often said.

Heavens, the mere idea caused Christina's stomach to clench. She had never been comfortable around people, let alone men. There had been no friends or family around during her childhood in London. Of course years had passed before she realized the problem was not *her*; it was her mother. Lady Barclay was widely disliked in society, even before their money disappeared. Still, this did not help Christina's confidence when it came to meeting people.

You have the beauty to attract a rich man if you would only smile, her mother said. *I had the eye of every gentleman in the room when I debuted. Of course, you are not as pretty as I was at your age . . .*

Christina dug her nails into her gloved palms. How she hated when her mother said that. What was there to smile about when you were being paraded about like a lamb for slaughter?

The bitter wind whipped across her skin as she ran a hand along the top of a short hedge. Even in winter, the carefully manicured paths were pretty, just empty plots where flowers would soon bloom. Trellises and arches abounded, the stone fountains dry and dormant. There was even a hedge maze. Perhaps she'd attempt it in the spring, if she were not married by then.

A shiver unrelated to the outside temperature went through her. Her American cousin, Patricia, told Christina not to worry, that marriage would not be so bad, but Christina doubted this. She brought no dowry to a marriage, no social standing. Instead, she would bring scandal and debt. What man in his right mind wanted as much?

She rounded the next bend and something large darted out from the bushes then stopped on the path. It was a dog. A very *large* dog. She froze. Suddenly, it spotted her, its head snapping up. Small dark eyes pinned her to the spot.

She had no idea what to do around a dog. The

countess had never allowed pets in the Barclay household. Was she supposed to speak? Run? Kneel?

"Good boy," she said, hearing the tremor in her voice. "I mean you no harm."

Unfortunately, the only way to reach her cousin's home was to cut through the gardens. She had to find a way to get around the dog unscathed.

There were iron benches along the path, hedges beyond that. No one was nearby. Perhaps she could lose the animal in the hedge maze. Legs shaking, she inched backward, never taking her gaze off the dog's large teeth. At her movement, the dog's tail started wagging. That was a positive sign, correct? "See, everything is perfectly well. I'll just turn around and—"

The dog bounded forward as if chasing prey. Panic shot through her limbs as fear clogged her throat. *Oh, dear Lord.* It was coming straight for her. She could not move, her muscles clenched in absolute terror. Just as the dog leapt to rip her to shreds, Christina screamed. Giant paws landed on her chest, pushing her down, and she felt herself tipping over, falling toward the stone path. Her arms flailed but came up empty.

A flash of pain erupted on the side of her head . . . and then everything went black.

OLIVER HAWKES WAS hard at work on his latest prototype when something nudged his leg. He glanced down and found Apollo, his dog, looking at him expectantly. Oliver signed for the animal to sit.

Apollo obeyed then prodded Oliver with his snout once more before trotting to the main door. That was odd. The dog had an entrance of his own that allowed him to come and go as he pleased. Why was he trying to gain Oliver's attention?

Putting down his soldering iron, Oliver rose and opened the door. He motioned for the dog to keep going, to show Oliver what he'd found.

Apollo darted through the door. Oliver followed, the frigid air slapping his face and blowing through his thin shirt as if he were naked. He hunched his shoulders and hurried after his dog. Hopefully, this would not take long; otherwise he might suffer hypothermia.

Shoving his hands in his trouser pockets, he watched as Apollo loped toward the maze. Oliver knew every inch of these gardens; he'd played in them often enough as a boy. His mother had loved it out here as well, taking him on adventures every chance they had, and the memory caused a dull ache in his heart. Even six years after his parents' deaths he missed them terribly.

When he rounded the bend to the sitting area, his stomach dropped. *Jesus . . .* A figure was on the ground, unmoving.

And it was a woman.

Oliver dashed forward, his heart pounding as

he fell to his knees. Her skirts had twisted around her legs, her body slumped under an iron bench as if she'd tried to catch her fall on the seat but had missed.

He reached out, desperate to assess how badly she'd been hurt. Blood streamed from a cut on her brow. *Damn it.* She must have hit her head on the way down.

Was she dead? With two fingers, he searched her neck for a pulse. Relief cascaded through him when he felt a weak, but discernable, heartbeat. Her chest rose and fell, her breathing even. She was alive.

He needed to send for Dr. Henry Jacobs. This woman could very well be concussed. Sliding his hands under her, he lifted her into his arms and started for the house. Henry would know what to do. The doctor would quickly set this woman to rights and then Oliver would send her on her way.

He did not care for strangers.

Oliver strode across the terrace and entered the house. A footman emerged from a side room, his eyes instantly popping open. It was not every day that the staff saw their master carrying an unconscious woman.

With his hands otherwise occupied, Oliver forced out a voice he himself had not heard since boyhood. "Ring Dr. Jacobs."

The boy nodded, running off to the telephone in the front entry. Oliver continued with the girl, twisting and turning through the labyrinth of rooms, until he reached the study.

He placed her on the long sofa then covered her wound with a clean handkerchief. Her cheeks were bitten with cold, her lips blue. Exactly how long had she been outside? After wrapping her in a wool blanket, he marched to the bellpull and yanked. They needed hot water and clean bandages, now.

Movement in the doorway caught Oliver's eye. His butler, Gill, stood there. "Sir, I understand there is an injured girl," the butler signed. Gill had learned how to sign along with the Hawkes family when Oliver lost his hearing fifteen years ago. It had taken time, but most of the staff had picked up quite a bit of sign language as well, though Oliver also excelled at reading lips. And when all else failed, he could write in the small ledger he carried in his pocket.

Oliver signed, "She fell outside. Her head is bleeding."

Gill's brows lowered in concern. "Oh, the poor dear. I shall bring clean water and bandages. Anything else?"

"Not yet," Oliver signed. "I sent Michael to ring Jacobs." Gill nodded and hurried from the room.

The wait seemed interminable. During his breaks in pacing the floor, Oliver placed a small pillow under the girl's head and adjusted her limbs to make her more comfortable. Some color had returned to her face, thank Christ. She was actually quite pretty, with chestnut hair and creamy skin. Classic features of strength and fortitude, like a strong nose and high cheekbones. Her clothing conveyed former wealth, the fine wool of her coat well constructed, if a little on the shabby side.

The young woman stirred. Panicked, he glanced toward the door. Where the hell was Gill? Better for her to wake with calming words from the butler rather than a silent, surly man looming over her. Unfortunately, the damn servant was nowhere in sight.

What in God's name was Oliver to do? Rub her forehead? Pat her shoulder? Tap her cheeks? He'd never cared much for society's ridiculous rules but even he knew there were boundaries as far as touching a strange young lady. He settled for standing a few feet away, just in her line of vision. It would have to do. If she wished for coddling and niceties, she had fallen outside the wrong house.

He had no idea how long he waited but it felt like forever, long enough for the fire to start dying in the hearth. Finally her lids fluttered open, and large eyes focused on his face. "Where am I?"

He hesitated. He rarely used his voice, well aware the sound came across as different. Not at all what he'd sounded like when he was still able to hear. A multitude of shocked expressions and cruel snickers from strangers in his late teens had made that perfectly clear. Instead, he reached into his pocket and withdrew the tiny ledger and pencil he carried. *You are safe,* he wrote. *You fell and hit your head outside in my gardens.*

He offered her the paper, but she just blinked and squinted at it. "I apologize, but the words are fuzzy. Please, tell me where I am."

She tried to sit and he held up his palms, motioning she should stay put. Thankfully, Gill entered at that moment, supplies in hand. Breathing a sigh of relief, Oliver signed to Gill, "You had better answer her questions and reassure her before she gets agitated."

Gill frowned as he signed, "What have you told her?"

"Nothing," Oliver signed. "She is your problem. I merely brought her inside."

The woman shrank further into the sofa and carefully watched the two of them. Her chest rose and fell quickly as if she was truly scared, so Oliver motioned for Gill to get on with it.

As the butler began to address the young woman, Oliver moved to where he could see both their faces, allowing him to read their lips. Gill told her Oliver was deaf and communicated by using his hands. She blinked a few times in response then cast Oliver a curious glance. Surprisingly, her expression held genuine interest, not the mocking derision he expected from the outside world. Well, at least not yet. *Give her time. She's had a nasty bump on the head.*

"You mean he cannot hear?"

"No, but he reads lips quite well."

She gave no outward reaction to that information, instead gazing about the study. "Where am I? How long have I been here?"

"Please, remain calm," Gill responded. "No one will hurt your ladyship here. And this is the home of Mr. Oliver Hawkes."

Ladyship? The girl was an aristocrat? Oliver hadn't expected that. "Ask her where she is staying," he signed.

Gill relayed the question. Unfortunately the girl stared at her lap while answering, preventing Oliver from reading her response. He snapped his fingers at Gill. "Tell her to look up when she speaks," he signed to the butler. "Otherwise I cannot read her lips."

Her cheeks flushed when Gill translated—was that embarrassment?—and she trained her gaze on Oliver's forehead. "With my cousins, the Kanes." She turned back to Gill. "Does he know them?"

Annoyance rippled across Oliver's skin. He snapped his fingers at Gill once more. "Tell her that *he* is able to answer for himself seeing as *he* is not an idiot," he signed, his hand movements sharp.

"She clearly meant no harm, sir," Gill signed, but Oliver held up a hand to stop him.

"Just tell her," he instructed.

Though Gill did not use Oliver's exact words,

he informed her that she could speak directly to Oliver, reminding her he could read her lips.

Her throat worked as she swallowed and her gaze landed on Oliver's forehead again. "I apologize."

Why could she not look him in the eye? Was she scared of him? Repulsed? He squared his shoulders and told himself he did not care. She'd soon be gone and he could return to his quiet life of experiments and learning. The people of this city could all go to hell, as far as he was concerned.

"Was it your dog that knocked me down?" she asked.

Apollo had caused this? Guilt swamped Oliver but he squashed it when she continued to avoid his eyes. He quickly signed, "I apologize for your injury, but he does not appreciate trespassers. Nor do I. What were you doing in my gardens?"

Gill flashed Oliver an unhappy look but nonetheless translated. The woman's bottom lip trembled. "I am sorry. I was not expecting to see a dog and I lost my balance when he approached me."

"That does not explain—"

A footman strode into the room, a tall blackhaired man behind him. Oliver immediately went over to Dr. Henry Jacobs, his hand extended in greeting. The two had known each other nearly two decades, since an illness took Oliver's hearing at the age of thirteen.

In fact, it had been Henry who taught Oliver to speak using his hands. Most American doctors and schools limited deaf instruction to speaking and reading lips, believing the deaf should assimilate to the hearing world whether they wanted to or not. The French, however, had developed a manual communication system using hands, and a school in Connecticut had adapted the system for American use. Because Henry's father was deaf, Henry had traveled to Connecticut to learn this signing system. He quickly became renowned in the city for teaching sign language to others, and Oliver's mother had hired him when the doctors finally gave up on saving Oliver's hearing.

Now he was the closest thing Oliver had to a friend.

"You are looking well," Henry signed after placing his bag on the ground.

"Must be all the whoring and boozing," Oliver answered. "Thank you for coming so quickly."

"Happy to help," Henry signed. "I was at the hospital uptown today." He turned toward the sofa. "And you are the injured woman I have been told about. Are you able to recall what happened?"

"I was knocked down by a dog. Apparently I hit my head on a bench when I fell."

"May I take a look at your injury?"

"Of course," she answered, fingertips gingerly touching her wound. "Though I cannot imagine there is much to see other than a bump on my head."

"Oh, you would be surprised." Henry gave her a kind smile, the one Oliver knew the doctor used to put patients at ease. Henry knelt by the side of the sofa and put his black bag on the ground. "What is your name, miss?"

Oliver wasn't certain he'd read her answer correctly so he glanced at Gill. His butler spelled each letter. *Christina*. A pretty name. It suited her.

Henry performed a quick examination, focusing mostly on her coordination and vision to look for signs of impairment. During this time, Gill had a tea tray brought up. Oliver helped himself to a few scones while he attempted to curb his impatience. It was not easy. The sooner she left, the sooner he could get back to his workshop.

Finally, Henry finished cleaning and bandaging her wound. "I cannot see there are any serious injuries, miss, but you should take it easy for a few days. You have a nasty gash on your head. Make sure to rest and drink plenty of liquids."

"Oh, I am certain there is no cause for concern."

Henry presented her with a card. "A head injury is not to be taken lightly. Send for me or your family physician if you start to see double." After she nodded and thanked him, Henry threw a meaningful look at Oliver. "May we speak privately?" he signed.

The two of them walked into the corridor.

Henry placed his bag down and began signing. "Why was she in your gardens?"

"I have no idea. I've never met her before today." At Henry's disbelieving expression, Oliver signed, "You think I am lying."

"I think there is a young pretty girl wandering about your estate. Dare I hope you have decided to secure future generations of Hawkeses?"

"I am not courting her. The idea is preposterous. And my sister is welcome to carry on the family legacy."

"I think it is a marvelous idea," Henry signed. "First, Sarah is only eleven. Second, you need to rejoin the rest of the world."

This was an old battle. Oliver's hand movements grew sharp. "I am perfectly fine just as I am."

This was not a lie. He'd tried to carry on with what gentlemen considered a "normal" life after school. It had resulted in being called "dumb" and "broken" at every turn. Why should he try to fit into a society that so readily dismissed him? That would sooner see him locked away in an asylum before allowing him into the Metropolitan Club? As far as he was concerned, the uptown set could go hang.

Henry's mouth tightened but he did not argue. "I shall send you my bill." He clapped Oliver on the shoulder and departed.

CHRISTINA WAS SITTING upright, drinking tea, when the man walked back in. So this was

Mr. Hawkes, the recluse her cousin had told her about. He was fairly young, which surprised her. Dark hair had been swept away from rugged features, showing off a Roman-type nose and broad jaw. Full lips and nice, even teeth. She noticed he wore only shirtsleeves and a waistcoat, along with dark trousers tapered to his long legs.

However, it was his eyes that drew her in. A vivid green, the irises were so unique and pretty they were almost difficult to look at. Right now, his eyes were focused intently, appreciatively, on her, as if he saw every flaw, every lie she'd ever told and did not mind a bit. As if he found her fascinating and beautiful—which had to be her imagination. She must've hit her head harder than she thought.

The butler signed to Mr. Hawkes and then disappeared, leaving her alone with the owner. Weirdly, that did not concern her. According to the butler, Mr. Hawkes had rescued her earlier when she fell. If Mr. Hawkes meant to do her harm, why bring her inside and call a doctor? Still, she had likely overstayed her welcome.

A gentleman is always less eager for a lady's company than she for his, her mother liked to say.

Christina set her tea on the table and started to push up, but Mr. Hawkes surprised her by motioning for her to remain seated. Even more alarming, he dropped down next to her on the sofa. She tried to remain calm and not fidget as he pulled a small ledger and pencil from his pocket and began writing in it. He held the words out for her to read. *How do you feel?*

Silly. Embarrassed. Tired. Where should she possibly start? She lifted her head so he could see her face. "Sore."

He nodded as if that was what he expected. *I am Oliver,* he wrote.

"Oliver." He could not hear her, of course, but he appeared pleased at her repetition. She wanted to . . . Well, she was not certain, but she wanted to know more about this man. She might never get the chance to ask him questions again and he seemed in no hurry for her to leave. "How does one say that in your language?"

His head jerked, brows dipping, before he bent to write. *Why?*

Had she offended him? "I was merely curious, but I understand if you would rather not show me."

His gaze remained wary, but he moved his fingers to spell his name. Christina lifted her hands. "Show me."

Slowly, he formed each letter, waiting patiently as she clumsily shifted to mirror him. Though the placement was unfamiliar, the letters made sense. She tried again, by herself this time, and he corrected her twice. When she finished, he smiled at her, and heat spread over her entire body. Goodness, he had a devastating smile.

She liked this exchange between them, a quiet

conversation without shouting or biting criticism. It was refreshingly easy to talk to him. She was not ready for their interaction to end. "Now sign mine," she said.

He obliged, again teaching her the correct letters. She practiced until she could do it unassisted.

His pen scratched over the paper. *Are you a lady?*

"Yes. My father is the fourth Earl of Pennington."

He wrote, *Benningson?*

She took his pencil and corrected the spelling. *Ah,* he wrote. *Would you care for more tea?*

His posture was relaxed, his expression curious. She was not nervous, she realized. Normally, she'd be searching for an escape when a man talked to her, palms sweaty inside her gloves. But Oliver was different than the loud and brash braggarts she had met in New York society. There was a confidence about him that she liked, a calm air of authority. "No, thank you," she answered. "Do you live here alone?"

He nodded. *My sister is away at school,* he wrote.

"I would love to live alone. People must think you are lonely but it sounds like heaven to me."

He frowned and she wondered if he'd misunderstood her. She reached for the paper but he stopped her, writing his own response. *I read your lips but I still do not understand.*

She lifted a shoulder, not intending on answering. All she'd wanted was to let him know that she envied him. That she did not care if he was a recluse.

In fact, there were days she wished to be left alone, not to be forced to hunt for a husband. Too bad her mother would never allow it. The best she could hope for was to marry a wealthy man who did not beat her and to survive childbirth. Such was a woman's lot in life.

Oliver bent his head and wrote, *I thought you felt sorry for me.*

"No, I do not. Should I?"

No, he wrote. *Of course not.*

Just then the huge dog that had knocked her down trotted into the room. Christina froze, uncertain what the animal would do. Did Oliver allow the beast to roam indoors?

Oliver snapped his fingers and the dog came right to his side, pushing his nose into his master's palm. The dog did not appear to be vicious, but one could never be certain. It hadn't hesitated to pounce on her in the gardens. Oliver petted the animal and she edged away, trying to put as much room between her and the dog as possible.

When Oliver noticed her reaction, he bent to write, *He will not hurt you.*

Before she knew what was happening, Oliver reached to pick up her hand. She had taken off her gloves earlier and the contact of his warm skin against hers sent a jolt through her. What was he about?

She tried to pull away, but Oliver did not release her, holding up his free hand to indicate she should have patience. Then he slowly dragged her palm toward the dog, placing her hand on the animal's back. The fur was soft and sleek, and she quickly forgot about the impropriety of Oliver's touch. She gave a few tentative strokes. The dog seemed to like this, his tail wagging, but when he tried to turn around, Oliver held him steady. She let out the breath she'd been holding and simply enjoyed the velvety sensation against her palm.

"It is soothing," she said, her eyes on her hand.

Oliver tapped her arm, and when she looked up, he pointed to his green eyes and then her mouth. Ah. He could not read her lips if he could not see her face. "It is soothing," she repeated.

They sat close to one another on the sofa and the intimacy of the situation struck her, especially because of how intently he was staring at her lips and mouth . . . almost as if he were thinking of kissing her.

All the moisture left her mouth and her tongue grew awkward and thick.

You are ridiculous. He is not interested in you; he is trying to communicate with you.

Embarrassed, she let her gaze fall back to the dog. Merely because she enjoyed this interaction with Oliver did not mean he fancied her in return. He was a recluse, after all, though she could not understand why. The man was ruggedly handsome and seemed comfortable in his own skin. Intelligent. Kind. Perhaps he merely needed a friend.

And why on earth would that friend be you?

She could almost hear her mother's voice saying this. No one could cut Christina quicker than her mother. Of course, there was some truth to it. He was being solicitous, end of story. He hadn't asked her in for tea. She had injured herself on his property. More than likely he was anxious to get rid of her but too polite to mention it.

She rose and wobbled a bit. Oliver's big hand shot out to steady her. "Thank you," she said once she'd collected herself. "For everything. I would have frozen to death if you had not found me and brought me inside."

You are welcome. He went back to his paper and wrote, *Are you able to find your way home safely or shall I find a footman to escort you?*

She noted he hadn't offered to escort her himself. "No, I will be fine. It is not far."

They stood for a moment, the silence stretching. Why was she so reluctant to leave? *Perhaps you are in need of the friend, not him.* Hard to argue that point; other than her cousin, she had no friends close to her age.

The Barclays were impoverished, so far in debt that London society had completely turned their backs on them. The only choice had been to flee to America. Who would want to be friends with a girl in such a situation? She was tainted, an outcast.

So she knew better than to ask. Instead, she said, "Would you mind if I continued the use of your gardens for my daily walk?"

His brows shot up, eyes round and wide. *You walk in my gardens every morning?* he wrote.

"I will not get in your way, I promise. And I will not fall again."

"No," he blurted, and they both blinked at the sound. He was able to speak?

She stuck to the topic at hand. "Why?"

He started writing once more. *Because it is my home and I do not wish to have strangers strolling about the property.*

The words irritated her. She was not usually one to argue, but those walks were important to her. Necessary to her sanity. Perhaps if she wrote it she'd craft a better case for herself.

She pointed to his ledger and pencil, which he promptly handed her. *We are not strangers, not any longer. And I swear not to disrupt anything. You will not even know I am there.*

I will know, he wrote, underlining the word "will" three times.

How? In nearly three weeks I have not encountered a soul in your gardens, she wrote then passed the ledger over to him.

A muscle jumped in his jaw. *Nevertheless, this is my house and I prefer to be left alone.*

She finished reading and bit back a sigh. He misunderstood, clearly thinking she would pop into the house and sit down to a chat. All she wanted was to continue her walks in his empty gardens. Instead of pushing the issue, she held up her hands in surrender. Let him think he'd won. "Thank you for your help today. Good-bye, Oliver." She signed his name as he had shown her then walked out into the corridor in search of the front door.

Chapter Two

Three days later, in the dull midmorning light, Oliver hurried to his greenhouse to begin working. He had not slept much last night, thanks to fitful dreams once again keeping him awake. He finally arose when the sun broke over the horizon.

Movement caught his gaze and he stopped. Good Lord, it was her. *Christina.* He sucked in a breath. She had returned, even after he'd instructed her not to come back. Yet here she strolled along the path in the same black overcoat, hair tucked under a thick hat, her gloved palm brushing over the barren hedges.

He clenched his hands and worked to calm himself down.

Why here? What was it about these plain sticks and shrubs that appealed to her? In springtime, when the blooms came in and the gardens overflowed with beauty, perhaps he could understand her interloping. But in the dead of winter? The space was downright macabre.

Not to mention she had been expressly forbidden from trespassing . . .

She hadn't noticed him standing there so he watched her, trying to decide what to do. Though he wanted to deny it, her perfect features affected him like a punch to the stomach. No longer pale and in pain, she looked vivacious and energetic. Mischievous, almost. Cheeks and nose rosy from the cold, her skin glowed like the purest cream. Silky dark hair blew around her face while her full lips were curled into a mysterious smirk. Quite a difference from the almost shy and skittish woman he'd met the other day.

At first, he had believed her repulsed by him, unwilling to even meet his eyes. Then he'd noticed her avoiding the eyes of the other men in the room, too.

People must think you are lonely but it sounds like heaven to me.

That comment had burrowed between his ribs to lodge somewhere in his frozen chest. What on earth could a society girl—an aristocrat, no less—have to complain about? The city was hers to conquer if she wished. No doubt the young men fell all over themselves to gain her favor.

So why did he sense her unhappiness?

And why did he have this ridiculous urge to make her smile?

A string of curse words paraded through his

head. Nothing good could come of this. Nothing good at all. His stance on visitors had not changed—especially unmarried, unchaperoned visitors.

Years ago, he'd felt differently. After returning from school in Connecticut, he had been determined to take his place in society. He'd refused to hide or restrict his social activity because of his deafness. He went everywhere: the opera, the theater, dinner . . . until he had realized what people were saying about him, not knowing he could read lips.

He is one of those imbeciles.

Have you seen the way he moves his hands?

His voice is so strange.

Even his lover, Adrianna, had turned on him. He'd caught her talking to her friends when she thought he was unable to see her. *Oh, Oliver is fine for right now, but we won't be together long. He is ridiculously rich, you know.*

He had been devastated. Was that all they saw, either an imbecile or a large bank account? Would his accomplishments and interests never count for anything? He'd worked so hard at school to fit in with the hearing world . . . and all that painstaking effort had failed. No matter what he did, they still saw him as deficient.

Then his parents died. First his mother from cancer, and then his father from heart troubles not even a year later.

Hurt and anger had embittered Oliver, and

he had retreated into a world of his own making. He sent his sister off to boarding school, ensuring she would receive a proper education instead of solely being groomed for the role of future society hostess. That had left him with the house, his laboratory, the staff . . . and those were the only things he needed.

The rest of the world could fuck right off.

And then this woman had injured herself in his gardens. The back of Oliver's neck prickled, an eerie sensation that things were spinning out of his control. He did not like it, not one bit.

There was no need for him to change . . . nor did he need change forced on him.

Therefore, it was imperative that Christina leave and not return—not even to meander through his gardens.

He strode toward her, his steps full of purpose and fury. She skimmed around a hedge and then her head snapped up, probably from the sound of his shoes on the gravel. Nearly stumbling, she came to a stop and gave him a shy wave. He narrowed his gaze. "Follow me," he signed, an easy enough motion to understand.

Spinning on his heel, he made his way to the greenhouse laboratory, not bothering to make sure she followed. He knew she would. Because if she didn't, he would chase her down.

He turned the latch and held open the door for her. She passed through and he closed them in, grateful for the warm humidity inside his workshop. Now they would not freeze when he took her to task.

"Good morning," she said, removing her gloves. Apollo bounded in behind her, his dog suddenly more interested in Christina than in his owner. The traitor.

Oliver withdrew his pencil and ledger. *What are you doing here?* He held it out to her.

She stopped petting Apollo to read the words. Then she passed the ledger back to him. "I did not intend for you to see me. I merely wished to cut through your gardens."

I told you not to come here again.

"No, you said you preferred to be left alone. I left you alone."

Semantics. You knew I did not want you to come back here.

"I had no intention of disrupting your day. I know you do not wish to be disturbed."

This is inappropriate. You should be chaperoned for visits such as this, even in the gardens.

Her brows lowered. "Are you planning to ravish me?"

If I were, I would hardly admit it to you.

She rolled her eyes when she finished reading. "You do not seem like the ravish type."

He blinked, uncertain he had read her lips correctly. Looking down at the paper, he wrote, *I am unable to ravish because I am deaf?*

"No." Horror washed over her expression. "I did not mean it that way. I am certain the deaf

are competent ravishers when the mood strikes.
I meant because you seem too nice."

Nice? Him? No one had ever called him *nice*, not
any of the times he had gone out in public. Prickly,
yes. Often dumb. Stubborn, most definitely.

But never *nice*.

"I am sorry," she said, shaking her head. "I
should go. I am quite awful at this and I have
already insulted you." She grabbed for her gloves
and hat. She kept talking, her mouth moving, but
he was unable to see enough of her face to make
out the words.

He touched her arm to stop her and then
started writing. *You have not insulted me. I am surprised, is all.*

"Does that mean I may continue walking
through your gardens each morning?"

A laugh bubbled up in his chest. The girl was
persistent, at least. She stood close to read his
ledger, her head barely reaching his shoulder.
He could see the fine hairs at her temple and the
sweep of her brown lashes. Her skin was flaw-
less, the features delicate and symmetrical. She
was absolutely stunning, a woman to turn heads
everywhere she went.

"I shall take a different path, if you wish. One
that does not lead me near your . . . whatever this
is." She waved her hand around the greenhouse
he'd converted into a workshop. "I won't bother
you. Please, Oliver."

He put his hands on his hips and stared out the

glass at the wide expanse of growth. Guilt nagged at him. He was being unnecessarily cruel. What had her trespassing harmed? If she stayed away from him, what did he care? She had appeared peaceful out there just now, almost happy. Did she truly like the place that much? He thought of his mother, leading him around the tall hedges when he was a boy.

This is my greatest joy, she'd told him, *seeing you enjoy a place I love so much.*

It would have made his mother happy to know Christina appreciated the gardens, too.

He went back to his ledger. *Use the gardens as much as you like. I do not mind.*

"Truly?"

Excitement brightened her expression, brown gaze sparkling, and his mouth dried out. He swallowed and looked down at the paper. *Why do you like them? It is not even spring.*

"It is quiet. I am able to be alone there." She bit her lip. "Well, almost alone."

He could understand the need for solitude. That had been his main priority in the past decade.

She pointed to the equipment resting on the counter. "What are you working on?"

Various wires and tools littered the surface of his workspace. He had been perfecting his design for an electric hearing device that would assist the partially deaf to hear. It would not help him, but it would change the lives of millions of people around the world.

Instead of attempting to explain it, he pointed at her with both hands. "Come here," he signed, curling his arms toward himself. Without any fear or hesitation whatsoever, Christina closed the distance between them. He picked up the earpiece and held it near her ear. Then he switched on the large battery and lightly tapped the microphone with his finger.

Her eyes rounded. "Oh, my." He tapped again. "How remarkable," she said, handing him the earpiece. "That will help people to hear?"

Yes, it will. Not the completely deaf, he wrote on his pad with a pencil. *It is not a cure.*

"How do you know it works if you cannot hear the sounds?"

Vibration, he wrote and put a finger on the earpiece. It was the same way he was able to enjoy music.

"Remarkable." Christina's gaze sparkled in genuine fascination. Oliver had not shown anyone this version yet, so her interest was a positive sign. "Have you sold it?"

It is too bulky and too expensive. This model would cost at least four hundred dollars.

Her eyes bulged at the figure, a number so high as to be impractical for most anyone. "And you are trying to bring down the cost?"

"Yes," he signed but did not elaborate. He doubted she came here to discuss his efforts to create a high-voltage dry cell battery.

"May I sit and watch you work?"

"Christina," he signed, spelling out the letters of her name, lingering on the last letter in frustration.

"Oliver," she signed back, the movements perfectly executed, and her expression was so full of fake exasperation that he nearly laughed.

You have been practicing, he wrote.

A slight flush crept over her cheeks, captivating him. "Just those letters. I hope you will teach me more someday."

He hung his head to hide a smile. He did not want to like her, but she was adorable and obviously intelligent. No pretension, as one might have expected with an English aristocrat. His plan to remain aloof seemed a losing battle, a coat that no longer fit. Perhaps if he showed her a few simple signs then she would leave. *I suppose I could,* he wrote. *Then you must go.*

She nodded eagerly. Using four fingers and a flat hand, he touched his temple, his elbow pointed at the ground, and then shifted his hand to the right. "Hello," he signed.

She performed it perfectly, so he showed her signs for *no*, *yes*, and *please*. She paid attention, her eyes steady and thoughtful, a slight pinch between her brows as she concentrated. It had been a long time since he'd taught anyone how to sign and he had forgotten the joy of discovery in another's face. In a different life he might've quite enjoyed the role of professor.

He decided to teach her a two-step sign. Touching his lower knuckles together, he arched his hands, thumbs out, then rolled his wrists until his thumbs nearly faced her. "How," he signed and pointed at her. "You?" He did both motions together. "How are you?"

She nodded, ready. She lined up her knuckles but closed her palms. Without thinking, Oliver reached forward to correct her hand position. When he touched her bare skin, he inhaled sharply. Soft. She was so damn soft. Sparks raced through him, a shimmering heat that he could almost taste, scorching every part of him. He recognized the sensation, though he had never felt it this strong. *Desire.*

She trembled, as if affected as well, and he jerked his hands away. Then he took a step in the opposite direction. Her eyes found his and he saw the question there, a curiosity that boded ill for them both. "I apologize," he said aloud before he could think better of it.

She cocked her head and considered him. "Why do you not talk more often?"

Suddenly self-conscious, he picked up his pencil. *I know it sounds strange. I try not to talk unless absolutely necessary.* He well recalled the startled looks and the comments.

What is wrong with that man? He sounds unpleasant.

Even his own cousin treated him as if he were stupid, a freak. Like one of Barnum's oddities.

Oliver refused to give them an opportunity to laugh any longer.

Christina tapped his arm to get his attention. "It does not sound strange in the least. You have a nice voice," she said, then picked up her gloves and hat. She signed *good-bye* and proceeded out the door.

He found himself grinning long after she had left.

CHRISTINA SIPPED HER lemonade and watched as the melting ice sculpture dripped all over the buffet table. Waterlogged canapés and soggy salmon were arranged in a morose line. Still, the dining room made an excellent place in which to hide from the other girls and their cutting comments. Most unmarried ladies never ate in public if they could help it, as this was considered bourgeois. Once her mother ripped a tart clean out of Christina's hands when she had foolishly attempted to eat in a crowd.

Someone touched her arm, startling her. It was her cousin, Patricia. Christina blew out a breath. "Oh, it is you."

"Did I frighten you? I apologize. You were staring at the ice sculpture." At eighteen, Patricia had just come out and, unlike Christina, seemed to enjoy the never-ending stream of parties and events. She linked their arms together and gestured a free hand toward the buffet. "That is the

most disgusting thing I have seen all day—and
that includes the dead frozen horse I saw lying
in the street this morning."

"It has certainly ruined my appetite."

"Well, I have a craving," Patricia said quietly,
"but it is not for food."

"What on earth does that mean?"

"Mr. Felton asked me to meet him in the gardens in a few moments."

"Patricia! Tell me you are not going."

Glancing over her shoulder, Patricia pulled
Christina toward the wall, away from the few
people gathered at the buffet. "Of course I am
going. I am mad for him. He is the sweetest, most
handsome man."

"Yes, but you must not act inappropriately.
What if your mother found out?"

Her cousin waved her hand. "Please. My
mother would jump with joy if Felton ruined me.
She's hoping I have a proposal within the month.
Gracious, the way he kisses . . . I tell you, I am
besotted."

"He has kissed you?" Christina could not believe it. She was both horrified and terribly curious. What was it like when a man pressed his
mouth to yours? It sounded messy. And weren't
tongues oftentimes involved? "Was it . . . Did you
enjoy it?"

"It was divine—and I am planning on doing it
again the second I have the opportunity tonight.

You know how hard it is to stay away when you fancy a gentleman."

Christina nodded and forced a knowing smile. Yet, she didn't know. She had no idea, actually, but admitting as much only made her appear foolish. Silly Christina. Such ignorance was the very reason she was a terrible conversationalist. The minute she opened her mouth she sounded like an imbecile.

No one wants to hear a lady's thoughts, her mother always said. *Just smile and look pretty.*

Yet Patricia talked all the time, laughing and smiling, and she was liked by just about everyone. A beautiful girl with cool blond hair, her cousin was unpretentious and comfortable in her own skin. Sort of like Oliver Hawkes, a man who hadn't even bothered to don a coat in the presence of a lady, propriety be damned. He was smart and resourceful, obviously unconcerned with how others saw him. How Christina envied them both.

Two young American heiresses strolled by, their gazes darting to where Christina and Patricia stood talking. "Did you see her dress?" one girl said in a not-so-quiet voice.

"I swear, that pattern went out with hoop skirts," her friend answered.

They both laughed. "God, the English are so *poor*," the first girl drawled as the two moved away.

"Ignore them," Patricia said. "They are unforgivably rude."

"But not wrong." Mercy, Christina wished the floor would open up and swallow her whole.

"Don't worry. I shall 'accidentally' trip them the next time I am dancing."

Christina clasped her fingers together and bit back a smile. It was nice to have a friend, one who would willingly stick up for her. "Thank you, but that is unnecessary."

Patricia waved her hand. "So what about you? Has any man caught your eye? New York City has the best-looking swells in the entire world, you know."

"I haven't noticed. It hardly matters anyway because my parents are determined to marry me off to the highest bidder."

"But why—"

"*Christina.*"

The single word went through Christina like a pike. She straightened, immediately wiping all traces of emotion from her face as she turned to find her mother. *Please do not let her embarrass me.* "Yes, Mother?"

Her mother's demeanor softened when she saw Christina's cousin. "Oh, hello, Patricia. I did not see you standing there. Don't you appear lovely this evening? How I wish my daughter could carry off that pale pink color as well. It is a shame her complexion is not as pale as mine and yours."

"I happen to think Lady Christina looks

smashing in her gown." Patricia squeezed Christina's arm.

The countess appeared unconvinced. "If you will excuse us, I require my daughter for a moment."

"Of course. Christina, I shall visit with you later."

"I cannot comprehend why you are hiding in here," her mother said as she towed Christina out of the room. "You should be dancing and flirting with the eligible men. Fortunately, I have been doing your job for you. There is someone you need to meet."

Christina's stomach dropped. She tried for a reprieve. "Must I meet him now? I had hoped to—"

"You will do as I say." Her mother's grip tightened, nails scoring through gloves and into Christina's flesh, and she pulled them to a halt. "Everything is riding on this, Christina. *Everything.* Our entire future depends on what happens in the next few weeks. You will *not* disappoint us."

Christina winced at the pain shooting down her arm, biting the inside of her cheek to keep from making a noise. Then her mother let go and rubbed Christina's arms affectionately, as if she were a doting, loving parent.

Christina knew better.

She'd been disappointing her mother since the day she was born. The countess never stopped telling Christina all she was doing wrong, all the ways she would never measure up.

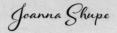

When I was your age, I was the most sought-after girl in England.

When I was your age, I'd already turned down three marriage proposals.

When I was your age, all the girls copied my coiffures and gown patterns.

"There," her mother cooed. "Now, are we ready to remember our purpose here?"

"Yes." The sooner this distasteful business was over with, the sooner she could return to hiding.

"Good. I am taking you to meet the wealthiest man in this godforsaken city. He is recently out of mourning and looking for a wife. I have already told him all about you, so merely smile and nod and you shall do fine."

Without waiting on a response, her mother pulled her into the ballroom, threading their elbows together as if they were lifelong friends out for a stroll. Her mother hated growing older and often introduced herself and Christina as sisters when encountering strangers. It never made any sense to Christina.

They made their way to the far side of the room, where her father stood next to a . . . Goodness. Was *that* the man? Stooped shoulders rounded into a crooked neck. Wrinkled, dull skin. Shorn gray hair. His black evening suit hung on his frame, as if he'd recently lost weight. He only came up to her father's sternum, which was slightly shorter than Christina.

Her lungs refused to pull in air. *Escape. You*

cannot do this. She stumbled, her feet as reluctant as her brain, and the man turned stiffly toward them. Spittle had gathered at the sides of his flat blue lips, which began to twist as he raked her body with a dispassionate gray gaze. She felt exposed, as if she were a prized stallion he was considering for purchase.

Her mother's hold strengthened, bringing her along. "Mr. Van Peet. Allow me to present my daughter, Lady Christina."

Pressure on her elbow forced Christina into a semi-curtsey. When she raised her head, a strange glitter appeared in Van Peet's eyes. "I see you have not understated your daughter's beauty, Pennington. Child, how old are you?"

"Nineteen."

"Slightly old for my tastes but I might be willing to overlook it."

She was the one too old? Christina fought to keep the horror from showing on her face.

"We waited a year to have her come out in New York," her mother explained in a blatant lie. The scandal had prevented a debut last year.

"You shall visit me tomorrow," Van Peet announced to her mother. "Bring your daughter."

"We would be honored." Her mother sounded positively euphoric and Christina's stomach roiled. Looks and age aside, he had not even been friendly or solicitous. He had been downright rude.

Van Peet shuffled away, leaving the three Barclays alone. "That went well," the earl said to his wife over Christina's head. A common practice, as they liked to pretend she did not exist. "Very encouraging."

"Indeed. If we are able to convince him to offer for her quickly, we shall have the money in a matter of weeks. Then we may return to London and retake our rightful place in society."

And leave her here? Married to that man? Christina said nothing, though she fought the urge to scream and shout, to run out of the ballroom and keep going.

"It will be a jolly good thing to get those creditors off our backs," her father murmured. "If this does not happen quickly, we shall lose the Mayfair house."

"Van Peet is desperate," the countess said in a reassuring tone. "He knows he does not possess much more time. That will work to our advantage."

A shiver went through Christina. They were discussing this as if the marriage were a foregone conclusion. What was she going to do? "Mother, I cannot—"

"*Christina.*" Her mother's hiss cracked through the air. "We shall discuss this at home."

CHRISTINA KNOCKED SOFTLY on her mother's door. They had arrived home from the ball moments ago and she would not be able to sleep until she voiced her concerns about Van Peet.

Her mother's maid opened the door, then

stepped aside. "Come in, my lady. I have just taken her hair down."

"Is that Christina?" her mother called.

"Yes, Mother." Christina walked into her mother's sitting room. The countess sat at the dressing table, still wearing her evening gown.

"Excuse us, will you, Gertie?" The maid bobbed a curtsey and then disappeared, shutting the door behind her. The countess turned to face Christina and folded her hands in her lap. "Well, what is it?"

Christina hated that impatient look in her mother's eyes, but she swallowed her nerves. This was too important. She drew herself up. "Mother, I will not marry Van Peet. I will find someone else—"

"Christina, you shall do what we tell you. Your duty is to marry the man your father and I select for you, regardless of his identity. Do you understand?"

"No. I cannot marry him. I understand we need the money, but surely there is a man not quite so . . . old."

Her mother's expression hardened. "You ungrateful girl, I am doing you a *favor* by selecting a man like Van Peet. He won't live much longer and then you shall have all that money for yourself. Heavens!" She threw her hands up and rose, her silk skirts rustling. "Think for a moment. Yes, he might be less than ideal, but you would remain married to him only for a short time.

Would you instead rather marry a younger man, one who might ruin your life for *decades*? When Van Peet dies, you shall be free, utterly in control of your own finances and happiness. Are you so dense that you cannot see the incredible gift I am giving you?"

No, Christina could not. Marriage to Van Peet did not feel like a gift; it felt like a death sentence. "There are plenty of wealthy men, Mother."

"Yes, a wealthy man who might live for years and years. Who might spend all that money and then leave you grasping and poor. Relying on the kindness of relatives. Do you honestly think I like coming here to New York, staying with my cousin? Selling off all my jewelry and discharging the staff?" She put a hand to her throat. "I am trying to save you from what I went through, Christina—from what I am *still* going through. This world is about two things for women: men and money. You must learn how to manage both, or you will end up miserable."

"But why not allow me to choose my own husband? I shall pick someone with money, as Patricia has."

Her mother sneered. "Yes, she's settled on Felton, who won't come into his trust until his father dies. God knows how long that will be. Your father and I do not have years to wait, Christina. We are destitute. If we return to England without the funds to settle our debts, your father will go to prison. We shall lose the house in Mayfair, the one his great-great-grandfather built. Is that what you want for your parents?"

Why is it my fault Father has a problem with gambling? Why am I being forced to suffer for his failings?

No matter how hard she tried, she could not picture Van Peet as her husband. Perhaps he wanted a marriage in name only. Would she really need to lie with him? A shiver racked her and she wrapped her arms around her middle.

"I asked you a question," her mother snapped. "Is that truly what you want for your parents?"

"No, Mother," she whispered.

"Good girl. Now, go get a decent night's sleep. Tomorrow, you shall meet with your future husband."

Chapter Three

Movement out of the corner of Oliver's eye startled him. The greenhouse door had opened and Christina's head peeked through, a question in her brown gaze. He squashed the small burst of happiness that expanded behind his ribs. Three days since he had last seen her. Still, it would not do to become excited at her return, not when he would much rather be left alone. He put down his tools and motioned her inside.

"Hello," she signed after slipping through the entrance and closing the door. It was colder today than previous mornings, frost coating every twig and branch in the gardens, so he was not surprised to see her teeth chattering.

He pointed to where a breakfast tray rested on the counter. "Drink," he gestured.

Nodding, she removed her gloves and poured herself a cup of tea, not even bothering to shed her coat or hat. She sat on the empty stool and sipped the warm liquid. He told himself he watched her mouth merely to notice if she spoke, but that did not explain the attention he devoted to the full lips hugging the porcelain rim, the pink tongue sweeping the extra droplets . . .

Stop, Oliver. Stop it right there.

He tried to look away, to concentrate on her hands, but then he saw her mouth move. She was trying to talk and he had not been paying attention, damn it. "What?" he signed.

She took another sip. "I have a question for you."

"Yes?"

She nibbled on her bottom lip. "It is difficult to explain."

He withdrew the small ledger and pencil from his pocket and slid them down the tabletop.

"No, I did not mean to imply you would not understand—"

She thought the issue was communication. He stood, went to her side, and picked up the pencil. *Writing can help to clarify one's thoughts*, he wrote. *Write it down.*

"Oh, I see."

After removing her coat and hat, she moved closer to him, their hips nearly brushing as she bent to write. He waited patiently, watching her hands instead of her face. He needed no reminders of her beauty and how it affected him. In fact, he'd thought of little else lately.

He started to read over her shoulder.

I am to pay a call to a gentleman this afternoon, she

wrote, *and I fear I shall not be able to fake civility.
He is entirely unsuitable. My parents are relying on
me to do my duty as a daughter but that grows more
difficult as the prospect of marrying becomes a reality.
To consider disobeying, however, fills me with guilt.*

Ah. Now he understood. He held out his hand
for the pencil. *Your parents wish for you to be happy.
Talk to them. Make them understand this man's un-
suitability.*

When she read this, she shook her head and
snatched the pencil back. *They only want money.
They do not care about my happiness.*

Oliver rubbed his chin. If their financial situation was indeed dire then her parents may very
well push her into a union, regardless of the suitor.
He'd been lucky; his own parents had wanted
the best for him, no matter the personal sacrifice.
When he lost his hearing at age thirteen, they had
hired every physician in the Northeast to examine him, hoping for a cure. Then there had been
Dr. Jacobs for sign language, followed by the best
schooling available for deaf students. Through it
all, he never doubted his parents' love or dedica-
tion, even after they died.

A shame Christina's experience differed.

He wrote, *Who is the man?*

Her hand wobbled as she gripped the pencil.
Mr. Van Peet.

Drumming his fingers on the wooden tabletop, Oliver tried to remember how he knew that
name. Hadn't the sons died? The father was still

alive, however, if memory served. *Wealthy? Owns the Upper Hudson Railroad Company?*

I am not certain what he owns but he is very wealthy. The wealthiest in New York, I am told.

Well, hell. Van Peet had to be eighty if he was a day. When Christina had said "old," Oliver had not thought quite *that* old. Though he never circulated in society these days, he could guess that marriages between nineteen-year-old girls and men in their thirties and forties—even fifties— were still common. However, a man in his eighties? It was distasteful. What were her parents thinking? Surely there were other wealthy men closer to their daughter's age.

She tapped his arm and pointed to the paper. *It is awful*, she had written. *I am able to tell from your expression.*

Oliver winced. *He is a bit older than I expected.*

"Me, too." Desolation shone deep in her eyes, unhappiness like a blanket surrounding her. *Is he cruel? What do you know about him?*

He was uncertain how to answer. Even in a city that revered capitalism above sense, Van Peet was vilified in the newspapers. His workers were constantly striking for better wages, living conditions, and benefits. Van Peet crushed the rebellions with a heavy hand, the bloodiest of the battles only three years ago in Scranton. Hundreds died and the union had not succeeded with their demands.

Then again, perhaps Van Peet had an altruistic

streak, like Carnegie. The old man could have a heart of gold for all Oliver knew.

Not much, he wrote, flipping the page to keep going. *But if you do not care for him, have your parents refuse his offer. He is far from the only wealthy man in New York.*

She grabbed at the pencil. *My parents are set on the match. How should I dissuade him? Is there a way to convince him we would not suit?*

Oliver considered this. Why would any man that old want a young woman? To bear children. As a showpiece. To gain a dowry. Christina could not provide the last but she could certainly provide the first two—if Van Peet's plumbing still worked, of course.

He wants a biddable young thing to give him children. To make himself feel young again. Show him you are not biddable.

She stared at the gardens, her bottom lip disappearing between her teeth again. He did not like to see her withdrawn, lost in her own unhappy thoughts. Tapping her shoulder, he pointed at the paper. She sighed and wrote, *I have no idea how to do that—and my mother will be present during the visit.*

Of course Christina would have a chaperone. *So?* he wrote.

I cannot. She will be positively furious.

What is worse: your mother's wrath or marrying Van Peet?

Honestly, I could not say.

He frowned. Was she so scared of her mother that she'd rather go through with the marriage? What sort of mother instilled such fear in a child? Without thinking, he reached out and gently brushed an errant strand of glossy brown hair behind her ear. His fingers touched the shell of her ear, so delicate and smooth. Something switched on inside him at the contact, a long-extinguished light that flared back to life. Sensation rippled through him, both hot and cold now coursing through his veins, causing him to shiver and break out in a sweat.

She froze, her confused gaze locking with his. A question lingered in her brown depths, one that he could not begin to answer. What in God's name had he been thinking? He had no right to touch her. Was his body so starved for companionship after six years that he forgot his manners and good breeding?

He forced himself to put distance between them. *I am sorry,* he wrote.

Color crept along her neck and over her cheeks, her skin glowing in the most innocent and fetching way. She really was incredibly lovely. Van Peet did not deserve her.

Yes, but neither do you.

"It is quite all right," she said with a delicate lift of one shoulder.

No. Nothing was quite all right, not since the

day she'd hit her head in his gardens. Now he was distracted and his mind disorganized, two things he hated and could ill afford. The last thing he needed was to be declared incompetent and have everything taken from him. God knew many people were committed for spurious reasons, let alone someone who was merely deaf. Oliver had read of several cases where the deaf or mute had been wrongly sent away to asylums. He had vowed to never let that happen, to keep to himself and focus on his inventions.

So the less he saw of Christina the better.

He wrote in the ledger, determined to put an end to this. *Convince Van Peet you have a backbone. Your mother might be angry, but she will come around.* He returned to his stool and presented her with his back, ready to concentrate on his work. Again.

A tap on his shoulder caught his attention minutes later. Her coat and hat were already in place. "I must return home. I shall see you tomorrow."

He tried to tell her not to return, but she had already turned away. He thought about using his voice but the words would not come. Frustrated, he watched as she disappeared out the door.

LONG SHADOWS DRAPED the empty corners of Mr. Van Peet's home, the gloomy interior doubling Christina's nervousness. Apparently Van Peet disliked electric lighting—and heat. The air was so frigid in the parlor that Christina was nearly certain she could see her breath. She clutched her gloved fingers tighter and tried to keep her teeth from chattering as they waited for Van Peet to arrive. Goodness, how did he stand it?

Her mother appeared unaffected by the conditions, which stood to reason, Christina supposed. Her mother would never live here. Christina put a hand to her stomach in an attempt to stave off the rising panic.

You cannot do this. You must not allow them to force you into this marriage, no matter the consequences for your parents.

She hated the guilt that followed those thoughts of rebellion. It had been eons since she had disobeyed her parents, not since she ran away from home at the age of twelve. Archery had been her favorite activity—until her mother declared it unladylike. Christina's bow and arrows had been taken away, leaving her devastated. That night, she'd stolen back her bow, packed some clothing, and departed in the darkness with no destination in mind.

The next morning, a groom found her sleeping in the village stables and promptly returned her to the countess. As punishment, her mother forced Christina to throw her bow and arrows into a bonfire. She'd been a dutiful daughter ever since, following every rule. Never complaining. However, this time she could not sit quietly and agree to something she knew in her bones was a mistake.

Convince Van Peet you have a backbone.

Oliver's advice seemed simple in theory, but she was not certain how to execute a show of independence in front of her mother.

"Sit up straight," her mother hissed. "Do you wish to develop a hunch?"

The question instantly reminded her of Van Peet, whose posture resembled a question mark. Christina lifted her spine and arranged the skirts of her pale pink gown. It was a dreadful color, but the countess had insisted on it, saying the shade made Christina look youthful.

"Today must go well. Smile and be charming. You must do all in your power to lure Mr. Van Peet into a betrothal."

The idea of luring Van Peet into anything soured Christina's stomach. She remained silent, however, still agonized over this visit. The trick was to convince him into thinking they were ill suited without her mother catching on. How on earth was she to manage it?

The door opened and Van Peet wobbled into the room, his gait stiffer than she remembered. The countess rose, as did Christina, her knees knocking from nerves and the cold.

"Bring us tea," Van Peet snapped at the footman by the door. "But not too hot."

"Good afternoon," the countess said. "Thank you for receiving us, Mr. Van Peet. You remember my daughter, Lady Christina."

"Of course I do," Van Peet snarled, thumping

his cane on the carpet. "She's the reason I invited you. Come here, girl. Let me see you."

Inhaling deeply, Christina approached him. His rheumy eyes peered at her bosom, modestly covered by fabric, and then moved down to her hips. "Pelvic area's a bit on the narrow side."

The countess tittered as if this criticism amused her. "She is still recovering from a cold last week."

"I hope she does not die on me, like my last wife." Van Peet lowered himself into an armchair, his head settling at an awkward angle. "Sit down, sit down."

The countess resumed her seat. "I assure you, she is normally the very picture of good health."

Christina's chest burned at the indignity of being discussed as if she were not even in the room. *Not biddable, Christina.* She lifted her chin and walked back to her seat. "Well, except for—"

"And she comes from a long line of healthy childbearing women," her mother said, talking over her. "Large families on both sides."

Van Peet nodded. "Good. I had three sons, but they've all died. My two daughters married wastrels so I have cut them off completely. I'd like at least two more children before I pass on."

Two children! Christina's mind reeled, her breath turning shallow as horror seized her lungs. She could not imagine reproducing once with this man, let alone twice. *I must find a way out of this. I cannot do this.*

"Perfectly understandable," the countess said. "Christina will make a fine mother. She has been trained in household duties befitting a wife her entire life."

Van Peet pursed his thin lips as if he doubted this. Before he could say anything, however, a young maid entered with a tea tray. The girl avoided Van Peet, walking around to the other side of the table, entirely opposite the old man. Was the maid afraid of him? Christina would not be surprised to learn he was a terrible employer. If his public demeanor was any indication, she shuddered to think of what his private demeanor was like.

The maid set the tray down. When she straightened, her gaze caught Christina's—and Christina registered the sympathy there, as if the maid was warning Christina away from this place.

"Girl, you pour for us," Van Peet said, waving his hand in Christina's direction. "Let's see your competence with tea service."

Christina had been pouring tea her whole life. Yet the countess's lips pressed tight, as if she suspected Christina would embarrass them.

An idea occurred. What would happen if she did embarrass them? Van Peet, appalled at her lack of manners, might very well order them from the house. He might lose interest in marrying her . . .

Her mother cleared her throat pointedly.

Snapping out of her reverie, Christina realized she had paused with her hand on the teapot handle. Hands shaking, she set to work on the strainer.

Van Peet thumped his cane on the floor. "Is she simple?"

"Of course not. She speaks four languages and plays two instruments." The countess's voice was smooth and confident, as if Christina was the perfect daughter. "She will make you an excellent hostess."

"I hope so. I have many business interests and prefer to entertain here. Easier that way for me."

Entertain? The idea filled Christina with dread. She hated socializing, was terrible at polite small talk. And here she had assumed this bargain could not get any worse . . .

She finished the pour and served Van Peet first, then her mother. She cradled her own cup for warmth, hoping her hands would soon thaw. When Van Peet noticed, he frowned. "You aren't hoping for coffee, I hope. Cannot stand the stuff. It will not be served in my home."

Backbone. Remember what Oliver said.

"I do prefer coffee," she lied. "It is far more flavorful than tea."

The countess's mouth fell open slightly, but she was too well-bred to argue in front of their host.

"You shall need to give it up, if I decide to marry you." He sniffed. "And is that perfume? I only allow unscented soaps here. I cannot stand any sort of strange scent in the house."

Christina's throat burned with the need to scream. To run. To leave all this behind and disappear. Why was this happening? Could her mother not see Van Peet's cruelty, comprehend the horrendous husband he would make?

Yet, her mother's expression had not changed since the visit began. *Do you not understand? I am doing you a* favor *by selecting someone like Van Peet.* In the countess's twisted mind, she saw this as the perfect solution for Christina.

Christina vehemently disagreed. This hardly felt like a favor. Almost anyone would be a better husband. Even Oliver, with his moodiness and proclivity for solitude, would be far, far preferable. She would rather be ignored than abused and belittled.

Though to be fair, Oliver had not completely ignored her today. He'd actually touched her, a gentle sweep of his fingertips over her skin, and the simple gesture had started a fire in her belly, an ache of some kind. She had not experienced that before, a strong physical yearning for another person. It had confused and excited her. She'd wanted him to continue, to let her drown in the green of his eyes and the soothing press of his fingers.

But Oliver had been appalled by the intimacy, recoiling as soon as he realized who he was touching. He'd ignored her for the rest of the visit. *How can you blame him? You are not a beauty, like your mother, or vivacious, like Patricia. You are plain and boring.*

"I am certain my daughter will be amenable to any household rules you have established," the countess was saying. "She is quite biddable."

Biddable.

Like a dog.

The burning resentment in Christina's chest spread to her throat and then her temples. *Do something, Christina.* Without thinking, she let the saucer in her hand slide and the cup teetered, liquid sloshing onto the fine carpet below. Her mother gasped and Van Peet uttered a choking sound. Christina righted the porcelain, apologizing profusely.

The countess put her own cup and saucer down with a snap. "I sincerely apologize, Mr. Van Peet. I do not know what has gotten into my daughter this afternoon."

Van Peet narrowed his gaze on Christina. "That was clumsy of you, girl."

"She is merely nervous," her mother rushed to say. "Young girls are quite excitable now and then."

A strange light came into Van Peet's eyes, one Christina did not understand but disliked all the same. "Well, do you have anything to say for yourself?"

Christina licked her dry lips and tried not to shrink in her seat. "I beg your pardon, Mr. Van Peet."

"That's better," Van Peet said, his lip curling. "And I have just the idea on how you shall make it up to me."

The hairs on the back of Christina's neck stood up. "How?"

"Return tomorrow afternoon for another call. Without your mother." He stood and lumbered to the bellpull.

"Of course," her mother said eagerly, not giving Christina a chance to refuse. "I am certain she'd be delighted to pay another call."

"Then you are dismissed. Let the maid come and clean up this mess."

A KNOCK SOUNDED on Christina's door that night. She had skipped dinner, preferring to stay in her room instead. Her arm still hurt from where her mother had pinched it on the carriage ride home, after telling Christina what a fool she was for not embracing this opportunity.

Embracing. This opportunity.

The idea of embracing a marriage to Van Peet sickened Christina. She'd rather throw herself in front of a streetcar. If it had not been dark upon their return she would have left to walk the city streets. Or perhaps visit Oliver's gardens. Instead she had been forced to hide in her room and wallow in her misery.

She opened the door to find Patricia standing there. Her cousin was resplendent in a mauve silk evening gown, the scoop neck trimmed with lace and fringe. Christina felt downright dowdy in comparison, her own simple dress over two years old and already out of fashion. "Hello."

"May I come in?"

"Please." She stepped back and her cousin breezed inside.

Patricia searched Christina's face as she shut the door. "You were not at dinner, so I wanted to check on you. Is everything all right?"

Christina was touched. In the past three weeks, she and her American cousin had grown close. Even though she had many friends, Patricia was always kind to Christina. "I am fine. Merely a small headache, is all."

Her cousin shook her head. "You are a terrible liar. Tell me everything, Tina."

A smile tugged at Christina's mouth. Patricia was the only person who used this familiar, shortened version of Christina's name. *This is your cousin, your family. Perhaps she will understand. Perhaps you finally have a friend in whom to confide.* "I've had an awful day."

"I heard you went to pay a call on Mr. Van Peet." Patricia's brow furrowed and she moved toward the bed. "Though I cannot imagine why."

The truth burned on Christina's tongue, but she was unable to push the words out. They were too humiliating, too unbelievable, and she did not want her cousin to feel sorry for her. "My mother thinks the connection may serve us well here."

Patricia dropped onto the mattress and rolled her eyes. "I've no idea how. No one is able to stand him." She pointed at the untouched strawberry tart on Christina's dinner tray. "May I?"

"Of course." Christina had lost her appetite since leaving Van Peet's house.

Patricia took a large bite of tart. "Anyway, Van Peet is the nastiest, most vile man in New York. His last wife died under suspicious circumstances. Fell down the stairs, they said, but no one believed it. She had lost two babies in a very short period of time."

Christina's throat closed and dark spots danced before her eyes. *Oh, no. Suspicious circumstances?* She wobbled, then reached out to steady herself on one of the bedframe posts.

"Tina!" Patricia came alongside and swept a gentle hand over Christina's back. "Breathe, cousin. Breathe."

Christina dragged in a ragged breath, her lungs finally filling. "Oh, God."

"What is it? What did I say?"

"My parents wish for me to marry him."

"Your parents want you to marry that . . . ? *Him?* No, your parents would not be so cruel."

Straightening, Christina made her way to a chair and sat. "My mother said she was doing me a favor. That Van Peet will soon be dead and I'll have all that money to myself."

Patricia's jaw fell open, horror in her gaze. "A *favor*? Goodness, he could live for years. And there's no guarantee you would get all his money upon his death—provided you outlive him."

That prospect sent a bolt of fear down Christina's spine. "What am I going to do? My parents need the money. I cannot disobey them."

Patricia came over and knelt on the floor by Christina's chair, then wrapped her arms around Christina. "Tina, I am so, so sorry. I hadn't any idea this was going on. I have been occupied with Felton and my own happiness and I never stopped to wonder about yours. Forgive me, please."

They'd only known one another for four weeks, so how could anyone blame Patricia? Christina sought to reassure her. "No need for apologies. I did not want to burden you—and there is nothing to be done for it."

"You are never a burden. Friends share their problems. Friends also rescue one another. I will not allow you to marry that man, no matter the reason."

Christina never had a friend before. Now, in the span of a few days, she had two. It felt nice. Strange, but nice. "I cannot see a way around it. My parents are destitute. If I do not find a wealthy husband, my father will end up losing everything."

Patricia straightened and began pacing. With her back straight and snapping blue eyes, she was a warrior preparing for battle. "It all makes sense now. Why your parents arrived unexpectedly in New York, why you never debuted in London . . . and why your mother hovers over you like a hawk."

And I am the mouse. Did that not just perfectly sum her up?

Patricia stopped and crossed her arms over her chest. "The way I see it, we merely need to find you someone else. New York is brimming with wealthy men. Locate one and your problem is solved."

"You say that as if it is easily done." Christina hadn't any current suitors; she had barely interacted with any of the young men of New York society.

"It is not impossible. You are lovely and charming. From a good family, albeit a bit misguided. Your lack of wealth won't matter here."

"There is no time!" Christina blurted. "I am to pay a call to Van Peet again tomorrow . . . alone."

"Alone?" Patricia's mouth fell open. "Your mother agreed to an unchaperoned visit? What if he . . ." She snapped her jaw shut. "No, he would not dare. Van Peet shall act gentlemanly, I am certain of it. At least until the vows are recited."

"Oh, Lord. You are not helping, Patricia."

"We need a plan. Is there any other man you met here, anyone at all?"

A vision of Oliver popped into Christina's

mind. He had touched her sweetly, so tenderly, the first man to ever do so. If only . . .

"There is someone! I can tell by that expression." Patricia pointed at Christina's face.

Christina held up her palms to quell her cousin's enthusiasm. "There is, but he would never marry me. We hardly know one another."

"Am I familiar with this man?" When Christina hesitated, Patricia pushed. "Come now, I have told you my secrets about Mr. Felton. You may trust me. We are family."

A smile tugged at Christina's mouth. Her cousin's generous nature and kindness were impossible to refuse. And really, how could she when Patricia had gone out of her way to help Christina at every turn? "Mr. Hawkes, your neighbor."

Patricia's brows shot up. "You have met the reclusive Mr. Hawkes? I am . . . I do not know what to say. I want to know everything. You must tell me all the details!"

"There is not much to say," Christina said. "I have taken to strolling his gardens each morning and have encountered him a few times." No need to mention her injury or what a fool she had made of herself. "He is quite nice."

"You are astounding. I cannot believe you have been withholding this information from me."

"It hardly seemed worth sharing."

"Liar. And you never know about marriage, Tina. Some men merely need a gentle push in the right direction."

This is my house and I prefer to be left alone. Her stomach sank recalling Oliver's words. "This man cannot be pushed. No, we must come up with another alternative."

"If you are certain he won't do, then we must find another way out of this. I shall help you think of something, I promise." She patted Christina's back. "You will not marry anyone unsuitable."

Chapter Four

Early the next morning, Oliver stood at the greenhouse windows instead of concentrating on his work.

He felt ridiculous. There were many more important things to do than to keep watch for her, so why could he not move? It was as if his feet were rooted here, bolted to the floor.

He did not care for how their last meeting ended—and the fault was entirely his own. He'd touched Christina inappropriately because he had not been able to help himself. Then he had ignored her like a petulant schoolboy until she departed. It seemed the control on which he'd long prided himself vanished in her presence. He had no concentration, no restraint at all when it came to her . . . and he hated it.

So why on earth was he waiting on her at the window?

Because you are scared she may never return after the way you treated her.

And would that be so terrible? He liked the way things were, with the same routine day after day and no one around to bother him, except when Sarah visited. He had no one asking stupid questions about his deafness or shouting at him, thinking the increased volume would somehow get through. No, other than the occasional visit by his idiotic cousin, Oliver had a peaceful, perfect life.

Yet that did not explain why his heart was pounding with anticipation at the moment.

Damn.

He was just about to turn away when she came into view, the same thick hat on her head. She looked down as she walked, her mouth pulled into a deep frown. Without waiting to see if she would come to him, he opened the door, went outside, and started toward her on the path. Apollo raced forward, tail wagging, and Oliver snapped his fingers and signed for him to sit. The last thing he needed was for the dog to startle Christina again.

Her head came up and she smiled at him. Warmth suffused his entire body, even to the roots of his hair. "Hello," he signed.

"Hello," she signed in return. "How are you?"

She'd remembered. "Fine," he signed. "Come inside."

She nodded and moved toward him. He considered holding out his arm to escort her, but that felt too formal. They were merely friends. He was not looking for a relationship—and certainly not marriage. Those things were not for him.

Better to not encourage her, then.

He was bringing her in to get warm, nothing more.

He gestured for her to lead the way and Apollo bounded along in front of them. The inside of the greenhouse was cozy, with a fresh pot of tea waiting for her. He went to his chair and got to work, twisting copper wire together, leaving her to get settled as she saw fit.

Time stretched as he kept busy. She did not interrupt; instead she sipped tea and read the Mark Twain novel he'd set out. Apollo nestled on the floor by her feet. It was all terribly domestic . . . but he didn't resent her presence in his space.

Far from it.

Every now and again, he noticed her biting her lip and staring off into the dormant gardens, brow creased in contemplation. When it happened once more, he rapped the counter with his knuckles to attract her attention. "What?" he signed when she glanced over.

"What, what?"

He took out his small ledger and wrote. *What is bothering you?*

Moisture had gathered in her eyes by the time

she finished reading, and he stiffened. Dear God, she was crying. How had he upset her? *Talk to me. Please.*

She looked up from the ledger. "He wishes me to pay him another call this afternoon. Alone."

"Who?" He had blurted it, unconcerned about the sound of his voice.

"Van Peet."

Ah, of course. He remembered their conversation from yesterday. She must have failed in convincing Van Peet to drop his pursuit. What were her parents thinking? He took back the ledger. *I cannot believe your parents have agreed to an unchaperoned visit.*

They exchanged the pencil. *Not only have they agreed, they encouraged it. My mother told me not to complain about anything that may happen, to let Van Peet do as he pleases.*

Oliver's insides went cold reading that, his jaw dropping open. What the hell? Her parents were forcing her to submit to whatever Van Peet had in mind, no matter how depraved. What if the older man raped her? Hurt her? He scratched furiously on the paper. *You cannot go.*

"I do not have a choice."

Everyone has a choice. This is your life. What if he injures you?

She bit her lip, looked away, and lifted a shoulder as if to say, *So what?*

He nearly fell off his stool. Did she not care? Had she given up? If she wanted to marry Van

Peet, fine. Oliver would not object. He'd wish her well and go on with his life. But clearly the prospect of the older man as a husband distressed her. So why go along with it?

He would not allow her to stop fighting. He was not foolish enough to believe women, especially young women, were always empowered to make choices for themselves. However, she was not altogether helpless.

Do you know how to fend off an attack by a man?

She frowned after she finished reading, her pretty pink lips turning down at the edges. "As in, hit him?"

Yes, but it is the location of the hit that counts. Has anyone shown you?

When she shook her head, he faced her and planted his feet. Then he beckoned with his hand. "Hit me," he signed.

She appeared appalled at the request. "No! Why on earth would I do such a thing?"

He reached over to write in the ledger. *This is important. I am going to teach you something useful. Now, where would you hit me first?*

Understanding dawned in her eyes after reading over his shoulder. Stepping back, she pointed a delicate finger at his face. "There."

"Wrong," he signed, also using his voice so he did not need to keep writing. "Guess again."

"Your stomach?"

"No."

"Step on your foot?"

He pinched the bridge of his nose. God save him from fathers who never bothered to prepare their daughters for the cruelty of men. It was shameful how little women were taught. "No." He pointed at his crotch. "Here. You hit here."

Christina's creamy skin turned crimson. "Oliver!"

He bent over to write. *I am not trying to embarrass you, but this is important.*

"Striking there"—she closed her eyes and threw out a vague gesture to his middle—"surely would not work."

Yes, it will, he wrote. *Testicles are the most sensitive place on a man.*

When she saw the paper, her blush deepened. "Are you certain?"

He could not help it; he laughed. *Yes. I am quite certain.* A blow to the stones could fell the strongest, biggest man on the planet. It was a pain like none other, a deep hurt inside one's belly that quickly shifted to debilitating nausea.

"With my hand?" She stared at her hand as if to wonder how that would actually work.

"Your knee," he signed and said simultaneously.

"Oh." Understanding dawned but she hardly seemed excited about the prospect, nibbling her lip as she stared at the floor.

Taking the paper, he scribbled. *Do not hesitate. Get as close as possible and then ram your knee into his groin as hard as you can. Try not to struggle or fight—some men enjoy that even more.*

She read over his shoulder, her skirts brushing his legs. The sweet smell of roses and vanilla stole through him and he drew in a deep breath. He never cared much for perfumes or soaps, but the scent of her made him dizzy. He suddenly longed to turn and take her in his arms, hold her close, and remove all this distress from her life.

He shook himself. *She is not yours. She will never be yours.* He had to keep reminding himself of that. The girl was here to find a society husband.

Still, the idea of Van Peet and Christina together, the older man fumbling between this woman's thighs . . . Oliver wanted to punch something every time he pictured it.

A light touch on his shoulder had him turning. Christina gripped her hands together tightly in front of her chest. "Do you think he will try to hurt me?"

He debated his answer carefully. There was no need to scare her unnecessarily, but she deserved honesty. He picked up his pencil. *I believe he will attempt something or behave in an inappropriate manner. Why else bring you there alone?*

She closed her eyes, as if she'd expected that answer. "I wish I could disappear."

Her lips barely moved, the words perhaps only a mumble, but he understood perfectly. He would help to hide her, if only he could. *You are stronger than you think,* he wrote. *You will find a way out of this.*

"Will you help me practice?"

"Practice?" he asked.

She pointed to her knee and then his groin. His brows shot up. She wanted to practice kneeing him in the balls? Did she believe the deaf were impervious to pain? *That is a bad idea*, he wrote.

"I won't hurt you, I promise. I just . . . want to understand how it is done."

Knee . . . testicles. Honestly it could not be simpler.

The flush on her face deepened and she waved her hand. "Forget I asked. It was silly of me."

"No, here," he said and signed. Without stopping to consider what he was doing, he reached for her. "I will show you." He held tight with both hands on her shoulders, angling his body closer into her space. He could smell her again—vanilla and roses along with something sweet and feminine—and his heart began kicking hard behind his ribs. Her palms landed on his chest, not pushing him away but resting there to touch him. There was such trust in her gaze, a trust he surely did not deserve, and heat wound its way through him, desire snaking along his veins in a slow, steady pulse.

He inched toward her, unsure for a moment about what he was supposed to be doing. All he could contemplate were the silk skirts rustling as he pressed in, the mounds of her breasts nearly meeting his chest. Her lips parted as her breathing increased, and satisfaction surged inside him. He affected her, which was damn gratifying considering the buzz humming along his skin at the moment.

Nothing escaped his notice at this distance, not the gentle bow of her upper lip or the smooth skin of her cheek, the sweep of dark brown lashes or the two tiny freckles on the bridge of her nose. He'd never seen a lovelier face, one so beautiful it made his chest ache.

Her eyes darted to his mouth and his breath caught. Was she hoping he would kiss her? God knew he could think of little else in this moment. She would undoubtedly taste glorious, warm and slick, her lips pliant and eager under his.

You need to rejoin the rest of the world.

Henry's words came back to Oliver, and he gave himself a mental shake. What was he doing, *seducing her*? To what purpose? He refused to marry a society girl and spend his time ignoring the sneers and insults at teas and parties. Time to get this over with.

Without the use of his hands, he was forced to use his voice. "Fight me," he said.

She blinked. "What?"

"If I were advancing on you like this, you need to fight me."

"Oh." She gave a weak shove of her arms but did not budge him.

"No hands," he said. "Your knee."

She nodded and then lifted her knee the tiniest of amounts. It came nowhere near the intended target.

"No, move in closer," he told her. "Make him relax and then lift your skirts to jam your knee up."

Her hands slid along his chest and around his neck, delicate fingers threading into his hair. Sparks raced down his spine, causing him to shiver, and he watched, fascinated, as she licked her lips. He felt his sanity slipping, his willpower evaporating, with each second this dragged on. *Damn it.*

His limbs grew heavy, his body drugged on her. If this were any other woman, any other situation, he would ask to kiss her mouth, her throat, the tops of her breasts—and he noted the subtle shift in her body, the transfer of weight. Then it dawned on him what was happening. He jerked to the side just as her knee flew up, thankfully landing on the inside of his thigh. It hurt like hell but did not unman him.

Releasing her, he bent at the waist to catch his breath as the pain receded. Christ, if he had not moved out of the way he'd be on the ground at the moment, writhing in pain. When the worst of it passed, he exhaled and straightened. Christina was gesturing at him, her mouth moving rapidly, saying words he could not hear.

He held up his hand. "I cannot read your lips if I cannot see your face. And speak slowly."

"I am so sorry." Her hand landed on her chest, gaze brimming with worry. "I never meant to hurt you."

"I am fine. You caught my thigh."

"Thank heavens," she said. "You had me worried. Do I need more practice?"

Any more practice might kill him. "No, I declare you more than ready."

"MOTHER, PLEASE," CHRISTINA breathed. "I cannot do it—"

"Stop that. You are being ungrateful, Christina." They were outside Van Peet's home, sitting in the carriage. Christina had hoped she could reason with her mother at the last minute, that she could somehow convince the countess not to force her inside.

She should have known better.

"Do not ruin this," the countess hissed, her eyes narrowed to slits. "You know our situation. You need to marry, quickly. He'll be dead soon and he has no sons. We shall have control of his fortune. What more could you ask for in a husband? Now, be a good girl and do as you are told. Above all else, smile and be polite."

Christina's stomach clenched, panic and unhappiness like a lead weight in her belly. Why hadn't she loosened her corset? She could hardly pull air into her lungs. Heavens, what if she passed out in front of Van Peet?

What if he hurts you?

Oliver's question had haunted her all day. Why was it a near stranger felt more concern for Christina than her own parents? She tried one more time. "Come in with me. I do not wish to go alone."

Her mother turned the latch and threw open the carriage door. "Off you go. Van Peet will send you home in his carriage. I expect good news upon your arrival."

Christina had no choice but to step out onto the walk. There had to be something she could say to prevent this. Legs shaking, she spun to face her mother. "What if—"

The countess's mouth tightened, lips white with anger. "Go, Christina. He is waiting."

The carriage door slammed and Christina watched in horror as the conveyance disappeared down the street. She swallowed and wondered if she could start walking and never stop. Just keep going until she disappeared. Would anyone miss her?

"Welcome, Lady Christina."

Van Peet's butler had pulled the door wide and was watching her. Dragging in a deep breath, she made her way up the steps and into the house. Her maid came in as well—a servant borrowed from the Kane household who had not acted particularly friendly toward Christina. Still, Christina longed to grab onto the girl and never let go. Not until it was time to leave, at least.

You will get through this. He won't hurt you. Remember what Oliver taught you.

The entryway was dim and gray. No flowers or artwork, just cold marble and bare plaster. A house as uninviting as its master.

"You shall await your mistress belowstairs," the butler told the maid in a tone that invited no argument.

A bubble of hysteria rose in Christina's chest, pressing in on her throat. Her maid was not to even wait in the hall? It seemed everyone wanted Christina at Van Peet's mercy, alone without a chaperone of any kind.

"I shall show you the way as soon as I return," the butler told the maid. Then he faced Christina. "Please, follow me, your ladyship."

She followed him deeper into the house, all the while examining the sparse and dreary rooms. Nothing appeared well used or lived-in. Barren and devoid of life, the space gave no impression that anyone lived here. The idea of this crypt as her home caused her stomach to roil.

The salon was blessedly empty and the butler instructed her to wait. She sat on a small sofa and repeated her inner dialogue. *He won't hurt you. It is broad daylight and there are others in the house. He is not your husband.* Not to mention, if he tried anything improper, there was always the knee-between-the-legs trick. *Thank you, Oliver.*

Heat went through her, a brief distraction from her terror. This morning something had changed between her and Oliver. Had he been about to kiss her? No man had ever stared at her quite so hotly, and there had been the way he inched closer, his breath hitching when she'd licked her lips . . . His reaction had sent her pulse pounding with sensation, her body becoming demanding in ways she had not expected. It was as if he had turned a switch inside her, electricity causing her to come alive.

The moment had quickly passed, however, with him returning to his instructions on how to fend off an attack. Still, she had ruminated on the exchange all day. Had she misread the situation? They were barely friends. His desire for solace had been communicated clearly.

Though it almost seemed as if he had been waiting for her this morning.

A thumping noise caught her attention. It grew louder, and she recognized it as the sound of Van Peet's cane. She braced herself, muscles clenched against the urge to flee.

Van Peet came through the doorway, his coat hanging awkwardly on his thin, bent frame. "I am pleased to see you are on time," he huffed in greeting.

She rose. "Good afternoon, sir."

Frosty gray eyes swept over her, the cold appraisal prickling over her skin. She fought not to squirm or cover herself.

"Other than wearing a very unflattering shade of pink, you appear healthy. You may sit."

Flustered, Christina lowered herself once more and arranged her skirts. Her mother had borrowed the pale rose dress from Patricia, insisting the color made Christina appear more youthful.

"You won't wear colors such as that if we

marry, of course," Van Peet said offhandedly as he dropped into an armchair across from her.

She would not marry this odious, rude man. Never. Backbone, she remembered. "Oh, but this is my very favorite color." She smoothed the fabric. "I have always had good luck while wearing it."

"Nonsense. There is no such thing as luck and you will learn not to test my patience."

Or what? The words hung there and she bit her lip. *Remain strong. Do not let him win.* She took a deep breath. "I am forever trying my mother's patience. Perhaps you'd be happier with another girl, one who is better behaved."

His mouth flattened, his loose skin pulling taut. "Have you no idea why I chose you?" He settled deeper into his chair, gripping the knob topping his cane. "I have need of a young wife. I want more children and God knows these American girls are too impolite. They do not possess the proper manners of you British girls. You will make me a fine wife."

She suppressed a shudder and gathered her courage. "What if I cannot bear children? After all, many women are unable to do so."

"The problem is not mine. I have sired half a dozen children. You will conceive."

That hardly answered her question, nor did it assuage her fears. "Sir, I cannot see how a marriage between us would work. Surely you want a more . . . well, someone else."

He sneered, his gaze downright chilling. "You do not seem to realize, Lady Christina, just how dire your circumstances are at the moment. I have done my due diligence on you and your family. You are all reviled in London society. Did you know they promised you to a man there for a large sum of money before taking the funds and sailing for America? Your parents are no better than common thieves."

Mouth agape, she rocked back in her seat. Events began to fall into place, things becoming clear in her mind. There had been very little money in the past few years until suddenly the funds for passages to New York had appeared. Had her parents actually promised her to someone only to renege and keep the money? "Who?"

"Avington's his name. Do you know him?"

She shook her head, unable to speak. Why would her parents do something so despicable, so dishonorable? Even with her father a stone's throw from debtor's prison, to steal from others was wrong.

Van Peet sniffed, his nose in the air. "I assure you I have no intention of allowing your parents to do the same to me. Whatever I purchase, I keep. And the poorer they are, the more desperate. No, I won't be handing over any money until I am assured you shall suit—and after your father helps me with a small matter in parliament."

She slumped in her chair as the idea sank inside her, deep in her bones, turning them cold and brittle. Was this it, then? Was this to be her future, marriage to a cruel and ruthless man? *You are a possession to be bought and sold. You are not a daughter or a lady. You are nothing.* She hung her head, fighting the urge to cry.

"Do not start sniveling, girl. I cannot abide tears and women's emotions. This house is not built for caterwauling."

Christina felt hollow, as if someone had scooped out her guts and thrown them away. There was nothing left. She was numb. "I beg your pardon," she mumbled.

"That's better. Now, go and tug the bellpull, will you? There is one thing we need to sort during today's visit."

As if controlled by strings, Christina did as she was told, rising and walking to the cord hanging by the mantel. After tugging it, she started to sit in a chair, not sure her legs could support her any longer.

"Return to the sofa," Van Peet said. "You shall be more comfortable there."

Comfortable? Oh, sweet heavens. What had he in mind? Her throat closed as she considered the terrifying possibility. Would he now force himself on her? If so, why were they ringing for a servant?

Perhaps he needs the servant's assistance?

She stood motionless, limbs frozen as she stared at the sofa, and a brief knock sounded just before the door opened. A portly gentleman in a brown suit strode inside, a black doctor's bag in his hand.

Christina's gaze swung from the man back to Van Peet, whose eyes glittered like dark stones in the dying afternoon light, almost as if he were anticipating what was about to transpire. Christina took a step back, putting more distance between her and the two men.

You are stronger than you think, Oliver had said. She braced her legs, ready to run. If escape failed, she would fight until her dying breath.

"This is Dr. West," Van Peet said. "He shall perform the examination."

She blinked. "Examination? But I am perfectly well. The illness my mother referred to has completely—"

"You misunderstand, girl," Van Peet snapped. "I have been lied to in the past, so Dr. West is here to ensure you are still in possession of your maidenhead."

Chapter Five

Oliver was enjoying an early dinner when a figure stumbled into his dining room.

Christina. Good God, was she . . . crying? What on earth had happened?

He pushed back from the table, shot to his feet, and hurried toward her. Tears streamed down her face, her mouth working as her chest heaved with the sobs. Gill trailed her, his butler every bit as unnerved as his master. "I apologize, sir," he signed.

"It is fine," Oliver signed. "Clear the room."

Everyone quickly departed except for Christina, who wrapped her arms around her stomach and hunched over. Oliver took her elbow and led her to his vacated chair.

When he tried to release her, she turned into his chest, clutched his shirt with both fists, and buried her face in his necktie. Her shoulders shook as she cried, seeming so small and fragile, a bundle of misery against him, and his heart fractured into tiny pieces. As if it were the most natural thing in the world, he enveloped her in his arms and held on. Never had he been more grateful for his lack of hearing. Seeing her upset tore him up; if he had to listen to her anguish, he'd likely murder the cause of it.

Then he stiffened. She'd gone to pay a call on Van Peet this afternoon, alone.

Goddamn it. If that old buzzard had harmed one hair upon Christina's head, Oliver would see him buried. Van Peet possessed a fortune, yes, but so did Oliver. He hadn't yet found a good use for all his family's money beyond his inventions, but he would happily use every cent to avenge this woman's wrongs, if necessary.

Occasionally, he stroked her back or hair but mostly he merely embraced her. She trembled, her small body tucked into his as she sought comfort. He held perfectly still, even though the anticipation as to the cause of her misery was killing him. A primal need welled up in his chest, a need utterly foreign to him. *Protection.* He wanted to shelter this woman from everything dark and unsavory, anything that might cause her pain.

That is idiocy. You hardly know her.

Yet he sensed something inside her, a quality that called out to a long-forgotten part of him. Sadness? Loneliness? Desolation?

It does not matter. You cannot keep her.

True, but he could still help her. They were

friends—even if he had been thinking about her all day. And his thoughts hadn't been of the tea and conversation variety . . .

After a long while, she calmed. More than ready to discover the cause of her distress, he slowly moved them toward the chairs and urged her to sit.

She dropped into the ornate walnut chair and he presented her with a linen napkin to clean up. As she collected herself, he pulled another chair closer and sat.

Even with her puffy and red eyes, her skin blotchy from crying, Christina remained breath-takingly beautiful. He curled his fingers into fists to keep from reaching for her again. He with-drew the ledger and pencil from his pocket, then slid them across the table and tapped the ledger with his finger. "Tell me," he signed. "Now."

Biting her bottom lip, she took the pencil and began writing. He leaned in to read as her hand moved, not content to sit back and wait to learn what had happened.

I went to Van Peet's home, to pay a call alone as he requested.

He ground his teeth together. Whatever was coming, he knew he would not like it.

He informed me my parents had accepted money from a man in London to marry me. Then they left town. That was how they afforded the passage to New York.

Christ, her parents were no better than charlatans. To swindle someone in such a reprehensible way—using their daughter—was unforgivable.

She kept writing. *Van Peet said he'd never allow my parents to cheat him, that whatever he bought he expected to keep. And he refuses to hand over any money until he is assured we shall suit.*

Oliver's fingernails dug into his palms. That bastard. Van Peet acted as if Christina was no more than a trinket, one to use and display, not a person to love and care for.

He—

The pencil began shaking, her hand unable to continue. Oliver reached out and tucked a long strand of chocolate-colored hair behind her ear, the backs of his knuckles brushing her cheek. *Take your time*, he willed her silently. There was no rush. He was not letting her leave anytime soon, not until he learned what had upset her.

She resumed her writing. *A doctor arrived during the visit. To examine me.*

Examine her? To ensure she was healthy? He leaned back in his chair, thinking, while studying her face. She would not meet his eyes, her gaze fixed on the table, cheeks flooded with color. She was embarrassed, which made no sense. He had watched Henry perform cursory examinations to injured members of the staff or—

Oh. This had not been a cursory examination, then. It had been personal.

Heaviness pressed on his chest, yet he had to

know. Not bothering to take the pencil from her, he forced out, "To what end?"

She shook her head and squeezed her eyes shut, a fresh tear leaking from one of the corners.

Damn Van Peet to hell. Oliver shot to his feet, the chair rocking behind him, as rage exploded within every cell in his body. The man had subjected her to . . . to an intimate *examination*? For what, to determine if she had any diseases his withered prick might contract? Good God, the very idea of it, the humiliation and cruelty, made Oliver want to howl with fury.

He stalked away, dragging both hands through his hair. The railroad owner would pay for this. Oliver would go to the old man's house and beat him to within an inch of his miserable, wretched life. He was no stranger to fights, having used his fists more often than not those first two years at school in Connecticut. Van Peet did not stand a chance—

A hand on his shoulder caught his attention. Emotions rioting, he spun to find her directly behind him. "I ran," she said. "I ran away before the examination."

"He did not touch you?" Oliver signed, using his voice as well.

"No. I ran fast."

Oliver shut his eyes, his knees almost buckling at the relief. *Thank Christ.* She had not been violated.

That fact did not absolve Van Peet, however. He had tried to subject Christina to the worst kind of invasion—and he would pay for it. Somehow, some way, Oliver would make him pay.

He motioned for her to sit at the table once more then joined her. "So you left?" he signed and said.

The pencil scratched as she continued writing. *I did not stay. I ran out as quickly as I could. I even left my maid behind.*

He finished reading then picked up the pencil to write, *What had your parents to say about this?*

"I have not informed them," she said. "I came straight here."

He was touched at that. He wrote, *At least now you shall not be forced to marry Van Peet. Your parents may decide on a husband but at least it will not be HIM.*

Christina started shaking her head before he'd even finished. *This will not change their minds about Van Peet. My mother told me before I went in to do as I was told, not to complain about anything Van Peet wanted or asked of me.*

Jesus, her parents had thrown her to the wolves—or wolf, to be precise. How could they be so cruel to their own flesh and blood? Her mother had basically said to put up with whatever happened, even if Van Peet raped her.

What kind of dashed world did this to a young woman?

He thought of his adorable eleven-year-old sister and his teeth ground together. Sarah would never enter society, not if Oliver could help it.

Christina tapped his arm and pointed at a new sentence on the paper. *They think they are doing me a favor by selecting him. My mother said he shall die soon and then we will be in charge of his fortune.*

"We?" he signed.

"Yes. They keep saying this marriage is for me, but clearly it is for them."

Her parents obviously meant to keep control of *her*. God, what a mess.

Moisture glistened in her eyes again. "I cannot go back there."

He agreed, but what did that mean for her? There were practical matters to consider. Where would she go? How would she survive? *Is there any chance they would understand, based on what happened today?*

She flipped to a new page in the ledger and snatched the pencil away from him. *No, they will be furious with me. My mother shall lock me in my room and agree to the wedding.*

The truth of the statement was there in Christina's steady brown gaze. The idea was not outlandish, based on what he knew of her parents. If they had instructed her to endure Van Peet's cruel whims today, then nothing would likely keep them from orchestrating the match. Especially if they expected Van Peet to soon die and leave Christina all the money. *What do you plan to do?*

Tears welled in her eyes and his chest twisted at the sight. "I have no idea."

He dragged a hand over the nape of his neck and stared at the back lawn through the dining room windows. Could he help her disappear? Give her a large sum of money and send her West? To Chicago or St. Louis, perhaps? Somewhere her parents would never find her. She could start a new life and change her name. Find a nice man to settle down with—

The notebook tapped his arm. Looking down, he read, *May I stay here with you? Just until I figure something out?*

His head snapped up and he spoke, too surprised to be self-conscious. "With me?"

"Yes, Oliver. Please. Let me hide here in your house."

CHRISTINA BIT HER lip and watched as the request sank in Oliver's brain. Hard to say what she would do if he refused. There was no returning home tonight. Her parents, in their desperation and fury, would eventually return her to Van Peet. If Oliver did not allow her to hide here, she would need to strike out on her own. Hop a train and attempt to disappear, with no money or clothing other than what she wore. She was ill-prepared for such an undertaking . . . but what choice had she?

You might marry Oliver instead.

No, definitely not. While she liked him quite a bit, she did not wish to marry anyone out of duty or obligation. She preferred to find someone who cared about her, who respected her. A man who did not mind that she hated parties and crowds, and understood that the idea of hosting a dinner party gave her cold sweats. A man who lived in the country where she could walk and not feel so closed in.

It went without saying that this man would also live far, far away from her parents.

"Christina . . ." Oliver used his voice, not bothering to finger spell her name. She liked the sound of his deep voice, uncertain why it embarrassed him. It seemed he used his voice more and more with her, a sign, perhaps, that he had grown comfortable in her presence. To her, each sound he uttered felt like a small victory. "How?" he signed.

Embarrassment flooded her and she could feel her cheeks heating. She had not planned for this eventuality, so she would need to rely on his charity. "I will hide here—but only until I find a way to leave New York and disappear."

He frowned, his vivid green eyes never leaving her face. Every second that ticked by in silence felt like an eternity. He gave no outward response and she could not read his thoughts. The urge to take the words back, to laugh this off, burned in her chest. It would be so easy to convince him she hadn't been serious.

But what then?

She was terrified of returning home. Terrified of her mother's anger and her father's indifference. They were not interested in her happiness; they merely desired the coin to dig themselves out of the creditors' clutches. Returning home meant putting herself in their hands—and Van Peet's. She could not do it. She would rather go live on the street and starve. Disappear and never see another soul.

She hurried to explain. Reaching for the ledger and pencil, she turned a new page and wrote. *I promise to stay out of your way. Nothing will change. I will not bother you and I promise it shall not be for long.*

He pinched the bridge of his nose with his thumb and forefinger upon reading that, his lids falling shut. She had no clue how to improve this offer to better appeal to a recluse who clearly had no want of a wife. However, she was desperate and, other than her cousin, this man was her only friend in this entire city—entire country, actually. Unfortunately, Patricia was unable to assist Christina with this mess, not unless her cousin planned on deceiving and angering their entire extended family. If they were caught, Patricia could suffer disastrous consequences for lying.

No, only Oliver could help her.

While she did not deserve his assistance, she had no problem begging for it. *Oliver, please. I will go away. To the West, like perhaps to Dakota or California. I will not stay.*

She underlined *not* three times.

He held out his hand for the pencil, which she relinquished. *I will give you money, then. You may go somewhere they will never find you.*

"I shall pay you back, every bit of it."

Shaking his head, he bent to write. *Not necessary. I have more than enough money. I am happy to help you.*

Relief nearly had her weeping once more. "Thank you, Oliver."

We should get you settled for the night. We may begin researching your escape in the morning. He rose and started toward the bellpull in the corner.

At that moment, the dining room door burst open, startling her. What on earth . . . ? She gasped as her mother charged into the room, with the earl fast on the countess's heels. They both still wore their overcoats and hats. Head spinning, Christina shot to her feet. "Mother, Father. What are you doing here?"

"We have come to save your reputation," her mother announced, every syllable clear and precise as if she were on stage.

"My reputation? I am afraid I do not understand." Gill and Oliver were currently signing with one another and Christina noticed one more figure slink into the room. Patricia. Their eyes met and her cousin mouthed, *I am sorry.*

Sorry? Sorry for what?

Before Christina could dwell on that curious statement, her mother pointed at Oliver. "You have ruined my daughter, sir. I understand she has been here, alone, with you for several hours."

Oliver's brow furrowed as he rapidly signed to Gill. "Mr. Hawkes would like for me to tell you," Gill said, "that her ladyship has not been harmed or accosted in any way."

"Of course he would say as much," her mother said, skepticism fairly dripping in her tone. "He is . . . deformed. An imbecile, I understand."

Christina gasped. "He is no such thing! Mother, do not dare speak of Mr. Hawkes in those terms again."

The earl folded his arms across his chest, his expression stern. "And what of the mornings you have been spending with him?"

Christina's mouth fell open and she shot a glance at Patricia. How could her cousin have betrayed her by telling her family about those visits? No wonder her parents had known to look here when Christina hadn't returned home. Mortification singed her insides, sending her skin up in flames. Good Lord, would the embarrassment of the day never end?

Patricia winced and mouthed another apology. Christina could not respond—the events now transpiring were all too terrible. Her parents had *found her.* How on earth was she to escape now?

"There has been nothing untoward about my

friendship with Lady Christina," Gill translated as Oliver signed. "You have my word on that."

"The word of a deaf and dumb man," Christina's father scoffed. "Forgive us if we are not reassured."

A muscle jumped in Oliver's jaw at the words *deaf and dumb*. "Stop it, both of you," Christina said to her parents. "Mr. Hawkes has been a complete gentleman at all times. I am not in the least bit compromised."

"That is not our understanding," her mother said. "And it hardly matters now. No decent man will have you with a tarnished reputation." She glanced haughtily at Oliver. "You have ruined her chances for a good match."

What was happening? Why were her parents so determined to paint Oliver as a cad and her reputation in tatters? "This makes no sense. You sent me to Van Peet's home by myself today without a care for my reputation."

"Do not argue with us, you ungrateful girl." Her mother's face turned red with fury as she stepped toward Christina. "Not after everything I have done for you."

Oliver suddenly appeared in front of Christina as he put himself between her and the countess. His arms moved as he signed to Gill. "You must calm yourself, madam, or you shall be escorted off the property."

Christina's chest expanded with gratitude and

something warmer settled in the neighborhood of her heart. Had anyone ever defended her like this?

Her mother clutched her chest. "How dare he speak to me in such a disrespectful manner."

"Now, let us all calm down," the earl said. "There is no need for anyone to become angry. We are here to arrive at a solution."

"A solution?" Christina peeked around Oliver's shoulder. "Whatever for?"

"Allow the adults to handle this, Christina," her mother said. "You have been ruined and your future must be sorted out."

Oliver's hands moved once again and Gill began to translate. "Christina is an adult and therefore should have a say in her own future. Furthermore, she has not been ruined—not by me."

"Her future was ruined when she decided to visit Mr. Hawkes every morning," her mother said to the butler. "Inform your master that he *will* be marrying my daughter as soon as we come to terms."

"With all due respect, your ladyship," Gill said. "You may speak directly to Mr. Hawkes. He is able to read your lips."

Her mother leaned forward and began shouting at Oliver, overenunciating each word. *"You . . . will . . . marry . . . my . . . daughter."*

Gill watched Oliver's hands and said, "I will not marry her or anyone else. Now I insist that you all take your leave."

"You have ruined our daughter's reputation, Hawkes," the earl said. "It will be all over Manhattan by morning."

Oliver signed to Gill, "If you think I am swayed at the prospect of being shunned by the uptown set, you are mistaken. Now, if you do not mind." Oliver gestured to the door.

"While you might not care about the consequences, I assure you that we do." The countess dabbed at her eyes with a linen handkerchief. "Our daughter will no longer be able to marry well. We shall be lucky to find her a husband at all!"

This was humiliating. They were discussing her as if she were not even in the room. And trying to force Oliver to marry her? Truly mortifying. "Everyone, stop." She stepped out from around Oliver. "Mother, Father, please. This is not Oliver's fault."

The earl ignored Christina and pointed at Oliver. "Are you saying you will not do the honorable thing, Hawkes?"

Oliver crossed his arms over his chest, his face devoid of any emotion. When the silence stretched, the countess sniffed and held out her hand. "Let us return home, Christina. Come along."

She hung her head. There was no way to escape, not now. Just as she took a step forward, Oliver put a hand on her elbow to stop her. His green eyes were full of concern—and for good reason. Leaving meant certain marriage to Van Peet, if the older man would still have her. *Please, God, let him refuse.* She tried to smile, to offer some sort of reassurance that she understood, but it was difficult.

Patricia spoke up for the first time. "Wait." Her cousin moved to the middle of the room. "I may have a solution."

"Who exactly are you?" Oliver asked through Gill.

"I apologize. I am Miss Patricia Kane, your neighbor and Christina's cousin. How do you do?" Oliver gave a brisk nod of acknowledgment. Undaunted, Patricia continued, "Mr. Hawkes, you must marry my cousin."

OLIVER THOUGHT HIS lip-reading abilities had deceived him. But when he checked with Gill, it seemed he had been right the first time. Christina's cousin was also attempting to force him into a marriage.

Had these people all gone mad?

"I beg your pardon," he signed at Gill. "But I believe I have made my position on the matter quite clear."

Patricia and Christina exchanged a meaningful glance—one Oliver could not read. Christina's skin had turned bright pink and he could only imagine how upsetting she found this entire scene. The earl and countess discussed her as if she were not even present, bargaining with her future and making demands. It was deplorable.

"May we speak alone?" Patricia asked him, her eyes never leaving his face.

Christina was shaking her head, her lips moving, but Oliver kept watch on Patricia. He sensed from the set of her jaw that she would not leave without saying her piece. "Tell her to follow me into the sitting room," he signed to Gill. "You had best come, too." Then he spun on his heel and moved toward the doors connecting the two rooms.

As he threw open the door, he noticed Patricia stopped to have a brief word with Christina. The earl and countess were locked in a serious conversation as well, huddled on the far side of the dining room. With everyone in profile, he could not read lips and annoyance tightened between his shoulder blades. It was his damn house and he hated feeling out of place here. These intruders were the ones who should feel out of place, not him.

He stalked into the sitting room, poured a half tumbler of whiskey, and tossed the liquor back in two swallows. Whatever Patricia had to say would not sway him. He'd let her speak, refuse to comply, and send them all on their way. Then his life could go back to the way it was a month ago, with no disruptions and rudeness from society types. Sarah would visit on school breaks and he would be left alone with his work.

Leaning against the sideboard, he waited. Patricia and Gill entered, the butler closing the door for privacy. "Well?" Oliver signed.

A tall blonde, Patricia bore little resemblance to her cousin. Nevertheless, Patricia stood straight and proud, unaffected at Oliver's brusqueness. Ready to do battle. "Have you gone mad?"

Oliver jerked, his muscles locked in outrage at the implication. "I assure you, I am of completely sound mind," he signed, his movements sharp and clipped.

"Have you no conscience, then?"

Was this woman angering him on purpose? "I have done nothing wrong," he signed. "Our visits were completely innocent." Well, not completely . . . but there was no reason to mention that now.

"This is not about you. Need I explain what shall happen to Christina if those two awful people drag her out of here?"

Guilt sliced through him, a prick under his ribs. Of course Christina's parents would try to force her to marry someone else—but he did not intend to give them the chance. "I plan to help her escape them. We were doing as much when the three of you barged in."

She glanced heavenward. "There is no *escaping* them. They are her parents and her legal guardians. Even if she were to leave the city, they could bring her back. Moreover, I heard them talking. They plan to keep her under lock and key until a marriage can be arranged. They do not much care with whom as long as he is wealthy. They said if you do not agree tonight, they shall sell her off to Van Peet."

"I thought Van Peet withdrew his consideration of marriage."

"Unfortunately, he has not. He was furious she ran away but it is about more than just acquiring a young wife. Van Peet has a railroad deal pending in Cheltenham and he needs the earl's help in getting it passed through parliament. The earl is to collect a fortune in exchange."

Damn, that was terrible news. At the very least, Oliver had assumed Van Peet would bow out, thereby buying them some time to arrive at a solution. However, if she was kept under lock and key he might not see her again, not until after she had married. God, the idea of her wedded to Van Peet turned his stomach. "Van Peet brought a doctor to examine her," he signed. "Intimately."

Patricia's hand flew to her throat, her brows rising. "Oh, my God," she said. "You must marry her, Mr. Hawkes. There is no other solution to be had, not unless you are willing to turn her over to Van Peet."

Oliver grimaced. It was an impossible situation. He did not want to marry anyone, but could he condemn his friend to a life of misery and heartache, especially when he had the power to stop it?

Every reason he loathed society and the idea of marriage returned to haunt him. The pity and the sneers in the clubs. Laughter and strange, blank expressions at the parties. He no longer cared to participate in that world, one of such limited scope and judgment. For a few years he had tried to fit in, to go where he pleased and fight for his rightful place in society. It had not worked. He had been treated like a joke, an oddity. Money and conformity were all those people cared about, and even his fortune hadn't been enough to shield him from cruelty.

This is not about you. Had Patricia not said that just moments ago?

She was right. This was about Christina, a kind, intelligent woman who had not shunned him or laughed in his face. No, she had treated him with respect and dignity. God knew she deserved better than those manipulative charlatans for parents and Van Peet for a husband. But must Oliver be offered as a replacement? "Surely there is another man, some potential suitor who has shown interest?" he signed.

"No, there is not. She . . ." Patricia paused and looked down, preventing Oliver from reading what she had been saying. Gill must have reminded her about Oliver reading lips because she quickly lifted her head and apologized. "She does not enjoy the society events. I found her hiding more often than not, off in a corner, miserable."

Something they had in common, then. "We hardly know one another," he signed. "How are you so certain I am not worse than Van Peet?"

Patricia's face registered her incredulity. "No one is worse than Van Peet. His last wife died under very suspicious circumstances, you know." Before Oliver could react to that, Patricia continued. "Also, I trust Christina. If you were an ogre she would not have returned here each day." She cocked her head and studied him. "Are you attempting to claim there are no tender feelings between the two of you? Because I shall not believe it."

He resisted the urge to drop his gaze, like a child who'd been caught in a lie. "You could help her escape," he signed as a last-ditch suggestion.

"No, I cannot, not easily. My mother and the countess are second cousins. I cannot disobey my family without risking my own future with Mr. Felton. Besides, I saw you and Christina in the other room, the way you looked at one another. You care for her, I would bet my life on it."

"It hardly matters," he signed. "I do not want to marry anyone."

"That may be so. But if you do not do the right thing, then who will?"

He was afraid he knew the answer to that question. "I shall make a terrible husband," he signed.

"I do not doubt it."

His jaw clenched. "Because I am deaf?" he signed and braced himself for the impact of her ignorance.

"No." Surprise must have shown on Oliver's

face because Patricia pointed at the closed doors that led to the dining room. "No one deserves that sweet and trusting young woman standing in there. However, I am starting to suspect you just may have a chance."

Chapter Six

Christina nibbled on her thumbnail and watched as her parents huddled together across the room, whispering. She could not hear them but understood they were agitated. Likely because they had assumed Oliver would roll over and agree to marry her. She had known better.

Oliver was strong and self-assured. He would never allow himself to be guilted or bullied into a marriage he did not want.

If only she were as strong.

You are a woman. He is a man. The world is built for men to have all the choices and for women to have none.

That reminder hardly reassured her. She glanced at the closed doors at the far end of the dining room. What was Patricia discussing with him? No matter their conversation, it would not change anything. In the end, Oliver would refuse the marriage and Christina's parents would wed her off to Van Peet. She pressed a hand to her stomach and tried to control her breathing.

The urge to flee flared to life in her chest, burning brightly until it could no longer be ignored. She did not wish to sit here meekly and await Oliver's refusal. The disappointment in witnessing said refusal firsthand would be a hundred times worse than merely learning of it later. She shot to her feet. "Mother, Father, let us return home."

"No, not yet. He is close to agreeing," her mother said in a low but stern voice. "We shall not depart until we have an answer."

"He will not agree, nor should he. Nothing untoward has happened between us and he does not deserve to have his life ruined."

"Ruined?" Her mother's brows rose. "He is a deaf imbecile and a young girl of marriageable age has dropped into his lap. How on earth is his life ruined?"

"He is not an imbecile," Christina said.

The countess shrugged as if the description was of no consequence. "What I know is that he is rich, Christina. As wealthy as Van Peet, from what I understand—and your recluse does not require any politicking in parliament."

The earl shuddered, mustache twitching on his face. "Cannot stand the long days in Lords. Would rather not sit through one dashed session, if it can be avoided."

Christina's heart sank. No wonder her parents had painted Oliver the cad and her the ruined debutante. A marriage to Oliver gained them everything they wanted, with nothing in exchange.

Well, nothing except Christina.

"You have done well, Christina, finding this desperate man and seducing him—"

"I have done no such thing!"

Before the argument could continue, the doors to the sitting room cracked and Patricia sailed through the opening. She wore a smug expression and Christina sent her a helpless look, one that silently begged for information.

Do not worry, Patricia mouthed and moved to the far side of the room.

Oliver entered, followed by Gill, and Christina could not read either of their faces. Oliver walked to her side but said nothing to her. Instead, he turned and signed to Gill. "I shall marry your daughter on two conditions."

The countess smiled broadly while the earl tried to appear serious, though his eyes were dancing with satisfaction. "And those are?" her father asked.

"One," Oliver signed. "After receiving your money, the two of you return to England. Immediately. And you are not welcome to visit unless expressly invited by your daughter."

"Fine," her father agreed, and Christina tried not to allow her feelings to be hurt. *You always knew the money was more important to them than you.*

"Two," Gill continued translating. "We marry tonight."

"Tonight?" her mother screeched. "But that is too soon. We must plan this event. She needs a dress and flowers, and there are guests—"

"Madam," Oliver signed. "This wedding shall be a private affair, taking place tonight, or it will not take place at all."

"But I wanted—"

The earl grabbed the countess's arm and said, "We agree to your terms, Hawkes."

Oliver inclined his head once and Christina stood there, shocked. So it was done, then? They were to be married? Tonight?

She glanced at him, this man who was to become her husband, but he was not looking her way. Instead, he was signing to Gill. The butler gave a brief nod. "I shall summon a judge, sir."

THEY WERE MARRIED that evening.

Standing in the drawing room, Oliver and Christina were bound together in matrimony by his father's old friend—who happened to be a judge. Gill had served as an interpreter throughout the ordeal, Patricia and Christina's parents acting as witnesses.

Oliver had no idea if they were doing the right thing. A hysterical Christina had arrived on his doorstep with a tale too horrifying to contemplate, and the same instinct he kept experiencing with her rose once more. It was a bone-deep desire to protect and care for her, an elemental knowledge that he and this woman were tied together somehow.

Patricia had been right: he did care for Christina. More than he wanted to admit, even to himself. He was unable to turn his back on her, not when the alternative was Van Peet.

Still, he'd tried to say no. He would not make a good husband. He remained at home, alone, for good reason. If Christina thought to change that, she would fail. She must accustom herself to the rules of the household and respect them if she thought to be happy here.

His agreement to marry her had not brought a smile to her face. On the contrary, Christina had frowned. Hard to blame her, he supposed. What young woman in her right mind would care to tether herself to a deaf recluse?

In that moment, upon seeing her reaction, he had arrived at a decision. The marriage was to end after one year. This way, no one felt trapped. He would return to his solitary life, focusing on his inventions, and Christina would be rich and independent, free to go wherever she wanted. The two of them would remain friends. It was the perfect solution to such an unconventional beginning.

It was best for everyone. She was young, an entire life ahead of her with adventures and heartache waiting. He had his inventions and his life here in New York, already settled into his future like a pair of comfortable slippers. He would never change, would never be a normal man, moving about society without attracting negative attention. Nor would he expect her to tailor her needs to his.

A year, then.

He turned his attention back to the room, where the judge was speaking with Christina, instructing her on signing the marriage record. Gill tapped Oliver's arm and signed, "They need you to sign as well, sir."

When it was over, Oliver shook the judge's hand and thanked him. The judge tilted his chin and studied Oliver. "You have turned into a fine man, Oliver. Your father would be proud."

"Thank you. I appreciate you coming on such short notice." After Gill translated, the judge smiled.

"Happy to help. You come see me anytime. It has been entirely too long." He patted his pocket where the marriage record had been secured. "I will get this filed with the Department of Health for you. Good evening."

The judge shook the earl's hand, nodded to Patricia and the countess, then turned to Christina. "A real English lady," the judge said. "He is lucky to have you, Mrs. Hawkes."

A becoming flush stole over her cheeks. Her mouth moved rapidly and Oliver could not catch every word, so he merely watched her. She really was quite lovely. He could hardly believe they were married.

The deed was done. She was Christina Hawkes.

He had a *wife*.

No, not really. *She is your wife, but for only a year.* How quickly he'd forgotten. This was not a true marriage and they were not a true husband and wife. There would be no wedding night. No consummation. No children.

No attachment of any kind.

Merely two people sharing the same space for fifty-two weeks.

At which point he would settle a large sum of money on her and send her on her way. She could then find a normal man who traveled, who left his home. One who was able to give her everything she'd ever wanted. Oliver would continue his research and his projects, where he did not have to deal with anyone other than Sarah and the servants.

The judge departed and Oliver told Gill, "Give her a few moments to bid good-bye to her family. Then I want them out of my house. The earl may expect to hear from Mr. Tripp, my lawyer, first thing tomorrow morning."

Gill related the instructions and Oliver watched as Christina first hugged her cousin. He could not see Christina's face but Patricia's mouth repeated, "It will be all right," several times while patting his wife's back.

He dragged a hand over the nape of his neck, not liking Christina's continued unhappiness. Perhaps one year was too long. He'd thought to give her enough time to acclimate to America and her independence. As far as he was concerned, however, they could start divorce proceedings when her parents sailed for England.

A fist-sized lump settled near his heart but he ignored it. Ending the marriage quickly was the right decision, he was certain.

The countess gave Christina an awkward embrace and the earl merely patted his daughter on the shoulder. Then the three members of Christina's family left and Oliver excused Gill.

He wanted a few moments alone with Christina to discuss what was to happen next.

When the door finally closed, leaving them alone, she met his gaze and bit her lip, her hands folded at her waist. He smiled at her, trying to put her at ease. "Hello."

She grinned, relaxing, her shoulders releasing their tension and muscles softening. "Hello," she signed. "Thank you—"

He held up his hand to stop her then removed his ledger and pencil. *No need to thank me any longer,* he wrote. *We are in this together.*

"Oh, you are the . . ." She dropped her head to stare at the floor as she spoke, which meant he had no idea what she'd said.

He closed the distance between them and put

a finger beneath her chin, forcing her to look at him. "Again," he signed.

"I said you are the kindest man I've ever met."

No, he wasn't. He was selfish and stubborn. Intolerant of fools, and utterly inflexible when he made up his mind on something. Unfortunately, she would learn as much in time. "Thank you," he signed.

The hour had grown late, according to the mantel clock. *Perhaps we should retire and then discuss how this arrangement will work in the morning.*

"Are you certain?"

Bluish circles ringed her eyes, hinting at her exhaustion. She had experienced quite a bit in one day. There was no reason for Oliver to keep her from her bed, not when they both needed a good night's sleep. He might as well take her upstairs to her new chambers. With a nod, he signed, "Follow me."

Chapter Seven

Married. She and Oliver were *married*. The very notion seemed ludicrous. Surreal. Christina wanted to laugh with the absurdity of it as her new maid, Shannon, brushed her hair. New maid, new bedroom, new home . . . Everything had changed and she was now forever tied to Oliver.

Nerves fluttered behind her ribs as she struggled to take it all in. At least she would no longer be forced to marry Van Peet. Heavens, she owed Oliver a debt she'd never be able to repay for preventing that.

You forgot about your wedding night. Your repayment shall come soon.

Though the idea of lying with a man caused her palms to dampen in terror, she knew her duty. A wife's job was to submit to her husband's wishes, especially in the bedroom. She was a vessel for his lust, the mother of his children, and the keeper of his home. Nothing else mattered.

Would Oliver remain kind and patient during the deed? It would hurt, of course, but she would bear the pain gladly, happily, because he had saved her. Besides, Oliver was easily more handsome than any other man she'd encountered in New York, with his broad shoulders and a strong jaw. He wore no pomade or puffed-up whiskers. Oliver was real and unpolished, comfortable in his own skin. At home, he dressed in shirtsleeves and no coat, so unlike the straitlaced swells who strolled about town with their noses in the air.

So despite her trepidation, tonight's duty would be endured willingly. As her mother had said, such was a wife's role and Christina was now a wife. She would request to keep the light switched off and for her nightclothes to remain on. He could lift the hem and do . . . whatever it was he needed to see the business done . . . all while under the covers, of course.

She drew in a deep breath and tried to slow her racing heart. *You shall survive. Oliver will not hurt you.*

"Would you like me to leave your hair down, ma'am, or plait it for you?" Shannon asked.

Christina paused. Normally she braided her hair for bed but she was married now. Which way would Oliver prefer? She glanced up at the maid. "What do you think?"

"Why not leave it down tonight? It looks shiny

and soft, like a cloud." Shannon continued brushing the long brown strands for a moment. "The staff here, we are all so happy you have married Mr. Hawkes."

They were? Christina straightened, eager to learn more about her new husband. "Why?"

"Mr. Hawkes is too young to be living alone. Miss Sarah does not come home often and he never looks happy. You know what I mean?"

She did. Perfectly. "Miss Sarah?"

"Mr. Hawkes's sister, ma'am."

Ah, yes. Oliver had mentioned a sister away at boarding school. "How long have you worked here?"

"For a few years now. Right after Mr. Hawkes started staying home and refusing to go out."

Oliver used to go out? She knew nothing of his youth, actually. His family and background were mostly a mystery. "I see."

"From what I understand, however," Shannon said, "Mr. Hawkes was quite the man about town after he left school."

Man about town? That surprised Christina. She could not picture him at the tedious parties, standing around dripping ice sculptures and signing his name on dance cards. He must have been bored to tears. Was that why he stopped and shut himself inside his house?

Perhaps he had grown tired of writing in his ledger to communicate. Or had he used his voice?

I know it sounds strange, he'd once told her. *I try not to talk unless absolutely necessary.* Had someone once insulted his voice? She hoped not. She quite liked the sound of it.

Suddenly, she realized how unfair it was to expect him to write everything down for her all the time. She would need to learn his manual language, no matter how long it took. She had practiced the few signs he'd taught her, but that would not be enough. "Does the staff know the sign language Mr. Hawkes uses to communicate?" she asked.

"Most of us have picked up a tiny bit," Shannon said. "Mr. Gill knows the most, seeing how Mr. Hawkes uses him to translate. I would be happy to show your ladyship what I have learned, if you like."

"Thank you, I would appreciate that." Maybe she would ask Gill to teach her as well. The idea excited her. She had never been much for talking, preferring to stand in the background and listen to others. Perhaps using her hands would be easier. Thank goodness Oliver had pushed for a private wedding with only a few guests. Reciting vows in front of hundreds of people in a big church would have caused her to hyperventilate.

Speaking of guests, she had another question for her maid. "Does anyone come to dine or visit with Mr. Hawkes?"

"No, ma'am. The only visitors I have ever seen

are Miss Sarah, Dr. Jacobs, and Mr. Hawkes's cousin."

Oliver had a cousin? She was not certain why she found that piece of news surprising, especially when she knew next to nothing about her new husband. Shannon had proved quite indispensable on Christina's first night in the house. "Do you know much about this cousin?"

"Only that Mr. Hawkes does not care for him. The two of them argue something fierce whenever he visits."

Servants were often privy to more than they let on about their employers. Christina hoped Shannon fell in this group. "Have you an inkling what the arguments were regarding?"

"It has to do with money, usually. Mr. Hawkes refuses to give his cousin a larger allowance. Makes his cousin spitting mad."

Interesting. It seemed they both had impoverished family members. Learning about Oliver's cousin made Christina feel a tiny amount better about her parents. "Thank you, Shannon."

The maid smiled. "No need to thank me, ma'am. Like I said, we are all so happy you have allowed Mr. Hawkes to sweep you off your feet. It is the most romantic thing we've ever heard."

Christina could feel her skin heating. Romantic? More like desperation on her part. She could not say why Oliver had agreed to the marriage. All Patricia had said was, *I shall make him understand.* Understand what, exactly?

Unfortunately she would not arrive at an answer until she could get Patricia alone.

Shannon excused herself for the night, a knowing look in her eye as she closed the door. Christina had no clue on what to do while she waited for Oliver. Would he expect her to be waiting under the covers? She tried to breathe through her nerves and uncertainty. People did this nightly, correct? She would be fine. Hopefully.

A small band of light shone from under Oliver's door. He was there. She'd heard him moving about not too long ago. What was he dawdling for? Her heart pounded as she stood there, watching the partition in anticipation.

When fifteen minutes passed, she sat on the edge of her mattress. After another thirty minutes, she smothered a yawn and brushed her hair again. Once an hour had gone by, she grew alarmed. Had she done something wrong?

He had bid her good night after taking great care in showing her the adjoining door to his suites. *If you need anything, anything at all, I am right here*, he had written.

Was she supposed to go to him?

Her knees knocking with trepidation, she glared at the door in the hopes it would suddenly provide answers. Lord, no one had told her a wedding night would be so dashed complicated. Obviously she'd gotten this part wrong.

You are a vessel for his lust. Go, do your duty.

And still she waited, praying for a miracle. A

sign. Locusts, a plague—anything to save her the embarrassment of having to enter his bedroom.

THE FIRE IN Oliver's bedroom blazed, orange-and-red shadows bouncing off the walls, as he relaxed with a healthy glass of brandy, trying to forget the evening's events. Christina's parents had been nothing short of awful.

No wonder Christina had been so eager to marry him, a man she hardly knew. Tomorrow, he'd send a message to the earl and offer him a tidy sum of money to take his wife and leave New York. Perhaps then Christina could breathe easier.

She had appeared exhausted so he escorted her to her new chambers, leaving the staff to see her settled. Tomorrow he would give her a tour and explain the way their marriage would work. It was best they respected each other's privacy from the start—

Movement along the wall caught his eye and he started, his body tense and ready. *Christina.* Oh, Christ. He exhaled, fighting the ever-present fear of never knowing when someone was sneaking up on him. She froze at his expression, instantly contrite, and he tried to keep from showing his irritation.

"Oliver, I am sorry."

"It is fine," he signed. He was unused to any-one other than longtime servants in the house.

The staff was well trained on not startling him. Besides, everyone should be abed at this time of night . . .

So what was she doing here?

He studied her as he came to his feet. A dark blue wrapper engulfed her from head to toe, dragging on the ground like a train. Was that . . . ? Ah, they had given her his dressing gown until her things were brought over.

Waves of brown hair cascaded past her shoulders. The long strands were lovely, thick and lush, as if recently brushed. His fingers itched to touch the silken length, to feel it on his skin. Bare feet peeked out from the silk edges of the dressing gown, revealing delicate, pretty toes. Merely seeing them was too intimate by half. It brought to mind the heat and wetness he could find higher between her legs . . . It had been ages for him, eons it seemed, since he'd last felt a woman's slick warmth. Tasted the sweet tang of her arousal on his tongue. And he had not missed it, not really, until this woman came into his life a week ago.

Yet he could not bed his wife. *She is not really your wife. She is living under the same roof with you for the next year. That is all.*

Even more reason not to bed her.

He set down his glass and clasped his hands. Why was she so pale? Even in the dim light he could see her pallor. "Are you all right?" he signed.

She pushed off the wall and straightened, her neck elongated. "Fine. I . . ." He saw her throat work as she swallowed. "I have been waiting for you."

Waiting for him? He searched his brain for anything he'd promised. What could she possibly think at this hour—

Oh, God almighty. She thought they would consummate the marriage tonight. No wonder she looked on the verge of fainting. "No, we are not doing that," he said, moving closer, his hands signing in time with his voice. He needed her to understand *now* and his pencil was nowhere close.

She cast a quick glance at his enormous bed and then frowned at him. "I am afraid I do not understand."

"Please, sit." He held out an arm toward the chairs by the fire. As much as he wanted her out of his bedroom, he needed to ease her mind first. Perhaps it was best to have this conversation now. "Please, Christina," he signed.

She glided gracefully to the chairs and lowered herself into one. Folding her hands, she waited patiently as he retrieved his ledger and pencil from the dresser and then settled.

"Brandy?" he asked, pointing to his glass.

"No, thank you."

He flipped to a blank page and wrote, *There is no need to consummate our marriage. I think it is best if we remain married for only a year. Then you may still find a decent husband after we separate.*

She accepted the ledger and read. He was not surprised when she reached for the pencil instead of speaking a reply. He sensed she was better able to communicate her thoughts this way, as when explaining about Van Peet. Her hand began to move quickly over the paper. *I do not understand. Married for one year?*

He nodded. *The point was to remove you out from under your parents. We have done that. Now you shall have some time to acclimate to America and decide where you would like to live. I am prepared to give you an obscene amount of money when we annul our marriage. You need not ever worry again.*

He was bewildered when her brow furrowed even further. Had she not found his statement reassuring? *I understand,* she wrote. *That probably makes the most sense. I know you never wanted to marry me. Patricia likely guilted you into it.*

Partially, but guilt had not been the only reason. No use admitting the truth, however, that he'd hated to see her given to another man, especially one like Van Peet. She deserved better. She deserved happiness and love, everything the world could offer. And when she and Oliver separated, she would have the means to find it all.

I never wanted to marry anyone. It had nothing to do with you. However, we are now married so we should discuss how to carry on.

After she finished reading, she wrote. *But I thought for it to be legal . . . ?*

No, he said. *This is not medieval Scotland. No one will inspect the bedsheets in the morning.*

Her skin turned a bright pink at those words. *Oh. You must think I am silly.*

"Absolutely not." He motioned for the ledger, which she promptly returned. *But while you are here, we should discuss our marriage honestly and openly. I do not expect you to cater to me as your real husband. Instead, while we are under the same roof for the next year, I think it best if we live totally separate lives.*

A flash of something crossed her face—annoyance? disappointment?—but then she quickly masked it. "How shall that work?"

He continued pouring his thoughts onto the page. *I keep odd hours and prefer to be by myself. You are free to roam about the house and the grounds, of course, while all I ask is that you respect the privacy of my chambers and the greenhouse. Also, we needn't schedule dinners or outings together. You may come and go as you please. I shall have a healthy allowance set up for you.*

She showed no reaction as she read. This puzzled him. He'd expected relief, to be honest. Especially since she'd come into his room a few minutes ago as if on a march to the guillotine. Clearly, bedding him was not something she yearned to do. So why was she not happy at this news?

"I understand," she said and pushed to her feet.

Something was off, he was certain of it. Over the years, he had learned to watch faces carefully and read into what people did not say. Christina was holding back, bottling up whatever thoughts and feelings she had. "Wait." He stood and took her elbow, turning her to where he could better see her face. "Tell me what is wrong."

"Nothing." She shook her head. "I am quite tired. I shall see you . . . well, at some point, I suppose. Good night, Oliver. Thank you again for rescuing me."

The back of his neck itched as she picked her way across the carpets toward the door. He thought about calling to her, taking it all back. Tossing her on his bed and throwing open her dressing gown. Dragging his tongue across her nipples and down her flat stomach . . .

But where would that leave them?

He hated that she'd been forced to defend him to her parents. *He's deformed. An imbecile, I understand.* The countess's words replayed in his head. How long before Christina tired of making excuses for him, grew tired of trying to force him into her world?

He was too practical, too different to flit about New York society. A deaf man who once possessed hearing was a bit of an anomaly, not quite fitting in anywhere. At deaf school, he'd been the odd one out, always reminded that his late-onset deafness made him different than everyone else.

He remembered sounds and tones, could speak when he wanted, yet he struggled in the hearing world, too. A few gestures and misspoken words would have others snickering at him, humiliation burning his insides.

No, he no longer needed their acceptance or approval. He liked his life, his pursuits. His home. Therefore, it was better to keep his distance from his new wife. They were friends who would separate after a year. He'd done her this favor, but he had no intention of making it permanent.

The sooner she came to terms with that, the better.

Chapter Eight

For the first time in her life, Christina overslept.

The morning after the wedding, she awoke completely on her own, without her mother or a maid rousing her. Oliver, she soon learned, had sent instructions to the staff not to disturb her. She planned to thank him—that is, if she ever saw him.

Perhaps not seeing him this morning was a blessing, considering the humiliation of last night. First, the incident with Van Peet, then her parents. Those paled in comparison, however, to bursting into her new husband's chambers and begging to consummate the marriage.

Lord above, she wanted to die from the embarrassment.

As if that were not awful enough, he'd turned her down. Not that she blamed him, considering he had married her out of pity. She let out a deep breath as she came down the stairs. Pity or not, Oliver had rescued her from a fate worse than death. So if the price was a lonely twelve months inside this huge house she would gladly endure it.

A footman was kind enough to point her in the direction of the breakfast room. As she wandered, she soaked in her surroundings. Oliver's home was stunning, the interior bright and cheery with gleaming wood and shining gold accents. French furniture and Eastern rugs, with flowers every which way one turned. He must have them brought in—unless there was another greenhouse hidden on the property somewhere.

A comfortable house, it was stately without being too ostentatious. The sort of place where children played and laughter could be heard throughout the day. Certainly nothing like her childhood home.

There had been no laughter in the Barclay residence or other children with whom to play. Dark draperies and old, worn furniture had comprised the decor. Anything of value sold off, it was a house in decline, its best years long passed, the only saving grace its location in Mayfair.

Gill was waiting in the breakfast room, along with another footman. "Good morning, madam. Would you care for breakfast?"

She replied in the affirmative and soon she had a steaming cup of tea in front of her, along with a plate piled high with food from the side-board.

"Was there any place in particular you wished to go today, madam?" Gill asked.

She sipped her tea and considered this. An entire city awaited her. She could do *anything*. Go anywhere. There wasn't a soul to stop her or tell her what to do. No one to criticize her or even keep track of her whereabouts.

So why was she not more excited at the prospect of leaving the house?

Her stomach clenched at the thought of aimlessly wandering through crowds and street traffic today. Was it wrong to stay in and explore inside instead? "I have a confession," she said. "I believe I would rather—"

A footman entered the room just then, a stocky older man on his heels. "Mr. Milton Hawkes, madam."

Milton Hawkes? Hawkes, as in Oliver's cousin, the one Shannon had mentioned last night?

"And just who are you?" Mr. Hawkes stopped short and put his hands on his hips. "Some doxy he hired who's overstayed her welcome?"

Christina's jaw fell open, but she quickly recovered. "I am Mrs. Oliver Hawkes."

The man's skin turned the color of snow as his mouth worked. "Did . . . did you say Mrs. Oliver Hawkes?"

"Yes. Mr. Hawkes and I are married."

He staggered and grabbed a chair back. "No, this cannot be. It absolutely cannot be. Oliver would not marry. He's quite determined to remain alone to focus on his inventions."

"The lady speaks the truth." Gill's voice cut through the elegant dining room like a blade. "Mr. Hawkes has taken a bride."

Milton Hawkes raked her with dull greenish-brown eyes that were similar to Oliver's but not nearly as beautiful. "What kind of game are you playing, madam?"

"I—There is no game, sir."

The man drew himself up, standing taller. "I am Oliver's oldest relative, his first cousin. And I am certain you would not have married him unless you have some sort of angle. What, do you hope to bilk him out of his fortune?"

She nearly snorted. If all she cared about was money she would have married Van Peet.

"Mr. Hawkes," Gill snapped. "You must speak to her ladyship with respect, or else Mr. Hawkes shall—"

"Or else Oliver shall what? Make a bunch of hand movements to frighten me?" Milton then sneered at her, his tone frosty. "You may think you are clever, but you will never get that money—"

The terrace doors flew open and Oliver rushed inside, his hair rumpled and windblown. He wore his customary shirtsleeves with the cuffs rolled over his forearms, and she took a moment to appreciate the dusting of dark hair atop rough skin, the muscles and tendons conveying strength. Her chest fluttered, even though she knew he was not hers to ogle.

You are not really married. He made his wishes perfectly clear last night.

His face flushed and taut, Oliver began signing, with Gill translating for Milton. "What are you doing here? We discussed my aversion to unannounced visits the last time you dropped by."

"I have something I wish to discuss with you, cousin. Yet imagine my surprise when I arrive and find that you have married."

The two men stared at one another intently and Oliver's jaw twitched unhappily. He obviously did not care for his cousin and the same could be said for Milton. Oliver's hands moved rapidly and Gill said, "My personal life is hardly your concern."

"Come now, is that any way to treat family? I am your oldest relative, after all. Should I not be friendly with my cousin's wife?"

That seemed to make Oliver angrier. "I do not want you talking to my wife. Do not even breathe her name. She does not exist. Do we understand one another?"

Christina deflated, her shoulders dropping. Well, that certainly illuminated the situation. *He wishes to live separate lives. What did you think, that he would show you off on his arm?* Not exactly, but she had not expected to be treated as a ghost, either. She rubbed her temples, the pressure behind them now thumping like a drum.

Why had she left the comfort of her new bed?

Perhaps she'd go lie down for a bit. Wait for the pain in her head to ease before attempting the remainder of her day. She lifted her chin and gave the room a wan smile. "If you will excuse me." She moved steadily toward the door, her feet heavy and awkward.

"Mr. Hawkes wishes to know if you are unwell, madam," Gill called after her.

"No, I am fine," she said without breaking her stride or looking back. "I am merely giving Mr. Hawkes his privacy."

OLIVER WATCHED CHRISTINA's retreating back, wondering over the sadness he thought he detected in her expression. She hadn't actually wanted to stay and talk to Milton, had she? His cousin was a pustule on the arse of the Hawkes family tree. Oliver would do anything and everything to keep them apart.

Milton Hawkes, his first cousin. Distaste curdled Oliver's stomach. The man visited every six months or so and, depending on Oliver's mood, he would either see his cousin briefly or refuse the visit. If memory served, he'd rejected the last two. When would Milton get the hint?

Milton treated Oliver as if he were a half-wit. In Milton's eyes, Oliver's deafness meant he could be manipulated. Lied to. Flimflammed. And Milton would do just about anything to get his hands on the Hawkes fortune, a fortune to which he had absolutely no right. However, for the sake of his late father, Oliver tried to be patient with Milton. Their fathers had grown up alongside one another and even started the family business together. It was after Milton's father backed out that Oliver's father had made his fortune, taking risks that his brother had forbidden.

Past history aside, however, Oliver would not allow Milton to harass Christina.

He glared at his cousin. "What did you say to her?" Gill translated Oliver's question, seeing as how Milton refused to learn sign language after all these years and Oliver refused to make anything easy for Milton.

"Nothing untoward," Milton said, hooking his thumbs into his vest pockets. "We were merely getting to know one another. Now, this marriage seems a bit rushed, Oliver. Are you certain this is best for you?"

Why was Milton addressing Oliver as if he were a child? "When was the last time you concerned yourself with what was best for me?" he signed.

"We are family. You know I always look out for you. Where did you meet her?"

This was absurd. "Why are you in my house?" he signed. "What on earth do you want?"

"I know you are able to speak, Oliver. Why do you insist on doing this?" Milton proceeded to do a series of absurd hand movements that meant absolutely nothing—other than as an insult to the entire deaf community.

Oliver seriously considered punching his cousin in the face. "Get to the point, Milton."

Milton rocked on his heels and cast a meaningful glance at Gill. "Perhaps it could wait until we are alone?"

"Gill stays. You have ten seconds to spit it out and then I am leaving."

When another few seconds dragged by in silence, Oliver clapped his hands once and started to turn away. As expected, Milton's lips began moving. "Wait! Do not leave. I was just trying to think how best to explain this opportunity I have come upon. It is a large alpaca farm in Kansas—"

Confused, Oliver looked at Gill. "What kind of farm?" he signed.

Gill spelled *a-l-p-a-c-a* with his fingers, mirth dancing in the butler's eyes. Oliver sighed and signed, "Absolutely not. I am not interested. And there are no alpacas in the United States. Whoever is trying to sell you on this farm is lying."

The butler relayed the message and anger flashed across Milton's face before he masked it. "I have seen the reports. The alpacas were imported from Peru. Their wool is stronger than a sheep's. Soon it will be in high demand."

Oliver signed, "The reports are false. Even if they were true, there is no market for alpaca wool here."

"All I need is a five-thousand-dollar invest-ment," Milton persevered after Gill translated.

Oliver plucked a blackberry from the sideboard and tossed it in his mouth. "My answer remains no. Was that all, cousin?"

Milton's cheeks flushed, his mustache twitch-ing in anger. "You know, I am the one who de-fends you, the one who says they are wrong when they call you insane. You might think about what happens if I stop preventing the Hawkes name from turning into a taproom joke."

"Those threats grow weary," Oliver signed. "I do not give a damn about the Hawkes name."

"You do not, but your sister might." Mouth pressed tightly, Milton stomped out of the room and disappeared into the corridor.

Oliver exhaled and selected another black-berry. Gill started to follow Milton to the door, but Oliver held up a hand to stay him. "What did he say to her?"

The butler shifted uncomfortably. "He called her a doxy, sir," he said. "Asked her what her an-gle was, if she was after your fortune."

"A doxy," he signed, certain his lip-reading must be incorrect. Gill nodded, his troubled eyes conveying his displeasure, and Oliver's body clenched, anger erupting behind his sternum like molten lava. *That miserable fuck* . . . Milton could call Oliver an imbecile and insane all he liked. But call his wife a doxy? No, absolutely not.

How dare Milton say anything distasteful in

this house? He avoided the poorhouse on Oliver's charity alone. Was his cousin so stupid as to infuriate his only source of income?

The question was clearly redundant. Milton was absolutely that stupid.

"I shall talk to her," Oliver signed. "In the meantime, ensure Milton is gone."

Certain Gill would handle his cousin, Oliver wasted no time in climbing the stairs and heading to Christina's rooms. He rapped on the door.

Within a few seconds the door opened. Christina stepped aside and he strode into her bedroom. Strange seeing his mother's old room in use again, but the sight did not upset him. No, the idea of Christina here, in these rooms adjoining his, appealed to him probably more than it should. His eyes were immediately drawn to the bed. *She'll be lying there at night, soft and warm, her big eyes drowsy with sleep . . .*

Heat spiked in his blood but he pushed those thoughts out of his head. Beautiful as she might be, this was a temporary arrangement. He was to protect her, not debauch her.

He faced her and signed as he spoke, "Are you all right?"

She nodded, though her expression remained guarded. "I am fine," she signed as he'd taught her.

Her efforts at signing twisted something in his chest. Sign language was about the face, the expression, of the person signing and Christina had the loveliest face he'd ever seen. He could stare at it for days and still find her fascinating. Watching her lips and mouth, her brow furrowed in concentration, was nearly like foreplay to him.

Christ, he was in a bad way over this woman. *All the more reason to stay away from her.*

"Milton is an idiot," he said while signing. "I apologize if he upset you."

She lifted a shoulder as if Milton's rudeness was nothing of consequence. "I had not realized . . . that is, I had not considered your family and what they might think of our marriage."

"Milton is more worm than man. I care nothing for what he thinks."

When she frowned, he grew worried. Had his voice betrayed him, his remark unintelligible? He withdrew the ledger and pencil from his pocket and started to write what he'd tried to say. Her hand on his arm stopped him. "I heard what you said perfectly, but I do not understand."

"Milton is angry and unbalanced," he said. "I had thought to spare you any distress from engaging with him."

"Truly?"

The side of his mouth hitched. "Truly."

Some of the light in her eyes returned, her shoulders relaxing, and Oliver smiled. She asked for the ledger and pencil. *I know we are to live separately and I shall try to stay out of your way. But I cannot hide or disappear—*

He put his hand over hers, stopping her. "I would never ask you to hide or disappear," he said. "This is your home for the next year. I wish for you to feel comfortable."

She glanced down at where their hands touched and Oliver realized he hadn't released her. "My apologies," he said and pulled away.

Color dotted her cheeks as she folded her hands together. "It is quite all right."

The moment stretched and he needed to return to his workshop. Why was he standing here, searching his brain for a topic to discuss with her? She likely had unpacking to do and—

"Your things," he said. "Have they arrived yet?" Oliver had sent a letter this morning to the earl to reach a settlement on the marriage. He'd also requested Christina's things be brought over.

"No, not yet. Have you heard from my father?"

"I have not." It had only been a few hours, but Oliver had assumed the earl would jump at the money. Oliver had offered Christina's parents a small fortune to go away and leave her alone. What were they waiting for?

"Perhaps I should go there, to hurry things along?"

He dragged a hand across his forehead. She should not go alone, in his opinion. He did not trust her parents. "Give it a bit more time. I will accompany you, if it comes to that."

"You will?"

From her shocked expression it was clear she had taken his separate lives speech last night quite literally. Perhaps he had been too harsh. "Of course. I would not want you to go alone."

A slow smile stretched across her face, and something shifted, amplified, in Oliver's chest, like he had been rewired from alternating current to direct current. His whole body became keenly aware of her. Aware of her movements, her sweet perfume, every blink of her long lashes.

He must retreat. Now.

Turning, he started toward the door. When he pulled on the latch he happened to glance over his shoulder. Christina stared off at nothing, looking vacant and lost. *She's in a strange house, in a strange room. Married to a stranger who told her to basically disappear.*

Guilt punched through him, an ache in the pit of his belly. "Have dinner with me tonight," he said, though everything screamed it was a mistake. They needed more space between them, not less.

You are falling for her.

Her eyes rounded, hope blooming on her face . . . and the tension inside him eased. "Yes," she said. "I would like that."

He dipped his chin and departed, closing the door behind him. Like an idiot, he had invited her to dinner. Just how in God's name was he supposed to remain aloof tonight?

BY THAT AFTERNOON, Christina's things had arrived from the Kanes' house—along with Patricia. Christina ordered tea and the two cousins settled into Oliver's drawing room.

"This is lovely," Patricia said, glancing around at the French antiques and blue-papered walls. "Really, who knew recluses lived so well?"

"I was not aware of his wealth when we met."

"Goodness, of course not. But Mother says his fortune rivals Mr. Morgan's—and Mr. Hawkes is certainly more handsome. Well done, Christina."

The praise was unearned. She and Oliver were not a love match. "I never intended to marry him."

"I know. I am teasing." Patricia reached over to clasp Christina's hand. "Honestly, I came today to apologize. I am truly sorry for inadvertently leading your parents here. They came with my mother, casually inquiring about your friends and acquaintances. They tricked me."

This sounded like something Christina's parents would do. "What did you tell them?"

"At that point, I had no idea you'd gone missing. I did not see the harm in mentioning your morning walks. If I had known, Christina, I never would have said anything about Mr. Hawkes. Please, forgive me."

"I do not blame you. I cannot even regret coming here because returning home equalled marriage to Van Peet."

"Things happen for a reason, cousin, and I am ecstatic for you. You deserve a good man, and you have found one."

Before Christina could reply, two maids entered, both carrying large trays. Soon she and her cousin were surrounded by tea and all manner of sandwiches and cakes.

Patricia placed two almond cookies and one cream puff on her plate. "You were saying Mr. Hawkes was quite handsome . . ."

Christina poured the tea. "I said no such thing."

"Well, I know his looks have not gone unnoticed. I saw the way you gazed at him last night."

"And how was that?"

"Like I am now staring at the cream puff on my plate."

Christina could not help but laugh. "You are incorrigible."

"True, but you love me."

"Yes, I do. So what did my parents say last night after you mentioned my visits here?"

"They were livid—up until the point when my mother explained about the Hawkes fortune. Then they began scheming on how to get him to marry you."

The tea turned bitter in Christina's mouth. She forced it down anyway. "That sounds like them." Undoubtedly they had thought it would be easy. Little had they known Oliver would refuse. "However did you get him to agree, by the way?"

"I wore him down. Adorable man wanted to do the right thing but merely needed a little push."

Christina frowned into her teacup. What a mess she had made of things. Poor Oliver. His entire life had now been upended, thanks to her.

"So tell me," Patricia continued. "What is it like being married to a person who cannot hear?"

"It has not even been a full day," Christina pointed out. "My insight into marriage is woefully thin, I am afraid."

"You know what I mean," her cousin said before biting into a cream puff. "What about in the bedroom?"

Christina choked on a bite of cookie and Patricia chuckled. "Come now. You are married. It is your duty to tell us unmarried types what it is really like. You know my mother never will. She keeps saying I will learn to like it. That only begs more questions in my mind."

"Oliver and I have not . . . That is, we are not that kind of married."

"Oh." Patricia wiped her fingers on a linen napkin. "He seemed perfectly healthy to me last night. Is he unable to . . . perform because of his condition?"

"He is deaf, not disfigured," Christina whispered. "Besides, he has not even kissed me."

"*What?* Oh, my dear Tina. You must do something about that. As in today."

"Why?"

"Why?"

"Yes, why do I need him to kiss me?"

Patricia's gaze went soft. "Because it is like breathing for two. You are inseparable. It is impossible to tell where you end and he begins, and your mind clouds over and all you are able to concentrate on is his mouth. Your body breaks out in a fever, like your clothes are too tight everywhere, and you cannot get enough, just need to get closer to him." She fanned her face with her hand. "Merely thinking on it makes me wish to track Felton down at his club and steal him away to somewhere private."

Christina had to admit the description seemed enticing. Would Oliver ever kiss her? He'd made it clear they would not consummate the marriage—but then he had also said they would live separate lives before inviting her to dinner tonight. So who knew where things stood? "I shall let you do the kissing for both of us. Oliver has no interest in me like that, not in a physical way. We are friends. He has agreed to marry me for a year, long enough to get me away from the earl and countess. Then we shall have the marriage annulled and go our separate ways."

"A year? Then annulment? I do not believe you."

"He considers me a friend in need of assistance. That is all."

Patricia threw her head back and laughed. "You cannot honestly think that."

"Why would I not?"

Patricia's brows rose, her eyes rounding. "I saw the way he looked at you last night. It was not the way a friend stares at another friend. Remember what I said about the cream puff? Trust me, he is attracted to you."

"That cannot be true." Oliver had no interest in anything romantic with her.

"Have you looked in a mirror recently?"

Of course, though Christina never liked what was reflected there. She always wished for different this and something else that.

"Tina, you are beautiful," Patricia said. "Have you not seen the jealous looks the other girls give you at parties?"

No, she hadn't. Those looks were daggers to keep her at a distance, more proof that she did not measure up as someone worth befriending. The men had stared as well, but in a way that made her uncomfortable. She had hated those gatherings.

Patricia slid closer and clasped Christina's hand. "I have never been more grateful to a recluse in all my life. Thank goodness you are away from your parents. Perhaps you will start to see yourself in a different, more flattering light. The way I—and your new husband—see you."

The reference to Oliver caused Christina to shake her head. "You are relentless."

"True, and I think all your situation with Mr. Hawkes needs is time."

Christina wished that were the case, that Oliver could be hers, if even for a moment. He was kind and intelligent. Handsome and strong. Had faced so much adversity and triumphed—unlike her, who had turned into a timid mouse. He could teach her so much, if only he would try.

She recalled the day he'd shown her to knee a man between the legs. The way he had held her and looked at her . . . Had there been something in his eyes, a hint of desire for her? It seemed so implausible, but her cousin might be right. Perhaps they merely needed time.

"I have two friends I wish for you to meet," Patricia said, setting her saucer down and rising. "They are clever and fun. You will like them, I promise. Would you join us for ice cream sometime?"

Christina thought about venturing outside the house. She might enjoy a short outing with her cousin in an intimate gathering, but she was terrible at meeting new people. "That is probably a bad idea."

"Nonsense. These two are close to our age and they have just returned from Paris. I swear they are nothing like those horrible girls you met during your debut." Patricia leaned in. "And if you refuse I will tell your husband of my cream puff theory."

"Patricia! You'll do no such thing."

"So you will come?"

Christina sighed. "Let me know when and I shall do my best to be there."

"Fine, but I expect you to show up. After all,

we must discuss ways to lure your new husband into kissing you."

"No, we absolutely will not."

Her cousin smiled sweetly. "Yes, we will. Indeed, if it is the last thing I do, I will have that recluse eating out of the palm of your hand."

Chapter Nine

She took extra care with her appearance that evening.

Shannon, Christina's new maid, was a pleasant change, with plenty of kind words and sound advice. Christina found the young girl's demeanor relaxing and the two were soon laughing together. She'd never had cause to laugh with a servant before, not even back in London, where the staff had been familiar but much more interested in currying the countess's favor than the happiness of a small child.

From Shannon's tales, Christina learned that Oliver cared about his staff, treating them much more like family members than hired help. It made sense, she supposed, that a recluse would come to appreciate those around him, as they were the only source of contact. Besides, Oliver was kind and generous, no doubt a fair employer.

"Mr. Hawkes, now he usually eats with Mr. Gill or by himself," Shannon was saying as she fastened the tiny buttons of Christina's evening gown. It was the best Christina owned, an ivory silk with a demure neckline and a coral under-skirt. Matching coral roses were sewn into the bustle and train. Of course, she had a harder time enjoying the dress since realizing Lord Avington had been duped into paying for it.

Shannon finished and went to fetch Christina's gloves. "It'll be nice to have a wife here to eat with him instead."

When the gloves were buttoned, Christina started for the door. "Wait, madam," Shannon called. "What about jewelry?"

Christina glanced over her shoulder. "Oh, I have none. My parents . . . well, the pieces are gone now." No use explaining how everything had been sold back in England.

"But Mr. Hawkes, he had a box of it sent up. Have you not seen it?" Shannon walked to the tiny dressing table and picked up a dark blue velvet case Christina hadn't even noticed.

When the lid opened, Christina's jaw dropped. There were hundreds of glittering stones staring up at her, jewels of all colors and sizes. Neck-laces, bracelets, ear bobs . . . she could not wrap her head around it all. Where had they come from? Had he purchased these things? "Did all this belong to his mother?"

"And grandmother, from what I understand. The Hawkeses are an old New York family. Would you like to try on some of it?"

"I couldn't . . . it is all too precious."

"Nonsense. Mr. Hawkes had them delivered for you to wear. And you are his wife. It is only fitting."

Even when she owned jewelry, none of the pieces had been this lavish. These jewels were meant to stun, to draw every eye in the room. She would feel foolish wearing them, even if she craved the attention. "I would rather—"

Before she could finish her sentence, Shannon dropped a diamond choker around Christina's throat. "There," the maid said. "Now you are perfect."

No amount of protesting would dissuade the maid, and Christina, helpless with her gloves on, resigned to leave the choker in place. The stones glittered garishly in the mirror, an unaccustomed sight to her eyes. She fought the need to cover the piece as she went down to dinner.

Oliver waited at the bottom of the main stairs, head bent as he stared at his toes. He wore just shirtsleeves tonight, no coat, with a slate-gray waistcoat covering his chest. A black necktie and trousers completed the ensemble. On anyone else the outfit would have seemed dark and somber, but somehow instead it came off sleek and elegant, as if he could step into the dining room of Delmonico's or Sherry's. How did he manage such effortless confidence?

Conversely, she felt like a fool. She had assumed he would dress for dinner, so she'd asked her maid to press her best gown. Had taken care with her hair. There was a fortune in diamonds draped around her neck. She was completely overdressed, acting as if this were a true romantic evening between husband and wife instead of two people merely sharing a meal together.

Idiot.

She stopped and decided to disappear back up the stairs—but Oliver's head snapped up at that moment, his gaze widening as it traveled the length of her. When he finally caught her stare, his eyes were dark, hooded, and filled with a heat that curled her toes in her evening slippers.

Patricia's words from earlier came back to mind. *Trust me, he is attracted to you.*

Based on this stare alone, Christina might be tempted to believe it. But if such a thing were true, then why turn her away last evening? If he desired her, refusing to consummate the marriage made no sense.

He closed his eyes and drew in a deep breath. Her skin burned with humiliation as she stood there. She longed to dash up the stairs, strip all this off, and forget the whole evening.

His lids opened, revealing familiar clear and bright green irises with none of the heat from before. Had she imagined it? "Good evening," he signed, then smiled and held out his arm.

He has already seen you. No use in hiding now.

She heaved a sigh and gestured to her attire. "I feel silly. I thought I was to dress for dinner."

"You look lovely," he signed and spoke at the same time. "You did nothing wrong."

"It will only take a moment to change." She lifted the hem of her skirts and prepared to turn around.

"There is no need for that. Come down and let us eat."

Admitting failure, she descended the stairs and placed her palm on his forearm. As they moved to the dining room, she could feel the strong tendons and powerful muscles shift in his arm, an intimacy that caused her heart to race.

He seated her at his right, not the opposite end of the table as was customary. She recalled he'd done the same last night. *Another example of the lack of formality here.*

He waved at the footman to begin service. "It is my fault for not telling you. I never wear a coat unless it is absolutely necessary."

She should have known. He'd worn a coat for their wedding but that was the only time in their acquaintance he had bothered. "I will remember for next time."

He winced ever so slightly and she could have bitten her tongue. Of course there would be no next time. They were to live separately, not as husband and wife. Yet another mistake on her part.

Silence descended as dinner service began. Gill poured the wine while a footman delivered a silver platter bearing the first course of oysters.

His brow furrowed, Oliver signed to Gill. The butler set the decanter down and signed back. No one spoke so Christina could not follow the conversation, however Oliver's lips were pressed into an unhappy line as his hands moved in response. Clearly this was a disagreement of some kind, but over what?

After their terse exchange, Gill threw up his hands and instructed Michael to place all the food on the table. Soon dishes of all types—from soup and roast duck, carrots and parsnips, to broiled salmon—covered the surface of the wooden table. She struggled to take it all in. Were they feeding the staff as well?

"Select whatever you'd like," Oliver said when they were alone.

She touched his arm as he reached for the oysters. "Were you and Gill having a disagreement?"

"No. I merely prefer to serve myself."

Ah. So the butler had wanted to serve à la russe, as was customary in England. It was more formal and required the help of the servants to move dinner along. Was Oliver so anxious to get this over with, then?

If he found her so repulsive, then what about that spark in his gaze earlier?

She gave a quick shake of her head, attempting to clear it. Married not even a full day and she could affirm that husbands were dashed confusing.

"Are you planning to eat?"

She looked up from her empty plate to find Oliver already scraping the bottom of his soup bowl. "Yes, of course. Though I daresay not as quickly as you."

He had the grace to appear abashed as he ladled soup into a bowl for her. "I apologize," he signed after passing her the bowl. "It is usually just me."

She tried the soup while watching his hands, the long, graceful fingers dusted with dark brown hair between the first and second knuckle. Competent hands. Not the hands of a gentleman or a laborer, but somewhere in between. He fascinated her, always had, yet they barely knew one another. She had so many questions about his parents, his childhood, losing his hearing, his inventions . . . Her life seemed positively boring in comparison. She vowed to get answers before this year was out.

"Would you like a tour of the house after dinner?"

Blinking, she tore her attention away from his hands. "Yes, I should like that very much."

FOR A SUPPOSED smart man, Oliver continued to
act the complete fool around Christina. At dinner, she'd been closed off, remote, barely eating
and staring strangely at his hands. Guilt had
again nagged at him—guilt and responsibility.
Perhaps it was the desire to crack the shell that
seemed to surround her, to help her feel comfortable in her new home.

*Or perhaps you merely want to spend more time
with her.*

Yes, he could admit it. There was something
about her quiet, reserved nature that intrigued
him. He needed to learn what drove her, what
interested her . . . all the various parts that comprised this complex woman. She was a puzzle
and he could not resist.

A gorgeous puzzle, if truth was told. When
he'd first spotted her tonight, a heart-stopping
visage in her fitted silk gown and his mother's
diamonds, his body had instantly reacted. *My
wife*, a voice deep inside him whispered, and
blood had started pumping, heat gathering between his legs to thicken his cock. Only closing
his eyes and thinking very bland thoughts had
caused the moment to pass. The whole thing had
been damned near embarrassing.

Then he'd foolishly suggested a tour of the
house. And after she had eagerly accepted, he
hadn't the heart to rescind the offer even though
it would prolong their evening together.

However, now they were nearly done, thank

God, with only one room remaining between him and the ability to excuse himself for the night. Then he could gain reprieve from her scent, the brush of her skirts against his leg, and the way she bit her lower lip when concentrating.

That lower lip had plagued him all evening.

Not that he had rushed the tour. He'd shown her the entire house, even the areas belonging to the staff, and saved his favorite room for last. The portrait gallery was a square space in the middle of the first floor, with four walls of stacked paintings in heavy gilded frames. Long sofas and deep chairs were strategically placed in the middle of the room to create a cozy spot, one he often employed to merely sit and contemplate.

The room was a bittersweet reminder of his parents. His mother had collected these paintings over years of travels and he knew the story behind each one. Not all were the works of great masters; some were from local artists peddling art directly on the street. His mother had often said that magic could be found in unexpected places.

Christina was moving slowly, carefully studying the sixty-six paintings, her lovely brow furrowed in concentration. He did not interrupt, just let her explore in peace. Eventually she stopped in front of a canvas with red-and-purple streaks, staring at it intently, and he was immediately drawn to her side. "What do you think?" he asked and signed at the same time. Even as he used his voice more and more with her, he still found it easier to sign as he spoke.

With her face in profile, he only saw her mouth move. He tapped her shoulder. "I need to see your face." She spun so quickly that she wobbled. He caught her shoulders, steadying her, and chuckled. "Easy."

She bit her lip once more and gave him an adorably sheepish smile, one that he felt in the pit of his stomach. "It is a bleeding heart, is it not?"

Distracted, he missed what she said. "A . . . I am sorry. What?"

"The painting. It looks like a bleeding heart."

He glanced at the painting over her shoulder. His mother had purchased it in Montmartre some twenty years ago. "It is called *Sunset over Cape Town*."

She craned her neck to see the painting and he realized he was still holding on to her. He dropped his hands but did not move away.

"I love it," she said when she faced him. "This painting could represent anything. The interpretation is up to the person viewing it."

He turned toward the image, trying to see the bold colors as something other than a sunset over water. He even squinted his eyes but could not do it. The artist's vision was completely clear. "It is a sunset."

She stepped in front of him, blocking his view of the painting. "Then you are not trying. Here," she said and then moved around, out of sight.

He started to follow, but she held his shoulders to keep him in place. Soft, slender fingers slid over his eyes as her front pressed against his back. The world went dark as his lids fell—and he tensed. He hated having his eyes covered, one more sense deprived him.

This is Christina. Breathe, Oliver.

He forced himself to relax, unclenching his hands.

With his vision hindered, his entire focus became her gentle touch, the swells of her breasts molded to his back as she balanced on the balls of her feet. He could feel the rise and fall of her chest, the warm breath on the skin of his neck. Her smell wrapped around him, a light and flowery scent that intoxicated him far more than the champagne at dinner. Desire raced through his veins, with his heart pounding so hard he could feel it in every part of his body.

Had she any idea of what she was doing to him?

Just when he thought it might be too much to take, her hands slid from his eyes and she waited, perfectly still, behind him. The painting was there, a blur of colors and shapes, his gaze unfocused, and then suddenly everything aligned into a heart on its side, the organ oozing onto the canvas in a trickle of deep purple. How remarkable. Never in his life had this painting arranged itself in such a fashion. It was like seeing the work for the first time, a complete revelation to an image he'd been quite familiar with.

Everything different. Everything rearranged. Exactly as she had done to him.

He nearly vibrated with excitement, his body alive with the thrill of discovery as well as an appreciation for this clever, unusual woman. Spinning, he stepped closer, not stopping until her front met his chest. Her gaze went wide with surprise, the gold flecks of her irises shimmering with heat. She did not retreat, merely stood as he crowded her, and the air suddenly left the room.

All that existed were the two of them, alone.

What he wanted in that moment nearly overwhelmed him, so much that he shook with it. He wanted to pull this woman, his wife, into his arms and kiss her. Tonight. Every night. Whenever he wished, damn it. Because the urge to kiss her right now was undoing him, building into a living thing he could almost touch and feel. This beautiful, clever woman who had endured so much, yet had not buckled.

She waited patiently to see where this led. Hell if Oliver knew the answer. Indecision rioted inside him, a cacophony of thoughts and desires he had not experienced in a long time. He was desperately hard now, his erection aching in the confinement of his clothing, yet he could not consider slaking his base needs on this innocent girl. She had been placed in his keeping for only a short time.

She does not belong to you.

The muscles in his arms strained at the effort to keep from touching her. He'd imagined it often in the past few days, the warm and soft texture of her skin. Her nipples, her backside. The slick folds between her legs. He desperately longed to discover those secrets for himself.

Her lips began forming words and he had to suck in a lungful of air before he could concentrate. "What are you doing?" she asked.

"I do not know," he answered honestly. "Being foolish."

"By staring at me?"

He dropped back a step. Staring at her was the least of what he wished to do at the moment. He'd rather start with removing all her clothing and finish by tasting her orgasm on his tongue. Swallowing, he closed his eyes and settled for some deep breathing instead. Clearly, he had gone far too long with only his hand for company. If he were not so starved for a woman, he'd be able to ignore Christina.

Liar, a voice in his head said.

Still, he absolutely could not sleep with her. She must remain intact to ensure a good match after the annulment instead of scandal.

A tap on his arm had him opening his eyes. Concern lined Christina's brow. "Did I upset you? With the painting?"

"No. I was astounded, not upset."

Her bottom lip disappeared between her teeth for a moment. Christ, he wished she would stop doing that. "Sometimes it is hard to tell what you are thinking."

"A common complaint, I am afraid." The result of spending most of his time alone. He had to work to communicate with others, an effort he often forgot to expend. "I shall try to do better with you."

"Because we are friends."

He nodded, a bit desperately. "Yes, of course. Because we are friends."

"If we are friends then will you always be honest with me?"

"Yes, of course," he answered without hesitation. Indeed, whatever she asked, he would not lie to her, not about her parents or Van Peet. No matter how distasteful the subject, she deserved the truth.

"Were you . . ." Another nibble on her lip caused his breath to catch. "Were you about to kiss me a moment ago?"

His jaw fell open. No wonder she had requested honesty—not that he could give it in this instance. He merely had to do a better job at hiding his own desires, burying them deep until they no longer arose at inopportune moments. Like now. "I promised I would not."

It was an evasion and he hated himself for it, especially when her shoulders fell slightly. Was she disappointed? All the more reason not to tell her the truth. They both had to remember what was between them for this to work.

She lifted her chin and straightened her spine. Her gaze fixed on his forehead. "I feel a bit tired. Would you mind if I cut our tour short?"

"Of course not. I shall show you to your rooms."

Chapter Ten

"Christina! Over here!"

Christina had just stepped into Morrison's Broadway Ice Cream Saloon when the feminine shout caught her attention. She spotted Patricia at a small wooden table near the back. The large room was packed with diners and tables, not an empty seat to be found, and all the moisture left Christina's mouth. She hated crowds. She also disliked meeting new people and making small talk, which was why she wished she'd never allowed Patricia to blackmail her into coming today.

Two young women were already sitting at Patricia's table. These were clearly the two friends her cousin had mentioned, the ones she'd wanted Christina to meet.

Was it too late to turn around and return home? Well, Oliver's home. At least there she could be alone and not have to deal with this cacophony. God knew Oliver wanted nothing to do with her.

Her husband had disappeared after the night of the house tour. In the two days since, he had not joined her for breakfast, tea service, or supper. She had considered going to the greenhouse to visit him, but remembered his request when they married. *All I ask is that you respect the privacy of my chambers and the greenhouse.* He'd made it clear those two places were reserved just for him.

Friend. He is only a friend. Yes, and if a little flutter erupted in the region of her heart every time she thought of him, it was best ignored. She could not allow herself to believe foolish things when it came to her husband. They were friends and she liked spending time with him. That was all. She could have sworn he felt the same about her, but she was obviously wrong. It was clear he preferred to be left alone.

Patricia appeared in front of her, clearly thinking Christina had not seen or heard her seconds ago, and several pairs of eyes were now watching them. "Hello. I am so glad you came," Patricia said, leaning in to kiss Christina's cheek.

"I know I am late. Perhaps I should go home and we may do this another time. You have probably already ordered and—"

"No, silly. We waited for you. No one has ordered yet." She reached for Christina's elbow. "Come along. I shall introduce you."

Short of tearing her arm free and making a scene, there was nothing Christina could do to prevent the inevitable.

Just go. It cannot turn out as terrible as you fear.
She hoped, anyway.

Patricia led them past table after table of well-dressed women. It was a gay scene, with every-one eating and laughing, waiters carrying trays bearing treats. Christina wished she could relax and that her tongue did not feel like a dry old carpet.

Patricia gestured to the two women at the table. "Tina, allow me to introduce Miss Kathleen Appleton and her cousin, Miss Anne Elliot. Friends, this is my wonderful cousin, Lady Christina—oh." Patricia covered her mouth, her eyes twinkling. "Mrs. Oliver Hawkes."

The two strangers nearly fell out of their chairs. "Wait—Oliver Hawkes?" The one called Kathleen gripped the table, her eyes round. "Hawkes, as in the big house right next to Patricia? Is he the recluse?"

"He is not a recluse," Christina said, for some reason feeling obligated to lie on Oliver's behalf. She lowered herself into the empty chair and settled her skirts.

"Oh, do tell." Anne put an elbow on the table and leaned in. "What is he like?"

"Before we start asking her a thousand questions, we must order." Patricia nodded at the waiter hovering nearby. "What is everyone having today?"

Christina studied the menu, frowning. The last thing she needed was to drop ice cream on her best day dress, giving everyone a great chuckle over her clumsiness. Once, she had sat on a chocolate bonbon, leaving an awkward brown stain on her dress. Her mother had refused to lend her a shawl to wrap around her waist on the walk home, saying the taunts from the other children would serve Christina right for being so inept.

"Pistachio for me," Anne said, waving away the menu.

"I like their tutti-frutti. Two scoops for me," Kathleen told the waiter.

"I shall have orange sherbet." Patricia held out the menu to Christina. "Tina?"

She shook her head. "No, thank you."

"You must order something." Patricia frowned. "It is tradition."

Make an effort. Try to fit in with the other girls. She thought of the plainest flavor, one that might disappear on her clothing. "Vanilla, please." The waiter nodded and then disappeared.

"Now, we were discussing your husband." Anne rubbed her gloved hands together. She had brown hair and blue eyes, with her afternoon dress a matching shade of blue. "You said he's not a recluse."

"No. He is deaf. I think he merely finds it easier to stay home."

"Deaf," Kathleen repeated. Her blonde looks were quite different than her cousin's, but she was dressed just as smartly. "Fascinating. How do you two communicate?"

"That is not the most important question to ask a new bride," Anne said to her cousin before turning to Christina. "Is he handsome and is he a good kisser?"

Christina felt her skin heating. "I . . ." She looked at Patricia for help.

"You must forgive Anne," Patricia said. "She is frightfully direct."

"Always," Anne confirmed. "I cannot help myself. Father says I shall never find a husband to put up with my smart mouth."

Kathleen elbowed her cousin. "Remember what Aunt Ada said: men like women with smart mouths."

"No, she said 'busy' mouths," Anne said, chuckling. "And we all know what *that* means."

No, Christina wanted to say. *I haven't a clue what that means.* Was it something prurient? Goodness, how she hated feeling stupid.

"You must forgive her." Kathleen patted Christina's arm. "She has never learned the ability to censor herself. You need not answer her."

"Especially since you do not know the answer," Patricia said.

Christina thought about the way Oliver's eyes had darkened in the portrait gallery, how he'd stared at her mouth so intently, and she bit her lip. He had been thinking about kissing her, she was nearly certain.

Not that he had admitted it when she asked.

Patricia gasped. "You do know! When did that happen?"

Several heads swiveled their way and Christina wanted to crawl under the table. "Shh, you are drawing attention to us."

"Let them gawk," Patricia said, though she did shift forward and lower her voice. "Wait, you finally kissed Oliver. I must hear the details."

The other girls leaned in as well, and Christina blinked. They had just met yet these two appeared equally invested in the conversation. She had not expected that. Clearing her throat, she said, "He did not kiss me, but . . . but I think he wanted to."

"I knew it." Patricia sat back, her expression smug. "Your husband is fond of you."

"Why would he not be fond of her?" Anne's gaze darted between Patricia and Christina. "I feel as though I am missing something."

"You need to seduce him," Patricia said, ignoring Anne's question.

Christina shook her head vehemently, memories of the wedding night returning to singe her skin with mortification. "I could never, not in a million years. I would die of embarrassment."

The waiter arrived with their orders and talk around the table switched to a comparison of the various flavors. The other three all swapped dishes to try each flavor. Christina kept to her vanilla, taking extreme care not to get any ice cream on her clothing.

"So your husband." Anne pointed her spoon at Christina. "What do you plan to do?"

"Nothing. I have not seen him in almost two days. He has disappeared."

Silence descended until Kathleen blurted, "He is a recluse. How far could he have gone?"

"He asked me to respect his privacy. I am attempting to do so."

"I had not thought husbands were allowed privacy," Kathleen said, glancing at the other two women for confirmation.

Anne lifted one shoulder. "Perhaps when it comes to their mistresses, but not inside their homes."

"Anne!" Patricia covered her mouth, her expression dancing with mirth. "I cannot believe you just said that."

"Yet you know I am right. Christina, you should corner him. Ask what is happening between the two of you."

"Unless you do not wish for anything to happen," Patricia said, watching Christina's face carefully. "But I think you do. I think you are sweet on Mr. Hawkes."

"I am not," Christina said. "He has been very kind, is all." His hot stare had been very kind indeed, kind enough to send her entire body up in flames. She had been close to melting into a puddle on the floor.

"Like a cream puff," Patricia muttered, eyes

assessing Christina's face. "So what would you do, Anne?"

"I would find him and ask why he is so hot and cold with me. Preferably at night, wearing something revealing."

"Yes, I like that idea," Kathleen said. "Or better yet, wear nothing at all." All three girls broke out into giggles.

Christina did not share in the merriment. She would rather die than confront Oliver about this. He had made his position quite clear and remained determined to resist whatever attraction was building between them. What else could she do but respect his wishes?

The three girls continued to laugh and discuss Christina's marriage, and the uncomfortable knot in the pit of her stomach grew larger. While they might not be intending to ridicule her, it also did not seem as if they were laughing *with* her. Instead, she felt excluded—again. Standing on the outside, not part of the joke.

The knot inside her twisted and burned until it wound up her throat, lodging tight. Her corset felt like a shrinking band, squeezing her ribs and preventing air from reaching her lungs. With shaking hands, she pushed her ice cream away. She needed to leave, now. Before the girls noticed her misery. Before she could no longer breathe. Before she ruined everything.

Pushing back, she shot to her feet. Patricia

glanced up, concern lining her face. "Christina, are you—?"

"I must go. Thank you for inviting me." Gathering her gloves and hat, Christina hurried out of the ice cream shop and onto the street. She took a deep breath and rushed along the walk toward Oliver's house. At least there she could be alone.

OLIVER STRUGGLED TO see in the dying afternoon light. He would need to switch on the overhead bulbs soon.

Shifting on the stool, he arched his back to stretch the sore muscles. He had been working since dawn in the greenhouse, taking breaks for only coffee and lunch. The tests on a smaller battery for his hearing device were promising. He preferred not to apply for a patent until everything was operational and mechanically sound, however. A deaf man patenting a hearing device would gain attention, but that could not be helped. All he could do was ensure the device worked properly.

Any public failure on his part was a surefire trip to the lunatic asylum.

And wouldn't his cousin love that? With Oliver incapacitated, his marriage annulled, and Sarah not reached majority, Milton would gain control of the Hawkes fortune. The very idea nauseated Oliver.

So he had to get the device working, as cheaply

and efficiently as possible. That meant a portable battery that would not corrode over time. And he was close.

Close, yes. But that does not explain why you are hiding from your wife.

Retrieving his soldering iron, he sighed. He was not hiding, per se. Merely giving the two of them distance. He had blundered badly the other night. After nearly kissing her, he had disappointed her by not being honest about it. Had she wanted him to kiss her?

I have been waiting for you.

He could not stop repeating her words from their wedding night in his head. She had been prepared to consummate their marriage. Was he the world's biggest fool for saying no?

It had been an offer born of duty, not lust, he reminded himself. Refusing had been the right thing to do, and he had to continue to remain strong. When she was ready she would find a society husband who would take her on trips, sing with her in the moonlight, and throw lavish parties in her honor. Everything Oliver could not.

The greenhouse door opened and Apollo jumped up from the floor, his tail wagging at the unknown visitor. Oliver's breath caught. Was it Christina?

Gill appeared, stepping into the workroom. Swallowing his disappointment, Oliver put down the tool he was holding and turned toward the butler. "What is it?" he signed.

"I apologize for the intrusion but I came to inquire about your plans for dinner."

Plans? He had no plans. Gill knew this perfectly well. "Why would tonight be different than last night?" He had eaten here, in his workroom. It was his usual routine when engrossed in a project. *Except when you are dining with your wife.*

No, no more of that. He had learned his lesson. Proximity to Christina meant wanting Christina. If he stayed away from her, remained busy, then perhaps these fantasies about her would cease.

"Because you are married," Gill signed. "And your wife dined alone last evening."

Gill had been closer to Oliver than almost anyone in the past decade, so it was not the first time the butler had taken Oliver to task. Though Oliver disliked being reprimanded, he tolerated it from Gill. Usually.

However, his wife was a subject not up for debate.

"We do not have that type of marriage," Oliver signed. "She agrees with me. Furthermore, none of this is your concern."

"The happiness and well-being of the household is my concern and I do believe Mrs. Hawkes is unhappy."

That news landed in Oliver's stomach like a lump of coal. He did not wish for her unhappiness. On the contrary, he had arranged for accounts to be set up for her at all the Ladies'

Mile shops. A carriage waited at her disposal. New York City was the grandest city in the entire world, with all sorts of entertainments and interests. "I thought I heard her leave earlier," he signed.

"She went for ice cream at one of the local saloons," Gill signed. "I believe her cousin and some other ladies were to meet them."

"Well, there you go," he signed. "She is probably stuffed and worn out from all the giggling and gossip."

"Hardly," Gill signed. "She returned in tears, dashing up to her bedroom, and we have not seen her since."

In tears? He straightened. "What happened?" he signed.

"I have not been informed. Shannon has not yet been admitted to her ladyship's suite."

Had something transpired with Christina's cousin? Patricia Kane was a bit like Apollo in that she was brash and determined, running at full speed rather than moving stealthily. Oliver would not be surprised at all to learn that Patricia had somehow hurt Christina's feelings.

Or it could have been these other ladies Patricia had invited. Oliver knew firsthand the cruelty society women could dish up. He had suffered through the sneers and strange looks, the biting comments, until he had walked away from that nonsense.

If they had dared to hurt his wife . . .

He made a quick decision. "I shall dine with Christina," he signed. "Make sure the staff knows. I will go up and visit her now."

Gill's face broke into a wide grin. "Yes, sir," he signed.

A KNOCK ON the adjoining door nearly caused Christina to drop her book. She had been wrapped securely in a blanket in front of the fire, reading, since returning from the ice cream saloon. She had not expected to hear a sound come from Oliver's bedroom. Was he there?

Of course he is there. Who else would be knocking?

But why knock when he could not hear her answer?

Throwing off the blanket, she hurried to the door. Sure enough, Oliver waited on the other side. His rumpled hair stood at various angles, as if he had run his hands through it repeatedly, and dark circles lined his eyes. He wore his customary shirtsleeves with no coat, and she made every effort not to stare at the sinewy forearms revealed by the rolled cuffs.

His green eyes searched her carefully, the moment stretching so long that she finally brushed a hand over her nose and cheeks. "Is something on my face?"

"No, not at all," he signed and spoke. "I apologize. Were you coming down to dinner?"

Dinner? She glanced over her shoulder at the clock. Oh, yes. It was nearly time for supper. When it had become apparent Oliver was avoiding her, she had taken most meals in her suite. "I had not planned on it. Were you?"

"I thought I would eat with you tonight."

This was quite a turnabout. He went from nearly kissing her to ignoring her, and now he wanted to share dinner again. This about-face exhausted her. On top of this afternoon's disastrous outing, she had not slept well the past two nights and was utterly drained. Going down to the dining room sounded like a Herculean effort at the moment. "I think I shall eat up here. Perhaps tomorrow—"

"Then I shall eat here as well. That is, if you do not mind?"

In her bedroom? Oliver planned to eat here, with her bed not even a few feet away? She blinked at him. "You wish to dine here? With me?"

"Yes, of course. May I come in?"

Anne's advice from earlier came to mind. *I would find him and ask why he is so hot and cold with me. Preferably at night, wearing something revealing.*

Christina considered her high-neck shirtwaist and long skirts. Not revealing in the least, unless bare earlobes and knuckles were arousing.

Not that she was attempting to arouse him. They were friends, nothing more. And that was fine with her. She did not have many friends—or perhaps *any* friends after running out on Patricia today—so the company was welcome. Oliver's presence might even distract her from her melancholy thoughts on how silly she had acted earlier at the ice cream saloon. "Please," she signed and stepped aside to give him room.

He strode in, Apollo on his heels. Stopping, Oliver snapped his fingers at the dog then pointed at the open door to his suite. The dog did not budge, merely stared at Christina with round curious eyes, his tail wagging slightly. Oliver tried one more time but Apollo did not pay him any attention.

"He may stay," Christina said, but then she realized Oliver was looking at the dog and not at her. She tapped his shoulder. "Apollo may stay."

"Are you certain? I would not want him to knock you down again."

The animal stepped toward her and nudged a cold, wet nose into her palm. She laughed, the feeling so foreign. Looking at Oliver, she asked, "What does he want?"

"He likes to be scratched behind his ears." He demonstrated and Christina quickly repeated the motion under the other ear. Apollo made some chuffing noises, apparently happy with the attention. He really was adorable, if one liked large domesticated animals.

"If we ignore him, he will lie down in front of the fire and nap for a bit." Oliver snapped his fingers to get the dog's attention and pointed at the floor. Apollo trotted to the place Oliver indicated and sat, his tail moving happily.

Christina went to the bellpull. "I will request food for us. Anything in particular you like?"

Oliver waved his hand before signing and saying, "Whatever the kitchen has prepared is fine with me." He lowered himself into one of the armchairs by the fire and Apollo came over to settle at his feet. It was so domestic, so right, that Christina's heart squeezed in her chest.

When her maid arrived at the door, Christina requested provisions. Shannon nodded and disappeared down to the kitchens. Christina then sat in the armchair opposite her husband and tried to make herself comfortable. *Husband.* It was such a strange concept. Did all married women feel that way, or only the ones who had not consummated their marriages?

"How are you?" Oliver signed.

She remembered the signs he had taught her weeks ago. "Well. And you?"

"Fine."

Silence descended, the only sound the crackle of the fire and the ticking of the clock. Her palms were damp, uncertainty skating down her spine. She had wanted the company but now could not think of a thing to say. He was so appealing, with his brilliant green gaze and strong jaw. Shirtsleeves rolled to his elbows, giving her a perfect view of his bare forearms, their sculpted strength apparent even in the firelight. No matter the circumstances, he seemed comfortable in his own skin. Confident. Endlessly fascinating.

"What are you reading?" he signed, using his voice for her benefit, then pointed to her book on the end table.

"The Portrait of a Lady." She picked up the book and showed him the cover. "Have you read it? Oh, that was a stupid question. The book came from your library. Of course you have read it."

The edges of his mouth curled. "I have read it. But it was not a stupid question. I haven't read everything in my library."

"No?"

"No," he signed. "I used to have more time for reading, among other things."

The way he said it had her dying to ask what those other things entailed, but she respected his privacy. His past was his own, unless he chose to share. That was how friends interacted, right? "I always make time to read."

"I did as well," he signed and said. "But then I chose to focus on my inventions."

She nodded and the silence descended once more. Questions floated through her mind, all the things she longed to know about him, but the courage to ask them eluded her. It was easier to use his pencil and ledger to communicate her deeper thoughts, honestly. Not that she could admit as much to him. What sane person found it easier to write to a person sitting across from them rather than use words?

"Would you care to learn a few signs?" he asked.

Relief filled her. "I would like that very much."

Over the next few minutes he instructed her on simple signs, mostly the objects in the room, such as the lamp, fire, and bed. She repeated them and he grinned. "You are a much better student than I was for Dr. Jacobs," he signed, still speaking for her benefit.

"Who?"

"The physician that looked after you when you fell. He taught me sign language."

Ah, that made sense. The two of them had signed quite rapidly with one another. "After your illness?"

He nodded. "I was fourteen when the doctors gave up on curing me. It was then my mother learned of Dr. Jacobs. His father was deaf and not an oralist so—"

She held up her hand. "What does that mean, an oralist?"

"At deaf school they teach students to speak and read lips. They believe that is the only way deaf people can function in society. To blend in with everyone else." He grimaced, his hands moving as he spoke. "I lost my hearing at thirteen, so I am able to still remember tones and sounds. As a result, my voice is more intelligible than it may have been otherwise."

She thought his voice quite intelligible but did not interrupt.

"But not all deaf people are able to speak easily, especially if they have been deaf since

birth. Verbal communication can be challenging in such cases. Henry knew there was a way,
a method they teach in France that allowed the
deaf to communicate with their hands. He traveled there, learned the language, and brought it
back to New York."

"And taught you."

"Yes," he signed.

She braved asking him a personal question.
"What was it like when you first discovered you
were deaf?"

He paused for a moment. "Terrifying. As if a
switch had been flipped and all the sound in the
world had been removed."

She could not even imagine. "Your parents?
What did they do?"

"Took me to the best doctors in the country.
When that failed, they threw money at every
quack, medicine man, charlatan, and medium in
the Northeast. They were determined to find a
cure."

Despite the toll that must have taken on him,
Oliver appeared to still hold a deep affection for
his parents. How lucky of him, to have experienced that unconditional love—even for a short
time. "And then?"

"When a cure could not be found my parents
threw themselves into helping me every way possible. Not only did they learn to sign, they forced
the staff to learn as well. Hired the best deaf
tutors. Found Dr. Jacobs."

"May I ask a question?"

"Of course. You need not ask permission first, you know. Just ask me."

"When you use your voice, why do you sign as well? Should not one replace the other?"

He lifted a shoulder as if this had not occurred to him. "Habit, I suppose. It is the way my brain thinks. Signing is not something I consciously force myself to do; I just naturally do it. Though speaking and signing together can slow me down at times."

That made sense to Christina, seeing as how this was two forms of communication happening at once.

"And for the record," he said, "you are the only person with whom I use my voice."

"I am?"

"Yes," he signed.

She ducked her head, more pleased by that bit of information than she wanted to let on. Oliver was remarkable, an incredibly intelligent person. Not to mention generous and handsome. How did all of New York not know this? Every single woman in the city should have fallen in his garden to gain his attention. Lucky for her, she supposed, they had not. Otherwise he would have married some other woman, leaving Christina to deal with Van Peet and her parents alone.

A knock sounded, causing Apollo to rise and hurry to the door, his tail wagging. "Ah, the food has arrived," Oliver signed.

Chapter Eleven

Four footmen hurried to set up an elaborate spread in Christina's room, complete with a small table, candles, and china. Oliver watched all this transpire with growing trepidation. The scene was intimate, designed for a new husband and wife. Not friends whose efforts to resist temptation were hanging on by a thread.

How was he to survive it?

Oliver narrowed his eyes at Gill. "I know what you are doing," he signed.

"I have no idea what you mean," Gill signed. "We are merely ensuring the master and his wife are comfortable."

"Utter nonsense—and you know it," he signed.

The butler's mouth pressed together, eyes dancing, and Oliver knew the servant was attempting not to laugh. Bastard.

Gill departed, taking Apollo and the footmen

with him, and Oliver and Christina were alone
once more. He held out a chair at the table and
she lowered herself into it. She wore a plain ivory
shirtwaist with a navy skirt, nothing fancy, but
she was the loveliest woman he had ever seen. A
hint of roses teased his nose, the feminine scent
stealing into his lungs and causing heat to un-
wind in his veins. *Stop it. This is a meal, not a pre-
lude to seduction.*

Determined to keep this about the food, he
reached for her round china plate. "I will fill
your plate with a little bit of everything." Without awaiting an answer, he walked to the covered
dishes on the sideboard. One of the benefits of
being deaf was you could not hear someone protest or argue behind your back.

He set the full plate in front of her, piled high
with a sampling of his cook's finest dishes. Once
he had his own plate, he lowered himself into
a chair. Christina sipped her wine, watching
his forearms through her lashes. He glanced at
himself, wondering what had her so mesmer-
ized. Was she horrified at his rolled shirtsleeves?
He hoped not. He'd rather attend Mrs. Astor's
Patriarch's Ball than wear a coat while in his
own home. "No need to wait on me," he signed.
"Please, begin."

Her lips curved into a shy smile and she
picked up her fork. He tried to focus on his own
plate but it was difficult. The room was full of
her, from the personal items on the dresser, the

rumpled coverlet on the bed, to the brush of her skirts against his legs under the table.

Additionally, an awareness buzzed between them now, one that had not existed before. He felt off balance and powerless around her, which was why he had ignored her since the portrait gallery. She had not backed down then, merely stared up at him with excitement and longing in her gaze, no hesitation whatsoever. Indeed, the doubt and insecurity had belonged solely to him.

He absolutely hated that feeling.

Focus on something else. Like the reason he had decided to dine with her in the first place. He placed his fork on his plate. "Are you happy here?" he signed and said.

"Yes," she said, her face emphatic. "I am very grateful, Oliver."

"I do not mean gratitude. I mean happiness. Have you everything you need? Is there anything more the staff may do for you?"

"No, everyone here has been very kind."

Her choice of words did not elude him. "Does that mean someone elsewhere was unkind?"

She looked down at her food, her bottom lip disappearing between her teeth. He gave her time by reaching for his wineglass and taking a sip. The Bordeaux was old and robust, one of his very favorites, and he savored the rich flavors before swallowing.

After a moment, she met his eyes. "No one was unkind. I am afraid I made a fool of myself, though."

"How?" he signed.

The way her lips pressed together signaled she was reluctant to share, but she answered nonetheless. "I left a bit hurriedly from an outing today with Patricia and her friends. It was silly of me."

He suspected she was making light of what happened. "Was something said to upset you?"

Color dotted her cheeks and she shook her head. "It was nothing."

"I disagree. Gill said you were crying when you arrived home," he signed/spoke. "You may tell me, you know."

An idea occurred to him. He withdrew the ledger and pencil from his shirt pocket and slid them across the table. She stared at the items for a long second before picking them up.

Her shoulders rose and sank with a heavy sigh as she wrote. When she finished, she slid the ledger to him. *Have you ever been surrounded by people but felt lonely?*

"Frequently," he signed. "Deaf, remember."

She cocked her head. "What do you mean?"

So she would not feel alone in writing instead of talking, he took the ledger and pencil back. *I tried for a long time to fit in, first at school with the other deaf students. But I was different in that I had not always been deaf. I was able to speak and remem-*

ber sounds. That sometimes made it difficult to relate to someone who has no similar references.

He turned the page and kept writing. *When I tried to join society, I hardly fit in better there. I was an oddity everywhere I went, treated no better than a sideshow act at times. I even had a gentleman ask if I would read J. P. Morgan's lips from across the room in hopes of garnering a secret stock tip. Women tolerated my deafness because of my bank account. After a few years I grew cynical, no longer interested in merely being "tolerated."*

When she finished reading, there was shock and comprehension in her brown gaze. He recalled Patricia's words the night he and Christina were married: *She does not enjoy the society events. I found her hiding more often than not, off in a corner, miserable.*

Had he found a woman who truly understood?

Indeed, he thought she might. There was an excellent chance this woman appreciated some of what he'd been through because of her own experiences in society.

They stared at one another, neither looking away. He could see her chest expanding rapidly, his own exhalations coming just as fast. Blood pumped hard, his skin alive with craving. He had been fighting the current between them, denying this connection he felt to her, but he could not do it any longer. Resisting this attraction was like attempting to keep the opposite ends of a magnet from coming together.

He was done fighting.

If she did not desire him, then so be it. He would not pressure or try to convince her. However, if there was a chance for them to occasionally enjoy each other physically during the next few months, he was dashed well going to take it.

Then she could find a normal man, one without Oliver's quirks and stubbornness.

Until then, she was his.

Mouth gone dry, he licked his lips. "May I ask you a question?" She nodded, so he went back to the ledger and wrote, *The night in the gallery, were you disappointed I did not kiss you?*

Her brows rose slightly as she read, clearly taken aback by his question, but she did not look at him. Instead, she took the pencil from his hand and turned over a new page in the book. *A bit.*

Heart pounding in his chest, he wrote, *And if I asked to kiss you now, what would be your answer?*

Her fingers gripped the pencil so tightly while writing that her fingertips went white. She bit her lip as she turned the ledger toward him.

I would say yes.

SHE HAD ACTUALLY written it.

Christina could scarcely believe she'd done it. Yet somehow it was easier to be truthful on paper than speaking aloud.

And it had been the truth. She wanted to kiss him. Badly.

Oliver placed his napkin on the table, pushed

his chair back, and stood. Nerves skittered throughout her chest, making it hard to breathe as he approached. The lines of his face had sharpened, the green of his irises dark and intense. It was impossible to look away.

When he reached her side, he held out his hand. She stared at it, beyond grateful that he was giving her a choice instead of pressuring her. Oliver was the most considerate man she'd ever met, and she knew in that moment this was the right decision.

She wiped her damp palm on her skirts and then took his hand. His skin was warm and rough, and he gently pulled her to her feet. Then he stepped closer, his hands sliding to cup her jaw on both sides. He surrounded her, so close that she could see the late-day whiskers on the lower half of his face, the faint lines at the corners of his eyes. His handsomeness stole her breath away.

He lowered his head and she waited, anticipating. When his lips brushed hers, a touch so faint she barely felt it, a shiver of excitement worked its way down her spine. His lids fell, dark lashes resting like crescents on his cheekbones, and she let her eyes close as well. Another featherlight touch swept the corner of her mouth before he continued over the bow of her lip and to the other side. When he finished, he finally—finally!—kissed her on the mouth, and she almost sighed in relief at the firm touch of his lips.

It was slow and sweet, an intimate joining of their mouths. His lips moved purposefully, coaxing as their breath mingled, and the world was reduced to just the two of them. This one single moment.

She tried to match his movements, to fit her lips perfectly to his, and he gripped her tighter. Her heart thrummed inside her chest, a beat that seemed to resonate everywhere in her body, her skin buzzing with a secret rhythm as the kiss deepened. The heat and strength of him made her dizzy, and her hands found purchase on his chest. She held on, feeling his heart pound beneath her palms, the rapid rise and fall of his breathing. His reaction thrilled her, blatant proof she was not alone in this.

When his tongue flicked her lips, she jerked in surprise. Her mouth parted slightly and Oliver's tongue drove inside. He filled her mouth, his tongue gliding against hers, twining and stroking, and then it made sense. This was what her cousin had meant, this deep connection, this intimacy as necessary as air. She felt drunk on his taste, desperate for more.

Her tongue touched his and the kiss turned eager, greedy. He tilted his head to change the angle, dipping farther into her mouth, while one hand moved around her waist to bring her flush to his body. Without thinking, she tried to get closer, moving her hands around his neck and into the soft hair at his nape.

He kissed her for a long time—at least she assumed it was a long time. Long enough that she could hardly breathe, with the ache between her legs growing urgent as her insides tingled and burned. Finally, he broke off from her mouth and rested his forehead against hers, both of them panting hard.

They stood, pressed together, for a long moment. Was this it, then? She was strangely unsatisfied, every cell in her body straining for more. She clung to him, unsure what would happen next.

"I should go," he said and placed a soft kiss on her forehead.

He started to step away but she curled her hands into the edge of his waistcoat to stop him. "Wait."

"I should leave. I—" He started signing as he spoke. "I do not wish to overwhelm you. We have plenty of time to explore this."

"Please. Stay."

"Why?"

She glanced away, too unnerved to answer, but he held on to her chin to hold her gaze. "Christina, why?"

"Because I would like you to stay." It was the best answer she could give at the moment. She had no knowledge of the specifics of what happened between a man and a woman in the bedroom but she knew enough to want this to continue. "Unless . . . unless you do not want to stay with—"

He pounced, grasping her shoulders, and his mouth took hers in a hard kiss. When they broke, he said, "I want to stay. I want to do every wicked and pleasurable thing under the sun to you."

Leaning back so he could see her face clearly, she said, "Then you had best begin."

Chapter Twelve

Then you had best begin.

Had one sentence ever affected Oliver so fiercely? His body went up in flames, blood pounding in every cell, his skin crawling with lust. He wanted Christina. Desperately. He wanted her naked and on the bed beneath him, writhing and gasping as he pleasured her.

He had to remember, however, that she was innocent. They must progress slowly. He needed her to be sure at every step, to accept—and enjoy—all that happened tonight. Because it would not stop with tonight.

No, he planned to have many nights of bone-rattling ecstasy with this woman.

Therefore, they had to start this pleasuring business gradually.

He lifted her hand and pressed his lips to the back. "If you need to get my attention, use your hand. Tap me, pinch me, tug my hair . . . If you do I shall immediately stop. All right?"

She nodded, and so he leaned over to kiss her once more, deep and thorough kisses designed to tantalize. As they kissed he steered her toward the bed until her knees hit the edge of the mattress. She did not seem to notice, her lids shut as she rubbed her slick little tongue across his. He lowered them into a sitting position, his mouth never leaving hers.

He took his time with her. Between the vigorous kisses, he explored the hard edge of her jaw with his mouth, the delicate shell of her ear. He gently nipped her throat above the collar of her shirtwaist. Dragged his nose over her cheek and relished the hint of roses on her skin.

Without the ability to hear her moans, he went by feel and sight instead. Her chest rose and fell rapidly, her skin flushed. The nails of her fingers dug into his clothed skin, keeping him close. She angled toward him, eager and excited, and his erection throbbed in his clothing. *Soon*, he reminded himself. Not tonight, but someday soon he would thrust into the warm clasp of her body.

Her hands began seeking, mapping his chest and shoulders, and she shifted restlessly on the bed. He gently pressed her back to the mattress until she was flat, and then rolled her until they faced one another. That allowed him to wedge his leg between hers, bringing her skirts up a bit. Then some more. Inch by inch he slid the silk and cotton higher until he could drape her leg over his thigh.

He stroked her stocking-covered calf, tracing the curves and angles of her leg until he reached her drawers. They were soft cotton edged in lace and had the necessary split in the middle. He trailed his fingers over her thighs and then dipped between her legs.

Slick warmth met his hand. She was wet, dripping with arousal, and he let it coat his fingers as he explored her. She put up no resistance, her hips still seeking, chest heaving, and he angled to kiss her throat as he stroked the swollen nub hidden in her folds. They were in no hurry, so he teased her, tracing her entrance. Then he worked her clitoris once more, switching up his pressure and speed to drive her wild.

He had forgotten this heady power, how much he loved to pleasure a woman. This was not any woman, however. Every touch, every sigh was a thousand times more powerful because it was Christina. She trusted him with her body, her gratification, and he would not disappoint her. Even if the demands of his own body were about to kill him.

He knew she was moaning by the vibration against his lips and hands, so he increased the pace, circling her clitoris faster. Within seconds, her hands clawed at him, pulling him closer, and then she stiffened, trembling as the orgasm overcame her. It went on and on, and he could not look away, her beautiful features lax with bliss.

When she sank into the bed, shivering, he pulled his hand out from under her skirts. He dropped beside her and closed his eyes to gain control of himself. He felt like one of those metal windup toys with a spring, turning tighter and tighter until the toy set off in a blur of motion. Still, he must hold off. There was no reason to penetrate her tonight. They had plenty of time for that, if she eventually chose.

He dragged her closer, tucked her into his side. She snuggled deeper, her lashes resting against her cheeks as she settled. Emotion welled in his chest, a tenderness that occurred more often in her presence these days. The feeling was new and disconcerting. He had never been so drawn to a woman before, not even ones he had bedded.

As he looked down at Christina's sweet and sleepy face, he found himself grinning like a fool.

What on earth was happening to him?

CHRISTINA TURNED HER face toward the winter sun, letting it warm her skin during her morning walk through the gardens. Though she was sore and tired today, she had never been happier. There were no words for what had occurred last evening between her and Oliver.

Transcendent seemed utterly cliché.

Life altering was not strong enough.

Yet it had been those things, and a hundred more adjectives used to describe something wonderful and momentous.

Yes, she had climaxed from his fingers. But it was so much more than that. It had been joy and light, like he had injected happiness into her veins. Oliver was some sort of magician, a sorcerer who knew exactly how and where to touch her.

She must have fallen asleep after because she had awoken under the bedclothes this morning, sprawled on her mattress and still dressed. Had Oliver tucked her in bed?

That filled her with guilt. Not only had she enjoyed herself immensely, she had fallen promptly to sleep. As a result, Oliver had not found his own pleasure last evening. While she had no practical experiences in these matters, she knew he had not climaxed. Would he blame her, then?

That thought dimmed a bit of her happiness and she kicked a pebble with her boot. At that moment, Apollo raced ahead to chase after a bird, distracting her. Oliver's dog had taken to accompanying her on these morning walks and she was surprised to enjoy the company. She wasn't yet entirely comfortable with the dog, but it was nice to have him around.

Without warning, Apollo began barking sharply. Christina could not see him, but he was somewhere near the edge of Oliver's property.

When calling him did nothing, she crept closer

to the stone wall near the Kane property. Perhaps he had spotted a cat or other animal. Just off the path, there was Apollo, barking at the wall.

"Apollo, come along. Stop that."

"Christina," a voice called. "Is that you?"

Was that . . . ? Her breath caught. *"Mother?"*

"Yes, it is I. Hold on."

A rustling noise sounded, the familiar swish of her mother's skirts. Then Christina heard a grunt an instant before her mother's face appeared over the top of the wall. "Are you . . . standing on something? Be careful, Mother."

The countess's hair was pulled away from her face, not a strand out of place, her eyes narrowed sharply. She gripped the edge of the stone to balance herself. "This is what I am reduced to," her mother said. "A peer of the realm forced to scuttle in the gardens like a common thief just to see my own daughter."

Christina's stomach clenched and she clasped her hands tightly. "What did you want?"

"Are you aware that your husband has forbidden your father or me from seeing you? Can you imagine the nerve? Your own mother, and I am not allowed to visit."

"He said as much the night of the wedding," Christina pointed out. "Were you not listening?"

"Do not take that tone with me, young lady, not after everything I have done for you."

Christina said nothing, merely pressed her lips

together and clenched her hands. Her mother would soon get to the point, whether Christina objected or not.

"Now, here is what I need you to speak to that man about," her mother continued. "The settlement he has proposed for the marriage is far too low. It might have been enough for some American family. However, we are English peers. We have responsibilities. Goodness, your father's title can be traced to the days of Edward II."

So this was about money. Again.

Christina smothered a sigh. Of course her parents were unhappy with what they had been given. She'd never known them to be satisfied with their lot in life. Her father had gambled to win a fortune; her mother constantly worried over appearances and what everyone else thought of them. They had married Christina off to a wealthy man. What more did they need?

"Mother, I am certain whatever Mr. Hawkes has offered is sufficient for—"

"It is absolutely *not* sufficient. Not for us. Furthermore, he can afford more. I have been asking as to the extent of his fortune and it is quite unbelievable. What we are asking for is merely a token for him."

Perhaps, but undoubtedly the amount was far more than they deserved.

Come now, Christina. They are your parents.

All the more reason she was able to see this ploy for what it was: another attempt to use her for their monetary gain. Would it never end? She rubbed the bridge of her nose and wished the ground would open up and swallow her whole.

"I expect you to help us, Christina. You must speak to your husband—or however you communicate with that man—on our behalf."

The condescension in the way her mother said "that man" scraped across Christina's nerves. She disliked how her parents had treated Oliver the night of the wedding, and apparently their biased opinion of him had not changed. He did not deserve to be looked down upon by anyone.

Her hands curled into fists and she once again longed for the courage to stand up to her parents, to voice her unhappiness. To rebel instead of giving in to their demands. To be strong and confident instead of the woman who would hide in a crowd.

Unfortunately, she was not that woman. She had learned a long time ago her parents would not relent, would not listen to her complaints. It would be easier to reason with Apollo than to change her parents' minds. Yet she had no intention of inserting herself into this matter and attempting to influence Oliver on their behalf.

Therefore, she would agree, placate them, and hope they went away.

"Of course, Mother," she said. "I shall try."

"Good." Her mother sniffed. "Really, these Americans know nothing of our history and way of life. They are practically barbarians. That they have all this money is completely unfair."

Christina was not certain the Americans would agree, but there was no pointing this out to her mother. A deep shout emerged from somewhere in the gardens and Apollo's ears pricked up. He turned and sped off toward the sound. Had that been Oliver?

The countess watched the dog disappear with growing alarm. "I expect to receive a new number today, Christina. Do not disappoint me."

Then she was gone.

Christina spun to find Apollo racing toward her. "Stop," she ordered, holding up her palms in hope of not getting knocked over again.

"Ho!"

Apollo instantly halted and sat, his tail wagging as he stared at Christina. She exhaled in relief and found Oliver striding along on the path. A young brown-headed girl of ten or eleven years of age walked next to him. Who was this?

Then she noticed the girl's bright green irises. Ah, this must be Oliver's sister, Sarah, home from school. Mercy, and here Christina stood in the bushes. Some wonderful first impression.

She moved to the path, smoothed her skirts, and patiently waited. Oliver slowly smiled as their eyes met, and her chest fluttered. "Hello," he signed.

She could feel her skin heating as memories of last night assaulted her. His fingers inside her,

his tongue in her mouth . . . It had been so intimate. "Hello," she signed back.

The side of his mouth hitched. "Is everything
all right out here?"

"Yes, of course," she answered quickly—perhaps
too quickly. "Merely enjoying the gardens."

He studied her hard, almost as if he did not
believe her, but he gestured toward the young
girl at his side. "Christina, allow me to introduce
Sarah, my sister. She will be staying with us for a
few weeks during her break from school."

Christina smiled at the girl. "Hello. It is a pleasure to meet you, Sarah."

Sarah's gaze narrowed on Christina's face.
"Oliver says you are a real English lady. Is that
true?"

"Yes, that is true. My father is an earl."

"Is that more important than a king?" Sarah
asked.

"No. Significantly less important, in fact."

Oliver touched her shoulder. "I thought perhaps you and Sarah might like to come visit my
workshop this morning."

Christina nodded. "I would like that. What do
you think, Sarah?"

Sarah turned to her brother and signed rapidly.
Oliver frowned and responded just as quickly.
He did not need to speak when signing to his sis-
ter, as he always did for Christina.

Christina's stomach tightened watching the
two siblings communicate. Were they discussing

her? She hated not being able to understand . . . Then it hit her. This frustration was what Oliver must feel like any time he could not read lips and the person was unable to sign.

Sarah lifted her chin and crossed her arms, no longer looking at her brother. Oliver faced Christina. "She would rather go shopping than spend the day in the workshop," he explained. "I have refused to take her."

"He used to escort me," Sarah told Christina. "Before he decided his work was more important than his sister. I do not suppose you would spend the day on Ladies' Mile with me?"

Christina? Shopping? In the most crowded part of the city? It sounded positively dreadful. "I . . ." She had no idea how to answer. How would Oliver feel if she refused his sister? And would Sarah then resent Christina?

Oliver must have read her thoughts clearly because he signed/said, "It is quite all right. You may say no."

"I apologize, Sarah. I would rather stay here, if that is all right with you."

"It's fine," Sarah said. "But do not expect me to give up. I will keep asking until you say yes, Christina."

Christina nearly laughed at the girl's tenacity. Had she ever been so outspoken at that age? "Thank you for the warning."

"Come," Oliver signed. "Allow me to show my two favorite ladies what I have been working on."

OLIVER HATED MEETINGS. It meant tending to business, which was the least enjoyable endeavor on the planet. Today, however, business could not wait. He needed to ensure that Lord and Lady Pennington accepted the marriage settlement and departed New York. Immediately.

Every instinct told him Christina had been lying this morning. He had found her standing near the wall separating the Kane and Hawkes properties, Apollo quite agitated. With no one visible on the other side of the wall, one could only deduce that person had not wanted to be seen.

It must've been her mother. Such was the only logical solution.

Oliver clenched his jaw. He had expressly forbidden the countess and the earl from entering his home, so they had taken to ambushing Christina in the gardens. Had those two no shame whatsoever?

Moreover, how could they complain over the settlement he had offered? It was a princely sum, way more than they deserved considering their treatment of Christina. Yes, Oliver could afford more . . . but it rankled to overcompensate those two. From what he had learned, the earl and the countess were appallingly irresponsible with money, spending and gambling every cent as soon as they acquired it.

Most of all, he did not like them putting Christina in the middle.

He pushed open the door of his study and found Frank Tripp, his lawyer, inside. Gill trailed directly behind Oliver, ready to translate. "Good afternoon," he signed when Frank stood.

"Hello," Frank signed. "Good afternoon."

Oliver shook the lawyer's hand. Frank was one of the city's top attorneys, recommended to Oliver when his late father's attorney had retired a few years ago. Oliver had liked the younger man straight off, especially when Frank had taken the time to learn a few simple signs. He also remembered to look at Oliver, not Gill, during their conversations, which Oliver appreciated. "Thank you for coming," he signed. "Have a seat."

Frank lowered himself into the chair opposite Oliver's massive walnut desk. "Congratulations on your marriage."

"Thank you. I appreciate you coming on such short notice today."

"That is what you pay me for." Frank opened his satchel and withdrew a stack of papers. "In addition, we've had a bit of a development I must discuss with you. But let us start with your matter first."

"Where do we stand with the marriage settlement?"

"Her parents are stalling. The reception to the amount was lukewarm at best, which was a bit of a surprise, honestly—especially as we know they are up to their eyes in debt."

"What did they say the last time you spoke, exactly?" Oliver signed.

"That they were still considering it and would not agree to anything rashly."

Unbelievable. "I have reason to think they have asked my wife to intervene on their behalf. To plead for more money."

Frank's eyes rounded. "I understood them to be estranged."

"Not estranged, per se," Oliver signed. "I have barred the earl and countess from seeing her unless she invites them. However, one of them, likely her mother, approached her outside this morning."

"What did her mother ask for?"

"I do not know, but one may only assume more money. Mrs. Hawkes mentioned nothing of the visit to me."

"You offered them a king's ransom. I would not advise adding to that amount."

"I have no intention of offering them more money," Oliver signed. "What I want now is leverage. Buy up every debt, every holding. Every piece of property. It is undoubtedly all in England, but I want everything down to the last farthing."

"That won't pose a problem." Frank scratched on his pad, making notes. "Creditors are likely desperate to unload the debt. I shall contact a friend of mine in London straightaway."

"Thank you. The sooner, the better. If they had accepted the money and gone quietly, I would have let this go. However, if they would like a fight I am happy to provide them with one."

"Then you probably will not appreciate to learn that the word *incompetent* was thrown about quite a bit in the meeting with her parents. They specifically asked if your mental state had ever been evaluated."

Oliver gripped the arms of his chair tighter, the wood digging into his palms as his chest burned. "They dared to question my competency?" Christ, it was his greatest fear. Tests, doctors, hospitals, asylums . . . He had lived with that threat ever since losing his parents. The deaf were often misunderstood and mistreated, thought to be insane or of lower intellect. He had tried to combat this by circulating in society, to prove he was "normal," but it had failed. His existence had only provided fodder for their gossip and, infuriated, he had turned his back on all of them.

Now he was even more resolved to fight Christina's parents, to acquire their debts and ruin them.

"A pointless endeavor, Oliver. They have no case, other than you have married their daughter in a bit of a rush and have refused to let anyone see her."

"I have not locked her away in a tower," he signed. "She has complete freedom. I merely wished to keep her away from her parents."

"Well, that will sort itself out when you escort her out on the town."

Oliver said nothing, knowing he would do no such thing. "If anyone's mental state should be questioned, it is theirs. They were planning to marry my wife off to Van Peet, you know." The idea still turned Oliver's stomach.

"Van Peet?" Frank's jaw fell open. "The old man? He's at least three times her age."

"More like four—which brings me to my next problem," Oliver signed. "I have the funds to buy out Van Peet's holdings but I would rather not make it quite so easy on him. He does not deserve full price."

Frank stroked his jaw, his gaze thoughtful. "We could drive down the stock price, then wrest control from him. Julius Hatcher is a friend and client. I could ask him for advice."

Oliver looked at Gill for clarification, certain he'd read Frank's lips incorrectly. After Gill spelled the letters, Oliver leaned back in his chair. "You know Julius Hatcher?"

"Yes, and if anyone is able to bankrupt Van Peet, it is Julius. Incidentally, he is married to an Englishwoman. Aristocracy. Might know your wife."

Oliver had not heard this, but it was welcome news. Christina needed more friends and someone from England might be a welcome reminder of home. If London society was as incestuous as

New York's, she most likely knew Hatcher's wife. "Are you able to get them both here?"

Frank ran a finger over his brow to smooth it, clearly hesitating. "You might be the only person more reclusive than Hatcher. I shall try." He held out his palms. "I cannot promise, but I will ask."

"Thank you."

"I must point out the obvious, Oliver. You pay me a fortune so I am not complaining, but using a lawyer for these kinds of things would be unnecessary if you'd only hire a secretary. Have someone come in once a week or so and manage your affairs."

"No." They'd had this conversation before. "I hardly require anything and I trust you. I do not want someone here underfoot all the time."

"Cannot say I did not try—and you might not be so grateful when you get my bill."

"Whatever you charge I shall happily pay it. You are worth every penny."

"Aw, you will turn a girl's head with all that flattery. Now, let us move on to the other piece of business. I received a note from Milton to request the funds for some alpaca farm in—"

Oliver sat up straighter. "I never agreed to that." He had expressly refused his cousin's request. Milton was trying to outright steal from him now?

"No?"

"No."

"I see. Five thousand for a bunch of big sheep seemed a tad crazy to me."

"Because it is crazy." Was Milton under the misguided impression that Oliver did not carefully scrutinize the family finances? That Frank would approve this expenditure without first checking with Oliver? He would need to set his cousin straight. In fact, a dose of punishment seemed in order. "Clearly I have been too generous with my cousin. Please inform him his monthly allowance will be reduced by ten percent."

"I will let him know." Frank slipped his papers and notes back in his leather satchel. "So when may I meet her?"

Oliver frowned at Frank. "Meet who?"

"Your wife. I am dying to see the woman that convinced the notorious recluse to marry her."

"I am not a recluse." Moreover, he did not wish for Frank to meet Christina. Frank was handsome, charming. A bon vivant who went out with a different woman every night. He did not need Frank flirting with her, causing her to realize how lacking Oliver was in every respect.

Well, that will sort itself out when you escort her out on the town.

He contemplated Frank's earlier words. Had Christina's absence from society really been remarked upon? He had not stopped to consider that gossip might spread about them. The last thing they needed was for anyone to believe he was keeping her here against her will.

Oliver could not escort her about town to quell the rumors. However, someone else could do the escorting. After all, this was not a real marriage. Though they had been intimate last evening they would still split at the end of a year. He had no hold over her, not really. She was free to pursue her own life, her own relationships. Why should she stay inside day after day, miserable, because Oliver would not show her around town? Better she go out and enjoy herself now and again.

And what better man than Frank to show her about? He seemed to know lots of people and was well familiar with the New York nighttime scene, if the newspapers were to be believed. He was the epitome of the perfect escort.

Every word burning a hole in his brain with its absolute wrongness, Oliver signed, "Actually, I need another favor. Have you plans this evening?"

"You wish for me to do what?" Christina could not have heard Oliver correctly. The request was ludicrous at best. At worst, insulting.

They were standing in the greenhouse, Oliver having summoned her here a few moments ago.

"My attorney, Frank Tripp. He wishes to escort you to dinner this evening. To Sherry's. He shall arrive at half past eight."

Dear God, she had not misheard him. "Another man will take me to dinner? Alone?"

Oliver nodded, his mouth flat as his hands moved. "You should enjoy the city. Go out. See the town. Frank is a lot of fun, I am led to believe."

Her heart squeezed painfully in her chest. She and Oliver had spent last evening in bed, intimate and close, sharing something wonderful and intensely personal. Then there had been the morning in his workshop, with her reading to Sarah while he tinkered. The companionship had been lovely, fostering a belief that perhaps this could be . . . more between them. She'd begun to think he cared for her, that he might desire her as a real wife.

How wrong she had been.

Now he was attempting to pawn her off on another man, a stranger. Men who cared for their wives did not send them off with other unmarried men. *You are so stupid. You thought one night of passion and everything would change.*

Separate lives, annulment after one year. She must never forget again.

Clasping her hands tightly, she stood and stared at him, thoughts swirling in her brain. She wanted to refuse, to tell him how the request pained her, but the words would not come. It was like facing her parents, where no one gave a fig about her wishes. It was another stark reminder that her life was not her own to control, not even after marriage.

"What are you thinking?" Oliver's brows dipped, his green eyes intense as he studied her expression.

As if he cared. If he had wanted her opinion, he would have asked her before arranging the evening's plans with Mr. Tripp. No, he had gone and planned this without her involvement, just like her parents.

"Christina, please. Talk to me."

You look absurd, standing here not saying anything. Tell him. Tell him what you think.

She pressed her lips together. Talking would not change anything; it never did. Yet she had to refuse this request. Perhaps she could sneak away and hide somewhere, just until Frank left—

Oliver let out a frustrated huff and withdrew his ledger and pencil. Then he slapped them on the table. "Write," he signed and spoke, his voice clipped.

She picked up the pencil and moved it between her fingers. Writing was easier than speaking, at least for her. Chances were high that her argument would end up more articulate on paper.

Opening the ledger, she found a blank page and wrote. *I have no need to see the town. I am quite happy staying here.*

"Nonsense," Oliver said when he finished reading. He took the pencil from her. *Every woman enjoys to be seen at the popular places. You shall have a gay time.*

I am not every woman, she wrote.

He frowned at this, and she thought she might have convinced him. Granted, they were near strangers, but he should know her well enough by now to understand that she would much rather hide than be seen. Moreover, if anyone was to escort her to dinner, it should be Oliver.

It would benefit you to be seen in public, merely enjoying a quiet dinner with a friend.

She took the pencil from his hand. *One could make the same argument for you.*

He waved his hand then wrote, *No, not me. It is better if I am not there.*

That made no sense. *I do not understand why you cannot come as well,* she wrote.

The answer arrived quickly, as if it were obvious. *Because I hate that sort of thing.*

She looked down at her shoes and mumbled, "So do I."

"What did you say? You were staring at the ground."

She did not repeat herself. Instead, she took the pencil and scrawled, *I do not wish to go.*

When he read the words, he looked at her earnestly. "It is important for you to be seen," he said, not bothering to write. "For people to see the recluse has not injured or corrupted you, that you are perfectly healthy. Then your parents cannot claim otherwise."

The words caught her by surprise and her head jerked slightly. "Have they . . . Have my parents threatened you in some way?"

"It is nothing you need worry over. However, it would be beneficial for you to be seen having a grand time with friends."

So her parents had threatened him. She rubbed her temples against the sudden ache building there. Would there be no end to the trouble her parents caused in her life?

"Please, Christina," Oliver said. "Will you go?"

It felt churlish to refuse, now that she knew the circumstances. Moreover, it was one dinner. She could survive one dinner in a crowded public restaurant, could she not? She had not yet dined at Sherry's, and everyone raved about the service and the view. Perhaps it would be nice to experience it once. Still, she did not care to be pawned off on a stranger. "I would prefer for you to come with us."

He shook his head, a lock of dark hair falling over his forehead. Her hands had caressed those soft strands last night, holding on as he performed wickedness all over her body. "I cannot."

"Why?"

His skin turned a dull red, the angles of his face sharpening. A large palm slapped the table, startling her. "Because I cannot," he said, his voice loud. "This is not a true marriage, Christina. We shall never take drives in the park and attend the opera together. I am not made for that—and I cannot allow you to bully me into it, either. So go with Frank. If not Frank, then someone else. Enjoy yourself."

The words knocked the breath from her chest. The pain inside her multiplied and bloomed until it threatened to crush her lungs. He could not have put their situation in any plainer terms. Even an idiot could see how he felt about her, which was that he had no intention of deepening their relationship—even after what they had shared last night. Oliver did not wish for more, as he'd made quite clear before, during, and after their wedding.

We shall live totally separate lives.

Everything he had said last night—the kind words, the tenderness—all a lie.

She hardened her heart, as she'd done before when the whispers and giggles threatened to crack her in half. *Feel nothing. Be hollow inside.* "Please inform Mr. Tripp I shall be ready at half past eight o'clock."

Turning, she left the greenhouse and started walking. It hardly mattered where.

Chapter Thirteen

By the time eight thirty arrived, Christina had resolved to go to dinner and not make a fool of herself that evening. She would stay quiet and soak in the atmosphere, not give the crowd cause to notice or remark on her negatively in any way. She'd been in New York for little more than a month and had not experienced much in that time beyond society dinners and balls. Tonight, she would visit one of the city's renowned restaurants. Not embarrassing herself or Mr. Tripp seemed of the highest priority.

"I hear you met Miss Sarah today," Shannon said, draping a sapphire and diamond necklace around Christina's neck. The deep blue stones matched the evening dress, an off-the-shoulder ensemble that Christina had only dared to wear once before. She thought it too revealing, but her mother had insisted, saying a little skin would cause the suitors to salivate. It hadn't, of course.

"Yes, I did. She is lovely. I can see that she may be a handful."

"Loads of energy, that one. Not a shy bone in her body. Miss Sarah's good at making this big house feel lively, that is for certain."

That would be nice, considering Christina and Oliver would no longer interact. Perhaps having Sarah around for a few weeks would give Christina someone to talk with.

"There," the maid said. "You look lovely, ma'am."

Christina studied herself in the mirror. Shannon had taken great care with Christina's appearance tonight. Her brown hair had been piled on top of her head in a complicated style, secured with Oliver's mother's diamond combs. In addition to the necklace, there were ear bobs and a thick bracelet worn over the elbow-length dark gloves. It was as if Shannon were trying to gain Oliver's attention on Christina's behalf. Christina did not have the heart to tell her not to bother.

"You shall be the talk of the restaurant, I've no doubt," Shannon said.

Dear God, Christina sincerely hoped not.

A knock on the door sounded and Shannon went to answer. Christina heard the footman relay the message that Mr. Tripp had arrived and was waiting downstairs.

Exhaling a long breath, Christina stood from her dressing table and smoothed her skirts. *Think of it as an adventure. One you neither asked for nor wanted.*

"Have a nice time, madam."

"Thank you, Shannon." She left her suite and started toward the stairs. There was no sound inside Oliver's rooms and she assumed he was busy elsewhere, living his separate life. Well, she would do the same.

No matter how much it hurt.

Lingering in the entryway stood a tall, dark-haired man. He was dressed in black evening attire, a black overcoat thrown over his arm as he waited, staring at a painting on the far wall. When he heard her approach, he turned and smiled at her. Goodness. She had not expected him to be so devastatingly handsome. Strong jaw, chiseled cheekbones, sharp blue eyes . . .

His perfect features made her feel worse. There would be no chance of hiding tonight or avoiding attention, not with this man along.

"Mrs. Hawkes, I presume." He bowed dramatically. "How lovely to meet you. I am Mr. Frank Tripp."

"Mr. Tripp." She descended the last step and held out her hand. "A pleasure, sir."

He took her hand into his large grip, holding tight. "The pleasure is most definitely mine. It is not often I am able to escort such a beautiful woman to dinner. Shall we?"

The compliment unnerved her and she could only mumble, "Of course."

Gill appeared from seemingly nowhere, a heavy woolen overcoat in his hands. He brought the garment to Christina and held it up, and she noticed the bright red lining inside. "That is not mine," she said. The garment was much too fine to be hers.

"Mr. Hawkes had this sent over from Lord & Taylor today, along with some other items."

"Oh." Oliver had bought her a coat? How was that living separately? Mercy, that man was the most perplexing creature on earth.

Gill slipped the overcoat up her arms and over her shoulders. Warm wool designed in the military style, the garment was absolutely glorious. It also fit her perfectly. How had Oliver managed it?

The butler opened the front door. "Your carriage is outside, sir."

Mr. Tripp extended his arm and Christina accepted it. As she passed the butler, she caught the sympathy in his gaze and wondered over it. Had he known her unhappiness over this excursion? Or how she wished it were Oliver's escort instead?

"Have a nice evening, madam," Gill murmured as she passed.

Once on the walk, she did not look back. Oliver was inside, somewhere, and if he cared about her leaving with another man, he would have made that plain before now. Mr. Tripp handed her into the fancy black carriage. After he joined her, they were off, the wheels turning and leading her away from her new home.

"I have to admit," Mr. Tripp said, "I do not quite understand what is happening between you and Oliver."

Christina had not expected him to put it so plainly, but she had no answers where her husband was concerned. "I am sorry you were forced to escort me tonight."

"Forced to escort you? My dear woman, it is my honor and my pleasure. Rarely have I been seen with such a beautiful woman."

Had Oliver asked Mr. Tripp to compliment her as well? The thought depressed her. "How long have you known my husband?"

"About seven years. Oliver is a good man. Misguided at times, yes, but he means well."

"What do you mean *misguided*?"

He crossed his legs at the ankles, stretching out in the carriage interior. "Thinks he knows people. That he knows how the world works. Happens to the most intelligent of men, of course. They have everything figured out and the rest of us poor fools are idiots. See, when you are right nearly all of the time, you refuse to believe the small percentage of times you are wrong. You are accustomed to believing you are right. That is Oliver."

This made a good deal of sense. Mr. Tripp was surprisingly wise as well. "Is this an argument you have used before, perhaps in court?"

A grin split his handsome face, his teeth white

and even in the dark. "Once or twice." He sobered, his gaze turning thoughtful. "Forgive me for asking, but were you happy with this suggestion? That I take you to Sherry's, I mean."

She had not the faintest idea on how to answer. To criticize Oliver felt disloyal, even if they were friends who led separate lives. "It is important for me to be seen in public, apparently."

"Yes, it is, but you needn't worry so much over that. The threat of incompetence has little basis in legal fact."

Christina stiffened, every muscle clenching. "Threat of incompetence?" This was what Oliver had alluded to in their conversation today.

Mr. Tripp blinked a few times. "I . . . That is, I thought Oliver would have told you. Challenging Oliver's competence was thrown about during the negotiations over your marriage settlement."

Her parents had threatened to have Oliver declared incompetent? What would that mean? Would he be sent away?

Confusion washed through her—along with fresh anger directed at her parents. Was this an attempt at blackmail to gain more money in the settlement? There could be no other explanation, at least none that she could discern.

She drew in a deep, fortifying breath. No matter what else happened, she could not allow her parents to ruin Oliver's life. He had married her out of compassion and decency, saving her the misery of marrying Van Peet. No, it was not a love match and, despite their mutual fondness for kissing, he preferred to keep the marriage short and impersonal. She would respect that and do everything in her power to keep him safe.

Even if it meant dining out every single night of the week.

OLIVER SAT ALONE in his bedroom, restless and distracted as he sipped a very fine French brandy. Light blazed from under his wife's bedroom door, a sign she was inside and preparing for her evening out with another man. A man who'd probably bedded half the available women in New York City—and a fair number of unavailable ones as well.

Both Gill and Shannon had already expressed their displeasure in tonight's plans, and Oliver realized he'd been much too lenient with his staff over the years. He was the master of this house, not them. Just because they were all fond of Christina did not mean he needed their approval in how he dealt with his wife.

So why are you feeling guilty?

He was still attempting to come up with an answer when Frank Tripp arrived in a sleek black brougham. Not a carriage, Oliver noted, which would have allowed for more interior room. His hand fisted where it rested on the window casing as the lawyer sauntered up the walk, not a care in the world. In that moment, Oliver hated Tripp. Hated everything about him, from his carefree attitude and dashing handsomeness, to his easy charm . . .

Christina would remain unaffected by all that, certainly. She was sensible. Reasonable. Practically shy. His wife and Tripp would share one dinner and then she would return home. To Oliver. She'd probably even be grateful for the quiet here after listening to Frank ramble all night. Knowing the lawyer, Oliver bet Christina would not get a word in edgewise at dinner.

Frank and Christina soon came into view, her hand on his arm as they moved down the walk. Her back was stiff and proud, glossy brown hair piled on top of her head and adorned with an elegant hat. She wore the new coat Oliver had purchased for her, a stylish black wool that would keep her far warmer than the threadbare garment she had previously owned.

He rubbed his chest, trying to ease the tightness there. *This is the right thing to do. Let her live a separate life.* It did not feel right, however, not at the moment. Watching her leave with Tripp felt very, very wrong.

He closed his eyes and thought of last night. He could almost feel her soft skin, the velvety walls gripping his finger. The way she had clung to him, holding on as if he were saving her from drowning. Her luscious mouth, the sweetness of her orgasm . . . His cock had grown half-hard several times today merely thinking on it. Never had he felt so lost in the moment with a woman before. She was like a drug in his system and he only wanted more.

When he opened his eyes, he saw Tripp hand Christina up into the brougham. She turned to sit and flashed the lawyer a smile—and Oliver's breath caught in his throat. That smile . . . it was too bright. Too genuine. Too similar to the smiles she gave *him*, damn it. Tripp did not deserve those smiles. Oliver needed them all for himself.

Heat spread along the back of his neck, an uncomfortable uneasiness. Christ, was he jealous? Would this burning desire to punch Tripp exist if Christina were not involved?

Gill appeared at Oliver's side, the butler's mouth set in a flat, unhappy line. Oliver returned to the window to watch the brougham disappear down Fifth Avenue. When only a desolate street remained, he turned to his butler. "You wished to say something?" he signed.

Gill's movements were sharp and angry. "You are feeding a lamb to the wolves."

"She is hardly a lamb. She can hold her own against Tripp." Christina may at times appear delicate and gentle, but he sensed strength in her. No one had parents like hers without learning how to survive. She merely needed space and time to grow more comfortable in her skin—and Oliver was prepared to give her both.

"Casting her aside will not endear you to her."

"I have not cast her aside," he signed. "It is one dinner, and Tripp will act appropriately."

"Are you certain about that? He complimented her beauty before they left."

Tripp had thrown compliments at her? To what end? Then there had been that smile as she settled into the brougham. Oliver's stomach clenched as he glanced at the clock. There were hours left to wait until she returned home, hours she would be spending with Tripp as they laughed and drank over dinner.

Perhaps their hands would brush as they sampled various plates of food on the table. Would Tripp order champagne? Of course he would. Not that Oliver thought she would do something inappropriate, but he certainly did not trust Frank Tripp. Outside of their work relationship all Oliver knew about Tripp was what the newspapers reported regarding the lawyer's wild nights, nights filled with parties, women, and recklessness.

Damn it. What had Oliver been thinking in arranging this outing? Maybe he truly had lost his mind. *You are feeding a lamb to the wolves,* Gill had said. Christina may not be a lamb but Tripp was definitely a wolf.

He started signing, "Dust off my evening wear and have the carriage brought around."

Gill briefly looked heavenward before answering, "About time, sir."

SHERRY'S TURNED OUT to be a grand and gay party with copious amounts of champagne. Seemingly everyone had a glass in hand, toasting and drinking, the waiters barely able to keep up with the demand. The food was impressive, a dizzying array of fancy plates with cleverly presented morsels.

"What do you think of your meal?"

Christina looked to the owner of the voice, Mrs. Julius Hatcher. Nora, as she'd insisted, also hailed from London. At first, Christina had worried Nora would act in the same manner as the other society women she'd encountered over the years. Thankfully, she had quickly been proven wrong. Nora was friendly, funny, and nothing but kind to Christina.

The kindness had come as a relief after arriving at the restaurant and discovering they were dining as a group. Christina had panicked for a few seconds when she learned Frank invited his friend Julius Hatcher and his wife along tonight. She had not mentally prepared herself for making awkward conversation over dinner.

Her trepidation eased, however, when it became apparent that Nora was genuinely open and gracious. There was no pretense that Christina saw; the other woman was very matter-of-fact. Christina liked that quite a bit.

"It is delicious." She forked another piece of fish into her mouth and then wiped her lips with her napkin. "Do you and Mr. Hatcher eat here often?"

"No, we mostly stay at home. We are both far happier that way."

Truly? As happy as the Hatchers seemed together, it surprised Christina that they chose to stay home. She wanted to hear more but knew it would be rude to ask.

This is not a true marriage, Christina. We shall never take drives in the park and attend the opera together.

Would Oliver's words never cease to hurt? Perhaps if they had not shared such intense intimacy last night she would feel differently. If he had not touched her so gently, so passionately, if he had not shown such care, then she would be able to breathe without this sharp ache in her chest. She would have lived separately without forming any kind of attachment to him.

However, last night had changed *everything*. In her bed, she had felt something for him, something deep and meaningful. A feeling he obviously did not share.

"You must save room for their chocolate mousse," Nora was saying. "It is divine. So how are you finding New York City? Have you been to all the shops on Ladies' Mile? Tell me, which are your favorites?"

This, combined with Sarah's request from earlier, illustrated that Christina was likely the only woman in all of New York who had no interest in shopping. She felt the tips of her ears burn. "Oh, I have not been there yet."

"No?" Nora quickly recovered from the shock and waved her hand. "Well, we must go. I shall take you to all the best shops and we will spend all your husband's money."

"That would be quite a feat," Frank said dryly.

Julius reached for his wife's hand and lifted it to his mouth for a kiss. "Nora loves to shop. You always have a willing accomplice, should you desire, Mrs. Hawkes."

The name startled her. "Thank you. And please, call me Christina."

"Yes, I think we are all familiar enough here." Frank leaned back in his chair and toasted them with his champagne glass before draining it. Christina liked the lawyer, though he was a bit too polished for her tastes. As she had anticipated, he drew nearly every eye in the room, with many of the ladies—and a few gentlemen—attempting to gain his attention during the meal. She would find it exhausting, but Frank seemed to thrive on the recognition, becoming more animated and winking at the matrons sitting around them.

"So tell me more about your husband." Nora selected an olive from the platter on the table. "I cannot say I have met Mr. Hawkes."

Not many have. "Mr. Hawkes does not often travel outside of the house."

"No? That is fascinating," Nora said. "And he is your client, Frank? Why have we never heard of him before?"

"I was not aware you needed my full client list, Lady Nora," Frank said. "Is there some sort of test I must pass?"

Julius snorted. "He will only tell you the reputable clients anyway. But rest assured that if you find yourself in the shadier sections of town, Frank represents those folks, too."

Frank adopted an expression of false outrage. "So I am supposed to be a stiff-neck? Shame on you, Julius Hatcher."

"Oh, shady clients?" Nora rubbed her hands together. "Give us some names."

Frank shook his head. "Those clients do not appreciate being mentioned, believe me. And I would prefer not to anger them as they always pay on time."

"And I do not?" Julius asked.

"You are one of the few—which is why I love you."

Julius chuckled and shook his head. "You love me because I give you stock tips."

"That, too, of course." Frank grinned, then he straightened, his attention wandering to somewhere over Christina's head. "As I live and breathe . . ."

"What is it?" Nora craned her neck to see what had caught Frank's eye. "Who is that man?"

Christina shifted to look as well—and her heart stuttered. No, it couldn't be . . . Here? Oliver was *here*?

Her husband. In the restaurant.

She blinked, certain her eyes were playing tricks. And yet there he was, walking straight toward their table.

Though his hair was slightly disheveled, he wore a black evening suit, complete with stiff white shirt and necktie. The coat was slightly too small in the shoulders and she bet he hadn't worn it in quite some time. Still, he appeared handsome and solid, certain of himself. A man who would let nothing get in his way once he set his mind to it.

He looked at no one but her, ignoring the multitude of eyes that tracked his progress across the floor, his determined green gaze holding hers as he approached. She could hardly believe he was here, that he was not an apparition or figment of her imagination. Had he not adamantly refused to join them tonight?

Something must have changed his mind—but what?

Frank rose when Oliver arrived and extended his hand. The two men shook and some secret message seemed to be communicated as they locked eyes for a few seconds. Oliver's expression remained grim while Frank grinned broadly. The lawyer then turned to the table. "Christina, I do hope you enjoy the rest of your evening. Julius, Nora, I shall see you both soon."

"Wait, you are leaving?" Nora asked. "We may pull up another chair—"

"No need to bother. I have merely been keeping his seat warm." Frank slapped Oliver on the back and gestured to the empty chair. "And, Julius, I promised Oliver you'd help him out with a little problem he is having with Van Peet. Do not disappoint me."

Van Peet? What had Oliver planned that involved Mr. Hatcher?

Oliver dropped into the chair, unconcerned with any of the people around them except Christina. His eyes never left her face.

"That sounds ominous," Julius said, rising to shake the lawyer's hand. "Good night, Frank."

"I have taken care of the bill, by the way. You are welcome." Frank bowed in the direction of Christina and Nora. "Good night, ladies. It has been a pleasure."

"Good night," Christina said. "And thank you for dinner."

Frank put a hand on Oliver's shoulder but addressed her. "He is a very lucky man, Christina. Never let him forget it."

Lucky? He had married her as a favor and had been threatened by her parents. Hardly seemed fortunate in her opinion.

Frank and Oliver exchanged a few signs Christina could not follow. She heard Nora whisper to her husband, "What are they doing?"

"I believe Mr. Hawkes is deaf," Mr. Hatcher replied.

Frank disappeared and silence descended at the table. Finally, Christina signed, "Hello, Oliver."

"Hello." He nodded at the other couple. "Hello."

Goodness, where were her manners? "Julius, Nora, this is Mr. Oliver Hawkes, my husband."

Handshakes were traded, Julius and Nora repeating their names for Oliver, and then Nora
asked, "How should we . . . That is, will he be
able to understand us?"

"He reads lips quite well as long as he can see
your face. I don't know if he will—" At that
moment, Oliver withdrew his ledger and pencil,
setting it on the table in answer to the question.
"He shall write his responses on paper."

"Oh, that is so simple."

The waiters quickly cleared Frank's place setting, silverware, and glasses, bringing Oliver
a fresh set. Once that was done, Julius lightly
touched Oliver's arm. "So you have an issue with
Van Peet?"

Nodding, Oliver grasped his notebook and
pencil to begin writing. Christina desperately
longed to read over his shoulder to learn more
about what he was planning but Nora began
speaking. "I understand you are cousins with
Patricia Kane. She is good fun."

"Yes," Christina answered. "My mother and
her mother are second—"

A heavy trouser-covered weight pressed flush
with her leg under the table, startling her. She
glanced at Oliver and noticed the edges of his lips
had curved into a small smile. Uncertain what he
was about, she slid her foot an inch away, leaving
him more room . . . only to have his leg flatten
against hers once again.

Heat washed over her and she reached for her champagne. Was he flirting with her, after sending her to dinner with another man? She did not understand it, especially after he had gone to such pains with his "separate lives" speech this afternoon. He had directly refused to attend tonight when she had asked him, repeating their marriage was not real.

Yet his presence here tonight was real. Not to mention the thigh pressed against her leg was quite real. She had no idea what any of it meant.

Even still, she did not move her leg for the rest of the meal.

Chapter Fourteen

The evening had not been nearly as miserable as Oliver had feared.

In fact, he had actually enjoyed it. Hatcher and Nora were polite and accommodating of his condition, and sitting next to his wife all night had started a slow boil in his blood, a simmering desire only she sparked within him.

Not that he could act on said desire. No, he needed to get her alone and apologize for his idiotic behavior earlier. Whatever happened beyond that was up to Christina.

Once Gill took their things, Oliver held out his hand to her. "A drink?"

She bit her lip, uncertainty plain in her eyes as she laced their fingers together. Still, he was encouraged that she trusted him enough to come along.

Instead of leading her to the salon or his study, he took her up the stairs. A fire had been lit in his room, warming the space, and he switched on the overhead gasolier. She began removing her gloves as he slipped out of his evening coat. "Brandy?" he asked.

"Yes," she signed. "Thank you."

He poured a healthy amount of brandy in two crystal tumblers and brought them to the seating area by the fire. When they were settled together on the sofa, he handed her a glass and set his on the side table. Then he angled toward her to better see her face. "Did you enjoy your evening?"

She nodded and sipped her brandy. "And you?"

"Surprisingly, I enjoyed it."

"Why did you join us? You had refused quite emphatically earlier."

"I know. I apologize. I should never have forced you to go alone."

"Then why did you? Furthermore, what changed your mind?"

"I thought it was for the best." He picked up his glass and downed a swallow of brandy, enjoying the burn along his insides. Once his hands were free, he continued to sign while also using his voice. "I did not like seeing you with Frank."

Her brows shot up. "You saw us?"

He pointed in the direction of the window. "I watched as you left."

"You were jealous."

"I was jealous." No use denying it. She deserved the truth after what he had done. "You were smiling at him and . . . I hated it."

She stared at the fire, sipping her brandy and not saying anything for a long moment. Nerves rolled about in his belly. Had he erred in being honest with her? Did she not feel the same about him?

When he left society, he had sworn never to allow himself to care about a woman this way. Yet somehow, Christina had slid under his skin, with her shy smiles and vulnerability. All his resolve about keeping her at arm's length and ensuring this marriage did not become real had crumbled in the presence of this one English lady.

His wife.

He could not lie any longer, not after last night—and especially not after chasing her down at Sherry's. She meant something to him, even if he had not planned for it to happen.

Gentle fingers swept over his thigh to gain his attention, and his skin broke out in a fever where she'd touched. Her expression serious, she said, "I was very glad you came."

"Was there a problem?"

"No, Mr. Tripp was a perfect gentleman . . . but he was not you."

Oliver's stomach jumped. He longed to savor this moment where she revealed something so personal. Most of their serious conversations had been concluded on paper, and he hoped this confession meant she had grown a bit more comfortable with him. "I am sorry I forced you to go, Christina. I should have given you the choice."

She cocked her head and regarded him thought-fully. "You know, no one has ever apologized to me before."

"No?"

"No one but you."

He shifted closer, unable to keep from touch-ing her. "Then I am outraged on your behalf." He held her jaw in his hand, the skin like silk against his palm. Flecks of green and gold sparkled in the depths of her brown eyes. She was beauti-ful, every inch of her, inside and out. "You are so lovely it takes my breath away. I am drawn to everything about you. I want to uncover every secret, learn all your hidden depths."

"I am afraid I shall only disappoint you," she said. "I am nothing special and you—"

He stopped paying attention to her words af-ter that. Was she arguing with him about what he wanted? "You could never disappoint me. If I had my pick of all the women on earth, you would remain my choice."

They stared at one another for a long moment and the world paused around them. Blood rushed in his veins, his skin alive with the need to do something. He leaned in ever so slowly to give her every chance to resist, but she melted into his grip, easing forward to meet him. Before their lips touched, he closed his eyes and held perfectly still, just breathing her in. This felt momentous, a corner turned, but he did not wish to go backward. No matter what happened, this was intentional.

Her lips met his in the gentlest brush, and lust punched through his gut, every bit of him on edge, and he kissed her long and sweet, his fingers tightening on her jaw. His functioning senses heightened, sharpened, to focus on her. He reveled in the softness of her skin, the way her lips nibbled and melded with his. The slide of her nose against his own. His tongue soon found hers and their mouths opened, where she met his strokes with a boldness and fervor that caused his cock to thicken.

As much as he longed to pick her up, toss her on his bed, and have his wicked way with her, Christina deserved better. He did not wish to scare her; rather, he needed to drive her wild, to have her crave this as much as he did. When they finished, she could have no doubt as to how much he desired her.

He broke off from her mouth and placed deep open kisses along her jaw and throat, using his teeth and tongue to taste her, gratified when her fingers clung to his shoulders. Her evening gown revealed a tantalizing amount of décolletage, the plump mounds of her breasts thrust up by her corset, and he wasted no time in exploring the luscious creamy skin.

He teased her with his lips and tongue, and one of her hands threaded in his hair to hold him in place. He slid a palm up her ribs and lifted her breast higher to expose more skin, and her back arched to push closer to his mouth. Still, it was not nearly enough. He needed every inch of her readily available.

He leaned back to ask, "May I undress you?"

She bit her lip, teeth sinking into the plump flesh. Then she nodded.

He stood and assisted her to her feet. "We may stop at any time." He clasped her hand and raised it higher. "Remember, use your hand to gain my attention."

Another nod. Her lack of audible response worried him. He stopped and peered into her eyes. "Am I . . . Is this what you want? I am probably overeager and pushing—"

"No, Oliver. I am merely nervous. Please, do not stop."

Thank God. He stepped in and pressed his lips to her forehead. "I will not frighten you or make you uncomfortable in any way, I swear. I only intend to give you more of the same pleasure."

"I believe you." She glanced over her shoulder. "Shall I lie on the bed? Like last night?"

His brows dipped. Was she in a hurry? While he was eager to taste and touch her, he had to be honest: he was also nervous. Before last night, he had not been intimate with a woman in years. Above all else, he must remain in control. Proceed slowly and not alarm her. "Not yet. I want to do this right."

"Is there a wrong way to do it?"

He stifled the laugh that rose in his throat, not wanting her to think he was making light of her questions. "No, at least not that I remember. Though it has been a few years for me."

She nodded once, understanding in her eyes. "I swear I won't complain, no matter how much it hurts."

She thought to spare *his* feelings? What had the world done to this woman that she thought of everyone else's happiness before her own? He stepped closer, close enough that her skirts brushed his legs, and he kissed her briefly. "Sweet Christina, I would not hurt you for the world. I only want to make you feel good."

He bent and sealed his mouth to hers. If he thought she would remain timid or withdrawn he was soon disabused of that notion. She responded instantly, her lips moving eagerly, intently, with no hesitation, almost as if she was relieved to return to kissing. Sparks ignited under his skin, every cell flickering to life, heat building, as their mouths moved in tandem. Her small palms rested on his chest, her fingers digging in to keep him in place.

When her tongue touched his lips, seeking entry, his knees nearly buckled. More than happy to oblige, he opened his mouth and found her tongue with his, tasting her, inhaling her scent. He tilted her head to the side and kissed her harder, desperate to get closer. Christ, he wanted her. His cock was painfully erect in his trousers and they were not yet naked.

Had he ever experienced this all-consuming fever with another woman? Certainly not that he could recall. Damn this clothing for separating them. Angling her shoulders away from him, he set to work on the buttons and hooks of her dress. She stilled his hand.

"Shall I stop?" he asked.

"No, but should we switch off the light?" She glanced at the overhead light fixture.

"That is not necessary. I would much rather see you."

"Why?" Panic flashed in her expression. "I thought . . . that is, I thought this happened under the covers."

"I am deaf, Christina, not blind. I wish to see every inch of you."

"No."

Had he misunderstood? "No?"

"Is it not proper for me to wait under the covers?"

He shook his head. "There is no proper here, not in my bed. There is just you and me, and whatever happens is between us. Furthermore, I shall stop anytime you wish."

"I do not wish to stop."

"Good. Now, allow me to demonstrate my ability to properly ravish you. I promise you will not regret it."

Shifting her away from him, he hastened to

unfasten the bodice of her evening dress. As the material gaped, he pressed gentle kisses to the newly exposed skin. She soon relaxed, her back resting on his front, allowing him to slide a hand over her shoulder and under her clothing. There he found her nipple, which he rolled and pinched until she dropped her head onto his chest, her mouth falling open in pleasure. Then he shifted to the other breast and performed the same delicious torture there.

His cock throbbed in his clothing, begging for friction. He could barely breathe from the desire for this woman. This ravishing needed to proceed at a faster clip, or else he might finally lose his sanity.

He pulled back to see her face. "I know I said we would not consummate our marriage, but I have changed my mind." More like he finally acknowledged the truth. He never had a prayer of resisting her. "I want you, Christina. In every way."

"Why?"

He traced the tops of her breasts with one fingertip, enjoying the raised bumps on her smooth flesh that followed in his wake. "Because you have bewitched me. Because I am delirious with desire for you. I cannot work, I cannot sleep. My body is no longer my own." He leaned down and dragged the flat of his tongue over the tantalizing mound visible above her underclothes. "It belongs to you, evidently."

Straightening, he felt her sigh against his

mouth right before she kissed him, her lips pulling him under her spell until he could not breathe. Soft fingers speared his hair as their tongues met and dueled with one another. Her mouth was hot and lush. Heavenly. He could kiss her for hours and never tire of it.

She tore away from him and rested her forehead on his cheek as they both struggled for breath. Air gusted over his jaw. Was she speaking?

He fixed his gaze on her mouth. "You said something?"

"Yes, Oliver." She bit her bottom lip briefly before releasing it. "I said yes."

THERE WAS NO opportunity for embarrassment over her agreement because Oliver immediately swept into action. He moved swiftly, surely, his hands going to the remaining fastenings and tapes on her silk bodice. Before she could help, he had the garment undone and falling down her arms. He placed the heavy piece on the sofa and then undid her overskirt. The rest of her clothing came off quickly—satin underskirt, camisole, flounced petticoat, bustle pad—until she was left in her undergarments.

You are standing in only your corset and drawers. In a man's bedroom.

Good God, what was she doing? Her skin went up in flames and she brought her hands up to cover herself as best she could. Was it too late to run toward the adjoining door?

The panic must've been plain on her face, because when Oliver turned from laying her things on the sofa he gave her a gentle smile. "You are contemplating running."

It seemed silly to admit to such a thing, especially when she had agreed to this whole business a few minutes earlier.

"Christina." He stepped forward and placed a finger under her chin, tilting her face up toward his. Dark green eyes glowed hot as he stared at her. "If you believe for a second that I am dissatisfied with the way you look, let me disavow you of that ridiculousness. I am burning alive with desire for you. I am seconds away from ripping all those tiny buttons and ribbons and throwing you atop my bed."

Her chest tightened, making it hard to breathe. Somehow Oliver always knew what to say, the clever man. Too bad she could not say the same of herself. She'd have to settle for a kiss.

Rising on her toes, she joined her mouth to his. He wrapped an arm around her waist and pulled her flush to his body—and she discovered the evidence of his desire against her belly. Mercy, a woman could hardly miss it.

He bent, clasped under her buttocks, and lifted her straight up. Gasping, she placed her hands on his firm shoulders and held on. Then she was falling until her back landed on the soft mattress. As he removed her shoes, she hurried to close her legs.

He stilled, studying her. "I see you require additional proof."

Additional proof? Her brow furrowed. "Of what?"

Instead of answering, he worked the buttons of his waistcoat free. He shrugged out of the piece and tossed it to the ground, much less careful with his own clothing than he'd been with hers. Braces and shirt followed, then he unbuttoned his undergarment and freed his arms, leaving him bare from the waist up. Before she could appreciate his solid torso and trim waist, he crawled onto the mattress and pushed her legs apart. "Relax," he signed and settled between her knees.

She had no opportunity to worry over how she appeared, spread below him, because he began unhooking her corset. "God above, you are lovely," he said when he uncovered her. Two large hands cupped her breasts through her chemise, squeezing the mounds gently, molding them as if learning the shape. When he rolled her nipples between his fingers, she gasped, the delicious pressure echoing in her womb.

Gathering fabric in his hands, he pushed her undergarment over her head, baring her breasts. He quickly dipped his head and took the tip into the wet heat of his mouth, sucking hard. She inhaled sharply. Had she ever dreamed her nipples were this sensitive? It was exquisite agony, with each swipe of his tongue and draw of his lips sending sparks up her legs and through her core.

She hardly noticed as he began working her drawers over her hips, too focused on what he was doing to her nipples. God, he must never stop his attentions. Ever. She could lie here for days and be perfectly happy.

Suddenly, he shifted, his mouth leaving her breasts as he drifted lower on the mattress, bringing her drawers and stocking down until her legs were bare. His head dipped and she felt electrifying kisses along the skin of her inner thigh.

Though it felt divine, she was uncertain what was happening. She levered up and pushed on his shoulder. Glittering dark eyes met hers. "What are you doing?" she asked.

"I swear you shall love this. Trust me, Christina."

She nodded, though her hands remained clenched in the bedclothes. Was he staring at her *there*?

"Lie back and relax." When she settled, he rested a hand on her sternum. The weight was comforting, as if he needed to remain connected to her.

His face came closer and she felt the swipe of his tongue across her most feminine flesh. She nearly leapt off the bed as a jolt of pleasure shot through her. Goodness gracious . . . had he licked her? There?

The question was answered when he did it again . . . and again, the sensation nearly overwhelming in its strength. She quivered and shook, her body reaching and straining, his tongue licking her core with purpose. After a moment, he dedicated his attention to one spot and her eyes nearly rolled back. The muscles in her legs locked, everything in her tightening, every nerve ending centered in that place.

Mouth and teeth worked on that nub, sucking and scraping, until she squirmed beneath him. Loud moans erupted from her mouth, guttural sounds she could no longer control. She was climbing higher and higher, the feeling so much more intense than last night's climax. When he inserted a finger into her channel, everything burst free, breaking, a thousand stars scattered into the heavens as release overcame her. The trembling went on and on as the sweet oblivion dragged her under.

After one more kiss to her sex, he stood and began tearing at the rest of his clothing. She watched, dazed, as he freed his erection from his undergarment. The shaft stood out proudly from his body, demanding and eager, the bulbous head slightly reddish. Blue veins ran down the sides under the skin. It was intimidating and so different.

"Christina."

She found his face. Oliver's right hand came up, his middle finger tapping the back of his other hand. "Touch me," he signed, his gaze wild. "Please." He stepped out of his trousers and undergarment then crawled onto the bed next to her.

"I cannot . . ." She reached tentatively for him, but snatched her hand back. "How?"

"Did you ask how?"

She looked up so he could see her mouth. "Yes. I do not wish to hurt you."

Curling his fingers, he signed by hitting one hand on top of the other. "Hard."

"Hard?"

"You cannot hurt me. Grab me as rough as you like." He took her wrist and led her hand to the shaft. "Wrap your hand around me."

She curled her fingers around him, surprised at the smooth feel. For something so hard his penis felt like velvet in her hand. She moved her fingers, sliding him through her palm. He gave a swift intake of breath, his big body shuddering. "More," he signed. "Please."

The quiet directions in his language emboldened her. She liked learning how to better speak to him with her hands, and he seemed to sign almost automatically, as if he was so far gone with desire he could not help himself. It made her less awkward about her own unclothed state and inexperience. "Keep signing. Tell me what you want."

He blinked at her, his chest heaving. "But . . ."

"Even if I cannot understand. Just talk to me."

His hands moved quickly then. She could not decipher the signs but continued to stroke his shaft with both hands, watching his reaction to see what he liked as she explored every part of him. The root, the underside, the tip . . . She did it by feel to keep her gaze on his hands and face. He was fascinating, lids screwed shut during her teasing, still talking to her.

Oliver shuddered and gasped. Suddenly, he caught her hand. "Please, no more. I am too close."

Pressing her hand to the bed, he rolled to partially cover her, his mouth finding hers. He kissed her desperately, as if he was nearing the end of his rope, and she loved it. She could feel the slickness between her thighs, an emptiness deep inside her. Despite her earlier release she was eager for him, eager for more.

"Tell me what you want," he said against her mouth then pressed up on his elbows to see her face. "I am trying to go slowly but I cannot last much longer. Tell me, my lovely wife."

Under no circumstances could she bring herself to actually voice her desires aloud . . . so she showed him instead. Distracting him with a kiss, she rocked her hips against his, along the length of his shaft. Oliver gave a quick intake of breath and his hands tightened. "Oh, Christ. Do that again."

She eagerly complied, the delicious pressure causing streaks of electricity all along her legs. On the next roll, however, it became clear this was not enough for either of them. He groaned. "God. I want to thrust inside you, but I do not wish to hurt—"

She loved that he thought of her comfort first,

that he would not rut like a mindless animal in heat. It gave her the courage to continue, to slide her legs apart and make room for him there. He shifted to line their hips together, the hard ridge of his shaft pressed between them. Without even knowing what she was doing, she angled her hips, asking for more. He lined the tip at her entrance and slowly pushed the head inside, panting against her mouth, his eyes screwed shut. Once there, he did not move, merely waited for her to take the lead.

Wrapping her leg more firmly about him, she shifted until the heavy weight of him slid in a little farther. Her body accommodated his length, the stretch of her inner tissues both foreign and thrilling. The pressure increased as he continued filling her, slowly and steadily, his forehead resting on hers, the sound of their breathing echoing around them. Finally, their hips joined, Oliver deep inside her.

She clutched his shoulders and marveled at the fullness, the way he was now a part of her. Oliver let out a moan, the tendons in his throat standing out in sharp relief. "You are so tight. I feel as though I might die if I do not hurry this along. Are you all right?"

"Yes," she said, and it was the truth. There had been no pain, only pressure, and she was now burning with the desperate need for movement.

"Thank God." He rose up over her and planted his knees between her legs, his weight supported by his arms. Then he withdrew slightly only to push forward, the head of his shaft dragging over her inner walls.

"Oh," she breathed, her toes curling with the shock of it.

His fingers threaded through hers, their palms pressed together, his gaze locked on hers as he thrust once more. "Christ, you are beautiful."

She closed her eyes, too delirious to keep them focused. He drove deep and her body trembled, heat and fire licking through her veins. Then he lifted one of her knees, stretching her open farther, and began to move fiercely, the thick length of him spearing her. She could not think, could not speak except in low moans as he worked himself in and out of her channel. It was even better than what he had done with his mouth—and that had been nothing short of life altering.

His thumb pressed between her legs, working the tiny nub with familiar magic, and her muscles soon trembled as the sensation built to a fever pitch. White-hot excitement built and built . . . until it crested, tossing her about like a wave. She shouted his name, dimly aware that Oliver had sped up, his hips now slapping against hers. Just as she regained her equilibrium, he gripped her tighter as his hips stuttered. He suddenly withdrew, his hand stroking his shaft twice before he ejaculated onto the bedclothes.

When he stopped shaking, he sagged on top of her, dropping down and crushing her into the mattress. She wrapped her arms around his sweaty back, liking this quiet moment of shared intimacy with no words necessary. Not even the weight of him bothered her. She liked supporting him, caring for him, and her heart expanded in her chest.

Oh. Was she falling in love with her husband?

There was no time to ponder that problem because Oliver began dropping kisses on her chest and throat. She had no idea if he was trying to reassure her or show his gratitude, but either way, she adored him for it. Her fingers threaded through his hair as she cradled him close.

When he reached her mouth, he kissed her softly, gently, with a tenderness she felt in her very soul. "Stay with me tonight."

"Here?" she asked when he had pulled back enough to see her lips.

He nodded. "I want you next to me. In my bed. Where you belong."

She bit her lip, so filled with happiness that she could not prevent herself from grinning. "I'd like that."

The next morning, Oliver was in his workshop when Christina strolled by the glass, bundled in her new black coat and thick black hat, headed toward the gardens. He smothered the insane desire to drag her inside the greenhouse and make love to her once again.

Last night was her first time. Let the woman catch her breath, for Christ's sake.

She gave him a blinding smile and lifted her hand in greeting. He waved, his lips curling at the sight. God, how had he become so fortunate? She was breathtaking. And the way she'd responded in bed . . . His cock jumped in his clothing at just the memory.

Should he send a groom to accompany her? He did not care for the idea of her mother reappearing and accosting Christina again. She was his wife and he needed to protect her from those charlatans. Keep her safe. Never have her want for another thing in her life.

Before he could decide, a footman shuffled from the house, bundled up and trailing Christina. *God bless Gill.* The old man knew Oliver so well. He lifted his hand to the footman, giving him an approving nod.

Time passed as he tweaked his new device. It was almost ready. One of the main issues continued to be the battery. He had been using a lead-acid battery but the thing was heavy and unwieldy for everyday use. Nickel, however, showed the most promise for a new type of battery, one that would be smaller and last longer. An improved power source was key in ensuring his hearing device would reach the largest number of people. Based on his latest tests, he should be ready to apply for a patent in a month or so.

Apollo jumped up, alerting Oliver to someone's presence just before the door opened. He expected to find his wife, but Gill was there instead. The man's face was paler than usual, the lines around his mouth more pronounced. "Sir, you have a visitor."

"Who?"

"Milton."

Oliver rolled his eyes. Why was his cousin here? Frank must have informed Milton of his reduced allowance. "Where is he?"

"In your study, sir."

"Sarah has not seen him, has she?" He wanted to keep his sister as far away from their cousin as possible.

"No, sir. She is still in her chambers."

"Good. See that she stays there until Milton departs."

Once inside the house, he made his way to the study, Gill not far behind. The door was ajar so he slipped inside, drawing in a deep breath for fortitude.

Milton stood when he saw Oliver. "Good morning, cousin." He was outfitted in a loud green check suit so flashy it actually hurt Oliver's eyes.

Oliver signed to Gill, who translated for Milton. "What do you want, Milton? If it is about the alpaca farm, I have not changed my mind."

"Now, listen. I was contacted by your lawyer and he led me to believe you are reducing my monthly allowance."

"That is correct. I have been much too generous with you, apparently."

Milton's neck flushed a dull red. "Generous? You are mad."

"No, merely wise to your schemes. Had you honestly thought Frank would not check with me before handing over a sum like that?"

His cousin appeared stunned but quickly recovered, adopting an air of indignation. "I do not see the problem. You can well afford the investment and I am your family. Perhaps I should help to manage more of our family's—"

Oliver started signing, not even waiting for that ridiculous suggestion to finish. "Absolutely not," Gill said, his eyes trained on Oliver's hands. "Even if you had not tried to swindle me for five thousand dollars I would never trust you with the family finances. All you have done is squander your own wealth over the years."

"That is because you are miserly with my funds. Your father cheated my father out of his rightful share of the money and now you are doing the same with me!"

Oliver rubbed his brow tiredly. When would Milton accept the truth?

Thomas Hawkes and his brother, Milton's father, had started a trading company during the war. The work had been dangerous and not highly profitable, especially once the blockades were put in place. Milton's father backed out, opting to open a dry goods store on Duane Street to provide for his growing family.

With only a wife and one child, Thomas had decided to embark on a risk. He went to England, bought war materials, and resold them to the Union army. When that turned a profit, he began investing in various businesses, such as real estate, railroads, and steel. His profits doubled every year once the war ended.

So no, Milton was not entitled to any of the Hawkes fortune.

Oliver signed, "Your father gave up his rights to the family business long before my father turned it profitable. The money was never *yours*, Milton."

"That is not true."

It was absolutely true, but there was no arguing with Milton. God knew Oliver had tried. "If you continue to disagree with me, I shall reduce your monthly stipend by half instead of just ten percent."

"Half! How dare you. The money I already receive is barely enough to live on. How am I supposed to get by with even less?"

"I could not say," Oliver signed. "Perhaps you should stop gambling or cut your mistress loose. Doing both would save you a considerable sum each month. All I know is that your lifestyle and the money to maintain it are no longer my problem."

Milton's eyes nearly bulged from his skull,

his lips white with rage. "You think you are so clever, sitting here in your giant house and tinkering on your inane inventions. You do not hear what everyone says about you, the names they call you. I have always defended you, told them they were wrong about Oliver Hawkes. What a fool I was to believe family meant something to you. What will happen, I wonder, when I stop defending you? Do you think you will finally be committed to one of those asylums?"

First outright thievery and now blackmail? For God's sake . . . "If anyone is starting those rumors it is you. You should know one thing, however. Even if something happens to me, my wife shall control the money in the family's interest—not you." He had not yet changed his will, but Milton needn't know that.

"Yes, your wife," Milton said with a sneer. "I have done some digging into your wife. Meek little thing, is she not? If you were not around I suspect she'd need advice, some guidance on how to best oversee the Hawkes fortune."

"Perhaps," Gill translated. "But that guidance won't be provided by you. Now get the hell out of my house, Milton. Any further communication between us may go through my attorney."

Milton huffed, his body vibrating in outrage. "This is not over." Jaw tight, he spun and stormed out of the study.

Gill hurried after Oliver's cousin and Oliver scrubbed his face with both hands. Milton was the lowest form of human being. A spineless worm who felt entitled to a fortune he had no right to claim. Christ, Oliver needed a bath after that meeting.

Or maybe he would find his wife and see if he could persuade her to join him upstairs for a "nap." A smile tugging at his lips, he thrust his hands in his pockets and sauntered outside.

Chapter Fifteen

Christina's fingers were numb from the cold. Normally she went straight to her apartments after a walk, but this morning she needed the extra warmth. The kitchens were hot this time of day, with food preparation well under way, so she headed there. Perhaps she could sneak a cup of hot tea to cradle in her hands to boot.

A small stone courtyard sat behind the kitchens, lined with pots for herbs and produce come summer. She entered through the heavy back door. Heavenly smells assaulted her, nearly causing her to stumble. Roasted chicken, bread, cinnamon . . . it was like a feast for her senses. Her stomach grumbled.

When she stepped into the kitchen, activity seemed to freeze, all eyes swinging her way. The undivided attention caused her pulse to race. Suddenly, she regretted not slipping into the house and going up to her room. "Good morning," she forced out, hoping they would ignore her and resume their normal duties.

Her eye caught on a small table and chairs off to the side and she noticed Sarah sitting there. Sarah's dark curls were piled on her head and she sipped from a china teacup. Christina came closer. "Good morning. May I join you?"

"Hello, Lady Christina," Oliver's sister said. "Please, sit. You look cold."

"I am." Christina lowered herself into one of the empty chairs. "And just Christina will do. I love your dress." Made of green cotton, the garment was adorned with lots of lace and ruffles.

Sarah frowned at the compliment. "It's baby-ish, which is why I wanted Oliver to take me shopping. None of the other girls at school wear dresses like this."

The dress seemed appropriate for the girl's age. "What sort of dresses do you want to wear?"

"Something sophisticated. Like what you wear."

Christina did not bother to point out the obvious, that she was almost ten years Sarah's senior. A maid set a cup and saucer on the table in front of Christina. She reached for the pot to pour herself tea. "When you are my age, after your debut, I am certain he will buy you whatever you wish."

"Doubtful," Sarah mumbled. "Oliver never cares about what I want. He always thinks he is right."

Christina had no idea how to respond. Negotiating sibling squabbles was far outside her realm of expertise. "What is school like?"

"It is mostly fun. I have lots of friends and my marks are high. I like visiting here and seeing my brother, but there is never much to do. That is why I am so relieved he has finally married."

Christina was happy to have Sarah's approval but she did not follow the reasoning behind it. "Because you want him to do more?"

"No. I mean, yes. That would be nice, but I do not expect him to change. I meant you." Sarah raised her brows meaningfully. "You and I shall become good friends. We will travel all over the city together."

Christina's heart sank. Oliver's sister wanted a friend, a companion here in New York. She had no idea that Christina was not suited for this role at all. Still, Christina hated to disappoint her. "I . . . I suppose someday we might."

Gill arrived. "Miss Sarah, Mr. Harris awaits you in the stables."

Christina latched on to the new topic, anything to evade discussions of exploring the city. "That sounds like fun. You like horses, do you?"

"Oh, yes," Sarah answered. "I plan to have a whole stable of them when I grow up. Would you like to come with me? I will show you my favorite one."

She cleared her throat. "I am actually afraid of horses."

"You are?" Sarah's eyes went wide.

"Yes, ever since I can remember."

"Were you thrown as a little girl?"

"No, nothing as terrible as that. I just never learned how to ride and the animals are quite big."

"I could teach you," Sarah said, her voice full of confidence.

"Miss Sarah," Gill said gently. "I believe the cook has carrots and apples set aside for the horses. Perhaps you would take them?"

"Oh, yes. They love those." The girl stood up from the table and raced to the other side of the kitchen.

Gill studied Christina's face. "If you care to escape now, madam, I am happy to give the young girl an excuse on your behalf."

"No need. I do not mind her exuberance. She is so different than I was at her age." Or now, for that matter. Christina never would have invited an adult to come to the stables with her or dared to ask personal questions of a near stranger. It was refreshing to see a girl being raised to speak her mind and act confidently. How much of that was Oliver's influence? "I have enjoyed spending time with her."

Gill gave a brisk nod. "Mr. Hawkes is fond of his sister but has always been a good deal older. I am certain she will like having another young woman around."

Christina looked over at where Sarah and the cook were standing. Something Sarah said made the cook laugh. "I have no doubt I shall like having her around as well."

OLIVER FINALLY FOUND Christina in the last place he expected. When a footman told him his wife was in the kitchens, Oliver thought he had read the man's words incorrectly. Sure enough, however, when he went below she was there, sitting at a small table and talking to his sister.

Christina had removed her heavy hat but still wore her black coat. Long brown strands of hair had escaped to frame her face, now rosy from the cold. She laughed at something Sarah said, and the sight of her joy was like a punch to his solar plexus.

He loved to see her happy.

Gill was the first to spot him. "Was there something you require, sir?"

"Merely looking for my wife," he signed, speaking at the same time for Christina's benefit.

She met his eyes and her mouth curved into a sheepish smile. "Hello, Oliver. Do you need me?"

Always, something deep inside him whispered. He shook off that fanciful thought. There was no place for silly romantic notions in his life. He believed in logic and reason, things he could see and examine. "Nothing serious. I merely wished to take a break and spend some time with you."

Even more color stained her cheeks, which he found absurdly charming. A hand tugged on his sleeve. He glanced down at Sarah. "Yes?"

"Christina is coming to the stables with me," his sister said.

Gill began signing and speaking. "Now, Miss Sarah. Mrs. Hawkes has already said that she does not like horses and has no desire to join you at the stables. You must not—"

Oliver stopped paying attention to Gill and faced his wife. "You do not like horses?" How had he not known this?

"I . . . I never learned to ride properly as a girl." She shifted in her seat. "As I grew older there hardly seemed a reason to start. The animals are big and . . . unpredictable."

He knew enough about her parents to suspect more to that story. Had they not owned horses for riding? Everything about her life in England remained a mystery to him. He resolved to spend more time talking with her, getting to know her in the rest of the time they were married. "I am happy to teach you."

Her face paled. "No, that is unnecessary. You are busy and there is no use—"

"Nonsense," he interrupted. "I am not too busy for this. You shall enjoy it, I swear."

Sarah jumped up from her seat and reached for Christina, pulling the woman from her chair. "Hooray! You and I will soon be galloping in Central Park—" His sister turned away and Oliver could not follow the rest of what she said. No matter. He started to follow the two out of the kitchens.

Gill's hand stopped him. "Are you certain about this?" his butler signed. "Your wife expressed a fear of horses a few moments ago."

It stood to reason she was afraid considering she hadn't spent much time around the animals, but they were harmless. Oliver had ridden nearly his entire life. No doubt she would come to love riding once she tried it. "She is only afraid because she has no experience with them. I shall show her and teach her. It will be fine."

Gill did not appear convinced. "Go gently with her. She has had a lot of change in a short period of time."

Oliver waved his hand. "She is stronger than she seems," he signed. "She survived her parents, after all."

He strode out of the kitchens, ending the conversation. People underestimated Christina: first her parents, then Van Peet. Gill. Oliver had witnessed glimpses of her bravery, the fortitude buried deep. All she needed was help to grow her confidence. As he recalled, she had been afraid of Apollo at first until he had helped her get used to the dog.

When he and Apollo caught up, Christina was standing in the mews, perfectly still, the breeze blowing her hair as she faced the stables. Sarah had disappeared somewhere inside the two-story building. Oliver placed his hand on Christina's lower back. She started then spun toward him, her eyes wide. "Oliver. You frightened me."

He gave her a reassuring smile. "Come inside. Let me show you around."

She was already shaking her head before he even finished. "No, I would prefer to wait here. I am able to see Sarah and the horses from this spot."

At several yards away from the three yawning entrances of the building?

Oliver moved closer and stroked his knuckles over her cheekbone. "Do you trust me?"

Her shoulders relaxed ever so slightly. "Yes."

"Then allow me to take you in and show you the horses. You shall soon see you have nothing to fear."

Her throat worked as she swallowed, her gaze bouncing between him and the entrances. "Oliver, please. I do not think—"

"Nonsense. I won't let anything happen to you." He took her hand in his and began gently leading her inside. She allowed it . . . barely. Her feet moved slowly. He did not rush her—but neither did he let up. She merely needed experience, and the only way to do that was to enter the stables.

The smell of horses and leather mixed with hay washed over him as they went in. The stables housed five full-time grooms and Oliver's fourteen horses. The building had been designed in the same French Renaissance style as the mansion itself, with the interior renovated three years ago to include a carriage elevator, electric lighting, and wider stalls for the animals. Terra-cotta and brass were used throughout, with carvings of horses as decoration. While he did not often spend time here, he loved the space.

The head groom, Mr. Harris, rushed over. Harris had been around long enough to pick up a few simple signs. "Sir, welcome. Did you plan on riding this morning?"

Oliver shook his head. He preferred to ride just as dawn broke, when the traffic was almost non-existent. Then he could ride in the park and not worry that he'd miss any warning sounds from other riders. "No," he signed. "I am showing the horses to my wife today."

"Very good," Harris signed, tipping his cap at Christina. "Welcome, madam. Please let me know if you need assistance."

"Thank you," Christina said. Oliver took her hand once more and brought her farther inside. Her head swiveled as she took it all in. He could not tell for certain, but he thought she appeared impressed.

"There are fourteen horses in the stables, kept for a variety of purposes," he said as Apollo darted ahead, down the row of stalls. "When we finally get you in the saddle it will be on one of the gentler mares."

Several horses walked to the front of their stalls to investigate the newcomers. Christina edged closer to him and he put his arm around her waist. Patches, the mare with the sweetest temperament, would probably fit Christina best. It was the horse Sarah was permitted to ride.

When they reached the correct stall, Oliver stopped. Patches immediately came over, and Oliver dropped Christina's hand to stroke the horse's muzzle. The glossy brown-and-white coat was soft beneath his fingers. He glanced over his shoulder to where Christina stood, her arms wrapped around her waist. "Come here," he signed.

She shook her head, wide eyes never leaving the horse.

"Please," he signed. When she continued to refuse, he decided some gentle prodding was in order. He took her hand and brought her near the stall. "I will not let anything happen to you. Just come and pet Patches."

"Patches?"

"Yes, because of her coloring. See for yourself."

He tugged her over. Patches sniffed and moved her head in Christina's direction. His wife tried to retreat but Oliver stood behind her, preventing an escape. "It is all right. She is just saying hello."

Christina stood frozen while the animal nudged her hand. When no treat was revealed, Patches grew bored and tried Oliver's hand.

"Here," he told Christina and produced two sugar cubes from his pocket. He'd grabbed them from a container near the entrance. "Put these in your palm and she will eat them."

Christina shook her head and tried to with-draw, but Oliver remained close, keeping his front to her back. "I swear, she will love it," he told her.

He could not hear his wife's response but she pressed into him, away from the horse. He understood fear, had lived with his own demons for years after losing his hearing. However, fears merely needed to be met head-on to conquer them. Taking his wife's hand, he placed the sugar cubes in her palm. "Now hold them out."

Christina's hand trembled as it inched forward. The horse smelled the sugar and opened its mouth, lips seeking, to get at the cubes. When the mouth brushed over Christina's palm, she jerked, which sent the cubes flying. Before he could say anything, she shoved past him and ran out of the stables, tears brimming in her eyes.

CHRISTINA DID NOT stop running until she reached her bedroom, cold fear like ice in her veins. Once there, she flopped on the bed and dissolved into tears. Part of her was disappointed in herself. It was silly to be afraid of horses and Oliver had only wanted to help.

The other part of her was angry with Oliver. What gave him the right to disregard her wishes and force her to do something like that? She had repeatedly voiced an objection to touching or feeding the horse. Even if he had not heard her protestations he should have been able to read her body language.

When would her choices be her own? At what

point would others stop forcing her to bend to their will?

And what was wrong with her that she allowed it?

You are weak. First your parents, now Oliver. They all profess to know what is best for you.

When would she gain the ability to speak up and decide for herself?

A gentle hand swept over her back and she tensed. Then the mattress dipped, signaling the presence of another person. It did not require a genius to figure out who had arrived. How had he entered without her hearing him?

"Christina," Oliver said. "Tell me why you are crying."

She pressed her lips together and remained silent. Oliver meant well. He was not a cruel person. For heaven's sake, he had married her to keep her away from Van Peet. Plus he'd given her parents a marriage settlement. There had also been last night, when they had shared beautiful intimate moments together. He cared for her, she was certain of it.

So it felt petulant to complain about having her choices taken away. What woman truly chose *anything* in this world? Christina was not alone in this. Young girls had been used as pawns in the pursuit of money and power since the dawn of time. Married women mattered even less, as everything they owned belonged to their husbands . . . including their bodies.

Oliver stretched out on the mattress, his presence warm and solid beside her. "I am so sorry," he said. "I thought I was helping you. With Apollo, you were initially scared until you grew accustomed to him. I erroneously assumed the same would happen with horses. I never meant to upset you."

The logic was sound, which stood to reason. Her husband was a very logical man. She wished she could also attack this problem logically, to arrive at some unforeseen conclusion that would cure her, but these fears were not in her control. They were silly and irrational, emotional reactions that had grown worse over time.

"When I first discovered I was deaf," Oliver said, "I was scared to death. I cried, I screamed. I threw things. I could not sleep because the constant silence terrified me. What if someone came into my room? What if the house caught on fire in the middle of the night and I could not hear the alarm? So I forced myself to stay awake, which did not help my adjustment."

Sniffing, she wiped her eyes and rolled to face him. She was eager to learn more about him, about his childhood.

His arms were folded under his head and he focused on the ceiling. "My mother was incredibly patient, however. She kept telling me there was no way backward, that we had to keep going forward. She had a strong will, much stronger than mine. She pushed me when I would have given up."

She studied his handsome profile, the sturdy jaw and straight nose. He seemed so strong, so capable. Yet it would terrify most anyone to suddenly lose his or her hearing. Putting her hand on his cheek, she forced his head to the side where he could see her mouth. "What does that mean, you would have given up?"

He said nothing, merely stared, but the truth was reflected in his bright green eyes. He did not hide anything from her, instead revealed the regret and misery he clearly carried over what he had contemplated. She could barely breathe thinking on all that would have been lost had he succeeded. "Oh, Oliver."

Letting out a long breath, he fixed his gaze on the ceiling once more. "I never wanted to be a burden or an embarrassment to them. To anyone, really. We come from a world that expects perfection. Any flaw or abnormality is unacceptable."

How well she understood. She thought of all the times the other girls had laughed at her, the biting comments that cut deep, often over something as little as a mismatched ribbon in her hair.

Unfortunately, cruelty never relied on rationality.

Yet those criticisms paled in comparison to what Oliver must have faced. She had not stopped to think of others with more difficult circumstances; instead she had selfishly focused on only herself. The world, she was learning, was much bigger than Mayfair or Fifth Avenue. No wonder a man with Oliver's intelligence and pride had lost the patience for high society. She rested her hand on his chest, needing to touch him in some small way.

He placed his hand atop hers and threaded their fingers together. "The first thing that significantly helped was a dog. I had been deaf for almost eight months when my father brought home a collie. I think my parents were worried I was lonely. They were not wrong, but I did not realize how much I needed that dog. I named her Diana because she was a hunter. She never left my side, alerting me whenever there was a noise. I was finally able to sleep through the night."

She squeezed his hand, content to listen.

"Then they found Dr. Jacobs, who was nothing short of a miracle. At the time, I had retreated, spending all of my time alone with my dog. I was frustrated, not to mention angry and scared. I had never even met another deaf person. My parents had started researching deaf schools but I refused to go. Eventually, after many long months of instruction and discussion, Dr. Jacobs helped me see that things were not so bleak. That I would have a completely normal life, just a life that was a bit different."

She swallowed past the lump in her throat, overcome with gratitude for his parents, Dr. Jacobs, and his dog. Oliver was the most remarkable man she had ever met, and everything he shared only made her adore him more.

He shifted onto his side so they faced one another, his palm cupping her jaw. "I am telling you this because I want you to understand that I know what it is to be afraid. My parents pushed me to move beyond the fear, but I should not have done the same with you. My problems were vastly different and we are not the same person. Meaning, what worked for me may not be what you need. I do sincerely apologize, and if you never wish to see a horse again then I will support you."

Her heart tripped behind her ribs. She had not expected such understanding. And he was letting her choose? "You will not make me ride?"

"Absolutely not. I shall buy you a velocipede to get about, if that is what you wish. Then you may ride a machine instead of a horse."

Emotion rose in her chest, like a hot air balloon rising off the ground. He was listening to her and taking her wishes into account . . . and that meant absolutely *everything*. She leaned in and kissed him, unable to keep from expressing her gratitude and appreciation for all he had shared. He seemed surprised and a half second passed before he kissed her back. Then his lips began sliding over hers as he worked her mouth with exquisite tenderness.

"I will not push you into doing anything against your will ever again," he said when they pulled apart. "But also know that I am willing to help should you change your mind."

"Thank you, Oliver." Her heart raced in a steady rhythm. She clung to him, her fingers knotted in his hair, their legs tangled on the bed. Desire hummed through her veins, buzzing and building, a reminder of their previous night together. She longed to stay here for the rest of the day.

"Good. That is settled, then." He kissed her nose and then started to roll away.

"Wait," she said, holding on to his waistcoat. He looked over his shoulder at her, his brows lowered in confusion. It was hard to meet his eyes so she stared at his forehead. "You said you were not too busy today. I thought perhaps . . . Well, I thought perhaps we could stay here."

His expression cleared, his mouth twisting in amusement. "Spend the day in bed? I am shocked by such a torrid suggestion. Have I already corrupted you?"

Chapter Sixteen

Oliver knew he had embarrassed his wife, yet he hadn't been able to resist teasing her. She was too adorable, staring up at him with a mix of desire and shyness. He understood her shyness but hoped, by making a joke, to demonstrate that their physical relationship should be fun. Mutually rewarding, and something they should both desire.

And really, would he ever refuse a request from her to stay in bed?

Her gaze slid away from his face, color darkening her cheeks. "You make it sound so . . ."

He waited for the word but it never came. "Tawdry?" He crawled toward her on the mattress. "Dirty? Delicious?" Her lips twisted as if fighting a smile and she began backing away from him. His hand shot out to capture her ankle and he dragged her closer, her skirts bunching around her legs. "Dashed enjoyable?"

She was laughing now, trying to shove her skirts down. "Oliver, stop! We should lock the door first."

"No one would dare enter with us both in here, not if they wish to keep their position."

"How can you be certain?"

"They know I am in here with you. Any fool would correctly conclude what we were doing in here, especially when we miss luncheon."

She craned her neck to see the clock. "Miss luncheon? But it is still morning."

"Yes, but this is going to take a very long time." Now on his stomach, he settled between her legs and moved her skirts higher. "A very, very long time."

She squirmed and he looked up to see if she was opposed to him using his mouth on her. "Objections?"

She shook her head. "My bustle was poking me but I am fine now."

Damned women's clothing. Reaching under her outer skirt, he began untying and shedding her base garments, one by one, until they were gone. He left on her stockings and pushed up her chemise and outer skirt, revealing long and pale legs, her sex so beautiful and ripe. The musky smell of her arousal caused his mouth to water.

"Remember to tap my shoulder or pull my hair," he reminded before dipping his head to taste her. He closed his eyes and swept his tongue through her slit. Her moisture met his mouth, a rich heady taste he could feed on for days. His cock swelled, his skin heating from the inside out.

Using his thumbs, he parted the folds and flicked her clitoris with his tongue. She jumped a little but did not tap or tug on him. Encouraged, he placed a palm on her sternum to feel her moans of pleasure and continued with this most delectable of tasks. He focused on the tight bud, slowly sucking and licking, drawing out the pleasure as long as possible.

The vibrations under his hand increased until her thighs began to shake, and still he continued to work the swollen nub, his tongue curling and flicking. The sweet taste of her was like honey in his mouth, and his erection strained inside his clothing. God, he could spend so easily like this, her scent and taste surrounding him.

When she tensed, her back bowing, he sped up his efforts. Soon she stiffened, her legs shaking as the orgasm washed over her. He eased up as her trembling tapered off, only stopping when her flesh became too sensitive.

He rose up on his knees and grinned at her. "More? Or have you had enough?"

"What about you?" she asked.

Hard to miss the erection tenting his trousers, he supposed. "There's no tit for tat between us," he signed and said. "I wanted to do that for you. Everything else may wait, especially if you are sore from last night."

She bit her lip, raised her hands, and began to unbutton her shirtwaist. His breath caught, hope rising fast. "Are you certain?"

After she nodded, he wasted no time, tearing at the buttons of his vest. Pushing his suspenders down, he whipped off his shirt, tearing a few small buttons in his haste. With her consent, he now felt frantic, absolutely mindless to get inside her. His balls were high and tight, the length of his shaft throbbing in time with his heartbeat. Next were trousers and his undergarment. He rolled to his back and worked as quickly as possible.

Once he was naked and on his knees, she had already shrugged off her shirtwaist and corset cover. He signed, "Turn over." When she was on her stomach, he quickly loosened the corset laces enough for her to pop the fastenings in the front and toss the heavy piece to the floor. Without bothering to remove her chemise, he rolled her over, lined up at her entrance, and pushed the head of his cock inside. Slick, wet heat gripped him and his eyes nearly rolled back in his head. Holy mother of God, she felt amazing.

He propped himself on his hands so as to not crush her and, gritting his teeth, pushed forward ever so slowly. It was both torture and pure heaven, his eyes never leaving her face, gauging her reaction.

Not that he needed to worry. With her head thrown back, lips parted in wonder, she held on to his forearms, keeping him close. After what seemed an eternity, he was fully seated inside her channel. Tight and hot, she gripped him like a fist. Pleasure rippled down his spine, and he had to suppress the urge to take her fast and hard.

Lowering himself onto his elbows, he kissed her and began to rock his hips, grinding into her pelvis as he pumped. After a moment she began to move as well, meeting his strokes. Tingles spread from his back along his legs to his toes, the familiar climb in the race to climax, and he knew it would not be long. Their tongues dueled as the tempo increased until she tore free of his mouth and buried her face in his throat. She stiffened, and he could feel her moans against his skin.

Oh, Christ. She was perfect, her walls milking his shaft as her nails dug into his flesh. The orgasm rushed up then, white-hot sparks that engulfed him. He quickly withdrew, pulling out to spend on her stomach, every muscle trembling in euphoria as his hand flew over his cock.

When the world stopped spinning, he dropped onto the bed next to her and closed his eyes. "I shall help you clean up in a moment. Allow me to catch my breath first."

A tap on his shoulder got his attention. Christina's head was turned toward him. "Do you think Dr. Jacobs would help me learn sign language, too?"

Oliver blinked. "I am certain he would love it, but I am perfectly capable of teaching you. Gill probably would as well."

"I know, but I thought it would be nice to learn from the person who taught you. Then you won't need to be bothered with me."

"You are not a bother. I like to keep busy, yes, but there will always be time for you."

That answer did not appear to appease her. She pressed her lips flat, her brows drawing together. His hands signed as he spoke. "You do not wish for me to make time for you?"

"No, it is not that. I just . . . do not understand."

"That I wish to spend time with you?" Was he misspeaking or slurring his words? Old fears resurfaced, ones he had hoped to never experience again. Frustration burned in his chest as he watched her mouth.

"I am making a hash of this." She shook her head. "Forgive me."

He rolled onto his elbow and stared down at her. "Christina, there is nothing to forgive. We must work a bit harder sometimes to communicate, but that is no different than any other married couple, I suspect."

"Are we a married couple, then?"

He did not understand this conversation at all. Reaching to the table by the bed, he found a pencil and a small ledger. He handed them to her.

While she wrote, he rose off the bed and went to his bathing chamber. There, he quickly cleaned off, and then he wet a soft cloth with warm water and returned to his bedroom. His spend coated her stomach and Oliver felt an absurd pleasure at seeing that. Like he had marked her somehow. Made her his. More and more he felt attached to this woman, her presence eliciting all sorts of emotions and thoughts he had never experienced before.

A week ago that may have frightened him . . . but no longer. This woman was meant to be here, with him, forever.

I will not push you into doing anything against your will ever again.

He had not forgotten his promise from an hour ago. Somehow, he would have to convince her to stay. Woo her into developing feelings for him. Turn this marriage into a real union.

Losing her was not an option.

She handed him the ledger. *You said we would live separate lives,* he read. *You also asked that I respect your private spaces. I agreed and have no wish to break that promise, but your offer to teach me sign language is confusing. What we are doing in this bed is confusing. It feels as if the rules are changing.*

Ah. He understood. The rules *were* changing. His feelings were changing, the world around him shifting and rewiring itself on a daily basis. No wonder she could not keep up; he could barely keep above water himself.

He set the ledger on the table once again, keeping it within reach if it became necessary. "The night of our marriage, I thought it was best if we distanced ourselves from one another. Then the separation at the end of a year would be easier. That has been much harder than I expected, however, and I now find the idea distasteful."

Her brows shot up. "You do?"

He smoothed errant strands of hair off her face. "I do. I like spending time with you. I like having you in my bed. I do not profess to know what any of that means for the future, but I have grown attached to you." He purposely did not raise the issue of postponing the divorce indefinitely. No need to scare her. Much better that she come to the realization herself, fully understanding all she would be giving up if she stayed his wife.

"I like spending time with you, too."

He tried not to read too much into that statement and willed his heart to stop pounding so hard. *Give her time.* "Good. Now, let us go enjoy spending time with one another in the bath."

She looked at him as if he'd sprouted a second head. "A bath? Together?"

Instead of explaining it, he slid his arms underneath her and moved to the side of the mattress. "Yes, a bath together. Trust me, you will love it."

"WATCH ME CLIMB these rocks, Christina!"

Christina watched as Sarah scampered away and began to climb a large stone outcrop. The two were on a walk today in Central Park. The girl had been bored and Christina took pity on her. A big house, no friends about to play with . . . Christina could certainly understand the loneliness in that. Besides, she liked to walk outdoors, and the park was big enough to prevent the crowded city from feeling overwhelming.

Sarah, it turned out, loved the park. The young girl had easily climbed every rock they passed, her small legs nimble even in a dress and petticoat. She seemed oblivious to the dirt or the possibility of injury. Christina tried to keep from wincing every time Sarah slipped.

Oliver's sister was a curious mix. She often seemed much older and wiser, and then there were times like this, a young girl out enjoying a bit of outdoor play.

"Too bad Oliver could not join us," Sarah said when she returned to Christina's side. They set off toward the main pedestrian path.

Christina's skin warmed. Memories flashed through her brain: naked, sweaty limbs and deep kisses. She and Oliver had spent each night together in the past week. *I have grown attached to you.* Mercy, those words melted her insides each time she recalled them.

"He needed to continue working."

"My brother is very smart. His speaker will help thousands of people hear. Do you think he is smart, Christina?"

Smart, not to mention handsome and kind. "I do," she said with a fond smile. Oliver's sister was adorable, a bright and brave child, so different from Christina at that age. Sarah said exactly what was on her mind, unafraid to voice her opinions. God, how Christina envied that.

"What did you like to do when you were my age?" Sarah asked as she kicked a pebble with her shoe.

"Well, I had a lot of lessons, so there was not much free time for play." Nor were there any children about with whom to play, but she did not bother to mention it.

"That sounds awful."

It had been, actually. Lessons on comportment, manners, dancing, instruments . . . Christina had hated them all.

"And you did not ride," Sarah added, her voice indicating what a tragedy she considered this. "So what did you do for fun?"

She snapped her fingers. How could she have forgotten? "One of the grooms taught me how to practice archery. I quite liked that."

"You mean a bow and arrow? Like out in the Dakotas?"

"Yes, a bow and arrow. You try to hit a target."

"Is it difficult?"

"A little. Points are awarded for hitting each ring of the target. The trick is to hit closest to the center. The person with the most points wins."

"I would like to try that one day," Sarah said.

"Perhaps you will. I have not practiced in years." Not since her mother forced her to quit.

When they reached a clearing, Sarah scampered ahead to chase after a bird, her arms raised wide. Then she discovered a group of children playing with a kite. As Christina watched, Sarah, without any reservation whatsoever, walked over and inserted herself into the mix. Within seconds, she was laughing and trying the kite. "She is so confident," Christina murmured to herself. Lord knew she never would have dared to interrupt a group in such a manner.

"Christina."

Her shoulders stiffened at the familiar hiss. Stomach clenching, she spun to find her mother barreling down on her, a maid not far behind. "Mother, what are you doing here?"

"I followed you." The countess's hair was pulled back from her face, her eyes narrowed sharply under the rim of her bonnet. "Have you any idea what that husband of yours has done now?"

"Wait, you have been following me?"

"I had no choice. I cannot approach you in the gardens any longer, not with the footman following you about. I must speak to you about that man you married."

You mean the man you blackmailed into marrying me? She did not say it, of course. Her mother would not appreciate the correction.

"Are you aware that he has purchased all the Barclay holdings, including the house in Mayfair and the Pennington estate? All the debts and property—even your father's club memberships. Everything we had left. He has taken it all."

Christina fought against showing a reaction, but it was not easy. Good Lord, that must have cost a fortune. What had Oliver been thinking? And had he been planning on telling her? She disliked secrets between them, especially when it came to her parents.

The hope and happiness of the past few days faded. Oliver had done all this without her knowledge or input. He had not even bothered to discuss this with her. As awful as they had been, she did not want to see her parents ruined. She'd much prefer they went back to London and resumed their old life without her.

"Christina." Sarah came to stand next to her. "Are you all right?"

Her mother's gaze raked Sarah from head to toe, the disapproval clear. Then she dismissed the young girl, turning her attention back to Christina. "Do you understand what I am saying?"

"Yes." She took a deep breath to collect herself. "However, I am not certain what you believe I can do at this point."

"You must talk to him—or write to him, whatever it takes—on our behalf. We want our belongings returned to us. He had no right to take those things."

"Mother—"

"Do not dare argue with me." Her mother's lips twisted into a snarl, the lines on her face deepening into angry slashes. "We sacrificed everything to bring you here and marry you to a man suitable of your breeding and . . . and this is how you treat us? Now, I am willing to forgive you if you help us. Your husband is very wealthy and he has no need for those properties. Tell him to sign them back over to us and we shall forget any of this nastiness happened."

Christina's shoulders slumped. She felt very, very tired all of a sudden. "I shall try, Mother."

"Good. You have a chance to redeem yourself, Christina. Do not disappoint us as you usually do." Without another word, her mother turned and strode away, leaving the maid to chase after her.

Christina chewed her lip and wondered what to do. Oliver now owned everything that had once belonged to her family. What did he plan on doing with it? She could not very well expect him to give the land back to her parents, who had mismanaged everything in the first place. Unless he did, however, her parents would be left without a home. What would they do?

She rubbed her temples. Once again, she was nothing but a means to an end for her parents. What an unholy mess.

Sarah was glaring at the countess's retreating back. "That was your mother? She is not very nice to you."

"She means well," Christina murmured, though there was little enthusiasm behind the words. "Come, let us finish our walk."

"Are you sure? We may head back, if you like."

The offer touched Christina. "No, let us enjoy the day."

At least this way, she would have some time to figure out what to do about her parents . . . and the fact that Oliver was keeping secrets from her.

Chapter Seventeen

Apollo bolted off the ground and raced to the greenhouse door, instantly gaining Oliver's attention. Oliver put down his pencil and waited for the unannounced visitor. Frank Tripp stormed in, Gill directly behind him, the lawyer's notoriously polished demeanor a bit harried.

"We have a serious problem." Frank dropped onto one of the small stools, making certain to face Oliver. He tossed his derby onto the counter.

"What is it?" Oliver signed and Gill translated.

"It is your cousin."

Oh, for fuck's sake. Why was Milton hell-bent on making a nuisance of himself? "What has he done now? Attempted to steal more money from me?"

"I wish it were that simple." Frank dragged a hand over his jaw. "I have a friend, one of the most well-known lawyers in town. He . . . well, he's not as scrupulous as other lawyers. He will do just about anything if the price is high enough."

"And how is that different from you, exactly?"

"Ha ha. I may twist the law as I see fit but I have never actively broken the law. This particular lawyer, however, believes rules do not apply to him. That he is above the law. Do you understand?"

"Yes. What does this have to do with Milton?"

"Your cousin has retained the services of this lawyer. The details are murky, unfortunately, and I was unable to find out the case Milton is pursuing. Have you an idea?"

Milton had hired a prominent attorney? To what end? And with what money? Oliver shook his head. "I have no clue. He came by last week and I confirmed his monthly allowance was being cut by ten percent."

"How did he take it?"

"About as well as you would expect. Nearly apoplectic with rage, spouting all sorts of nonsense. I told him to leave or I would reduce it by fifty percent."

Frank's brows dipped, his gaze turning wary. "Nonsense? Like what?"

"Just idle complaints and threats," he signed. "Nothing to be concerned about, in my opinion."

"He has no claim to your money so he cannot possibly think to sue you for it. I wish I knew what he was planning. My gut tells me we should be worried."

"Dig harder. See what you can find out."

"I will. In the meantime, perhaps you should tell me about these idle complaints and threats." Oliver started to sign a protest but Frank put his palms up. "Humor me, Oliver."

Oliver recounted the conversation, including the bit about the asylum and Christina's meek personality. A muscle jumped in Frank's jaw at that bit of information. "Are we to assume this is something about your marriage, about your wife?"

"He shall have a hard time getting the marriage annulled, if that is what he plans."

"Does he possess anything to blackmail you with? Any secrets or skeletons?"

"No, not a one."

"The asylum, then. Does he have the influence to—?"

"Absolutely not," Oliver signed. "Milton has neither influence nor funds. I have no idea how he is compensating this lawyer."

"The lawyer may have agreed to work pro bono for now, if he believes a big reward awaits. That is precisely what makes me nervous."

Oliver stroked his jaw. He was not afraid of Milton. Yes, his cousin perpetually angled for more money, but Milton was not cruel. He was full of bluster, an inept nincompoop completely incapable of carrying out any of his threats against Oliver or Christina.

"Might it have something to do with this?" Frank

gestured to the workspace. "You are close to finishing your invention, which stands to gain you a measure of success. Is he hoping to capitalize on those profits somehow?"

"How?"

"Have you discussed the plans with him or shown him the device? He could claim some right to the idea, especially if you have not patented it."

Oliver grimaced. No, he had not yet filled out the patent application. The device was nearly ready, but he would much rather wait until it was perfect before he filed for a patent. "That would only work after the invention is sold and I have profited, correct?"

"If he has seen this"—Frank pointed to the hearing device and battery on the counter—"then he may have applied for his own patent. He could sue you for infringing."

"No one has seen the device," Oliver signed, "except for Gill, a few staff, Christina, and Sarah."

"Your sister?"

"Yes. She is home from school for a few weeks."

"We must be prepared for anything. If Milton snuck in here one night and sketched out your prototype, we have no way of knowing."

"My plans for this go back years," Oliver signed. "I have proof and Milton would never win in court."

"I still think we should submit the patent application quickly to be safe."

Oliver did not like it but he supposed Frank was right. "Fine. I shall draw up the current design and send it over to you."

"Good—and if you think of any other reason Milton has hired this lawyer, let me know. I will keep digging, see what I can learn. The good news is that Sarah's trust is completely safe. Milton could never touch that money."

Oliver had set aside a large sum of money for when Sarah reached majority. No one but Sarah—not even her future husband—would have access to that money. God forbid, if something happened to Oliver, at least his sister would be well provided for.

Yes, but what about your wife?

Apollo ran back to the door, his tail wagging. Christina's face appeared in the crack of the door. She was buried under mounds of winter clothing, her cheeks red from the cold. Oliver's chest tightened, a visceral reaction to her he could not control.

Her eyes widened when she saw the lawyer. The color on her face heightened and she edged away from the door. "Oh, I did not realize . . . I will return later. Hello, Frank."

Oliver frowned. Why was she flustered all of a sudden? "It is quite all right," he signed. "Come in."

Frank rose and bowed. "Christina, always a pleasure." He swiped his derby off the counter and said to Oliver, "I must be going. We'll be in touch."

Oliver nodded and the lawyer departed along with Gill. Christina then moved to follow. "Wait," he said to his wife's retreating back. "Stay a moment."

She stopped but did not turn. He closed the distance between them until her skirts brushed his legs. When she remained facing the door, he stepped in front of her to better see her. "Is something wrong?"

"I should not have intruded. I apologize."

It was not lost on him that she had evaded his question. "Tell me, what happened?" Must've been something today. She had spent the night in his bed yet again last night. This morning he'd awakened her by licking and sucking her nipples, and her enthusiastic response had led to a damn energetic bout of lovemaking. They had parted on good terms after, with her saying she planned to spend the day with Sarah. "Was it Sarah? Did she upset you?"

"No, it was not Sarah."

"So someone else upset you. Who?"

She closed her eyes briefly. "Do not worry about it."

He did not like this. His wife would not confide in him. He reached out and tucked a long strand of hair behind her ear. "You are my wife. It is my sworn duty to worry about it because I care about you. I . . ."

I am obsessed with you. I think about you nearly every second. I am beginning to think I love you.

She pushed away from him, took a few steps deeper into the workshop, and turned. Her lips had compressed into a tight, angry line. "Why did you not tell me you decided to ruin my parents?" A hand flew up to cover her mouth, her eyes now as round as saucers. "Oh, goodness. I apologize. I did not mean to yell at you."

"You have the right to yell at me if you wish, especially if you feel I deserve it." He pointed to his ear. "Besides, deaf, remember? I cannot hear how loudly or softly you speak."

"Of course. I had not thought of it that way."

"Talk to me. Tell me why you are upset."

She swallowed but did not look away. "My mother followed me into the park. She said you have assumed all their debts and belongings. That you now own everything."

"Yes, I do."

"And you did not think to inform me of this? Or ask if I had any objections?"

He opened his mouth, then closed it. Was she actually angry over this? "Do you have any objections?"

"Of course!" She threw her hands up, as animated as he had ever seen her. "They are my parents. Why did you not ask what I wanted to do about them?"

Standing there, he could only blink as he tried to think of what to say. He had no idea why she would defend these people after all they had done. Hell yes, he had ruined her parents. He had wanted to do a lot more, in fact. "I cannot see how you are defending the two people who wanted to marry you off to Van Peet. The two people who trade your happiness for money at every turn."

"They are still my parents. I do not wish to see them without a home."

"I have no intention of kicking them out on the street. However, they should suffer a bit for all they have done to you. Those two do not deserve your forgiveness."

"We do not grant forgiveness based on whether someone is deserving of it or not; it is granted for ourselves, so that we may sleep at night knowing we have done the right thing."

"And yet I shall sleep perfectly fine knowing they are completely at my mercy."

"Oliver." She drew closer, her face softening. "You are a good, kind person. Do not let my parents rob you of that."

Putting his hands on her shoulders, he pulled her in and pressed their foreheads together. Then he closed his eyes and breathed her in for a long moment, the now-familiar scent of roses stealing into his lungs. He was not particularly good or kind. Over the course of twenty-nine years, he'd been pretty damn selfish at times. "I cannot forgive them for how they have treated you. Do not ask it of me."

She put her hands on his chest and leaned back so he could see her face—a move that aligned their hips together. His body instantly reacted, blood heating in his veins. "Then do not forgive them," she said. "Give them the use of the house in London and send them home."

"Provide them an allowance?" Even giving her parents a nickel would chafe, let alone hundreds of dollars a month.

"They will hate it, knowing they have you to thank for the very food on their table."

He blew out a long breath. Logically, there was not much difference between her parents and Milton—they were all despicable human beings—and he had been financing his cousin as long as he could remember. "Fine—but I want them gone. Tonight. I shall cable Frank and have him handle it. Do you want to see them before they go, to say good-bye?"

"No." Her brows came together. "Does that make me a horrible person?"

"Indeed not. It makes you human." He kissed her nose and then took her hand. "Come with me. I'll contact Frank and then give you a special treat in my bedroom."

She smiled. "Will this treat cause us to be late to dinner?"

"Most definitely."

A FEW DAYS later, Christina was having breakfast when Oliver and Sarah arrived. "We have a surprise for you," her husband signed.

He wore a heavy overcoat instead of his usual

shirtsleeves, which was odd. Sarah had on her coat as well, grinning at Christina while bouncing on her toes.

"You do?" she asked.

"We do," Sarah confirmed. "But you must get up, close your eyes, and come with us outside."

What had these two done? For a brief moment, she feared it might have to do with horses. *No, Oliver promised he would not force you to ride.* Her shoulders relaxed. "Well, then I cannot wait. Lead the way." She rose and put a hand over her eyes, holding out her free hand for them to take.

They began guiding her through the house and then outside to the terrace. Her eyes remained closed, but it was a struggle not to peek. What kind of surprise had they planned? No one had ever done anything like this for her before. The frozen ground crunched under her boots as Oliver and Sarah led her to the side of the gardens.

"Keep going," Oliver said, his hand warm in hers. "There's a turn to your left. Good, now stop."

A beat passed and then Sarah said, "Open your eyes, Christina."

She blinked into the glare of the late morning sun. Was that . . . a target? Good heavens. Then she saw the longbow and arrows. Her jaw dropped. "Is that . . . ?"

"I told Oliver how you used to practice archery," Sarah said proudly. "He insisted we find the perfect equipment so you could start again."

She remembered telling Sarah about enjoying archery as a girl, but she never thought anything more about it. She looked over at Oliver, who was watching her carefully. Emotion threatened to overwhelm her, and she struggled to maintain her composure. "I honestly cannot think what to say. This is the nicest thing anyone's ever done for me—other than you marrying me."

Oliver lifted Christina's hand to his mouth and pressed a soft kiss to her knuckles. "I hope you like it."

"I love it. Thank you, Oliver."

"You are welcome," he signed, one she understood without translation. He gestured toward the set. "Try it out. The bow should be perfect for your height. If not, we may easily have it adjusted."

She stared at the pieces, her brain buzzing with excitement. Could she still do it? She recalled the thrill of the execution, of trying to remain perfectly steady before releasing the string. The precision of the strike. She'd been quite proficient at it all those years ago. "It has been a long time."

"We do not mind if you are terrible," Sarah said. Then the girl ran to grab the bow and one arrow. "Here you are." She handed everything over to Christina. "Will you shoot for us? Please?"

Christina saw there was even a leather cuff to protect her arm. "I shall try, but only if you'll assist me. Deal?"

"Deal." Sarah clapped her hands. "What should I do?"

"Here, help me put this on." Christina slid the leather cuff over her wrist and adjusted it for comfort. Then Sarah pulled the strings tight and tied them off. "Thank you. Now, where shall I shoot from?"

"Back there." Sarah pointed to a reasonable distance away. Christina nodded. She should be able to hit the target from that spot.

She took her place and steadied herself. Strange to hold a bow after all these years, but it felt familiar. Right. She nocked the arrow, raised her arm, and used three fingers to grip the bowstring. Then she drew the string back and took aim. Her arm muscles began to shake and she tried to keep steady. Slipping her fingers from the bowstring, she let the arrow fly.

It was not even close.

Frowning, she watched the arrow plummet to the ground well shy of the target. Hmm. It had been much easier when she was younger. "I guess I am sorely out of practice."

Nevertheless, Oliver and Sarah broke into applause and Christina's heart melted into a puddle. "That was excellent form," Oliver said. "With practice you shall strike the center of the target in no time."

Sarah came running over. "Will you teach me, Christina? I want to learn how to shoot, too."

"Of course. I'll show you now."

"That is my cue," Oliver signed. He pressed a kiss to Christina's cheek. "I will leave you to it. See you at dinner."

She put a hand on his arm, stopping him from walking away. "Thank you, Oliver. This is a truly wonderful gift."

The side of his mouth hitched, and she could've drowned in the tenderness reflected in his gaze. "I am glad. Enjoy it, ladies." He walked in the direction of his workshop, leaving Sarah and Christina alone.

"We should move a little closer to the target," Christina told the girl. "Then I'll teach you how to hold the bow."

After each shooting more than two dozen arrows, they went inside to get warm. They entered and found Gill waiting. "Luncheon awaits in your suite, madam," he told Christina. "Miss Sarah, your apples and carrots are downstairs for your afternoon visit to the stables."

The young girl shook her head. "I do not wish to go to the stables anymore."

Gill appeared utterly shocked at this revelation. "No?"

Sarah slid a glance at Christina then raised her chin. "Horses are mean. I have decided I no longer want to help take care of them."

Had something happened in the stables? Sarah had loved the horses up until today. "Were you injured?" Christina asked.

"No." Oliver's sister studied her shoes. "They are just big and sort of scary. I could get hurt very easily."

"Nonsense," Christina said, trying to put the girl's mind at ease. "You have nothing to worry about. These horses are gentle and well trained. Think of all the mornings you have spent with them. Almost every day for three weeks. Besides, the grooms would never allow you to be harmed. You are perfectly safe out there."

"But you said horses were big and unpredictable. You do not like them."

Christina's mouth fell open slightly. Indeed, she had said exactly that to Oliver the other day. Only, she had not expected Sarah to remember it word for word. Nor had she thought voicing her opinion would negatively influence the girl or ruin something Sarah genuinely loved. Her stomach sank. "You should not listen to me."

"Why not?" Sarah cocked her head. "Were you lying when you said those things?"

"No, not lying. Those were just my own silly opinions. They are illogical and you should form your own opinions."

"If they are silly and illogical then why do you believe it?"

A lump formed in Christina's throat. She wished she had a clever answer. She caught Gill's gaze in a silent plea for help.

Nodding, Gill motioned for Sarah to follow

him. Christina watched them disappear, her feet rooted to the floor. She heard bits of their conversation, like the words *daring* and *brave*, which was how she knew they were not discussing her.

Sarah had loved horses until recently—until she began spending more time with Christina. Now she was afraid of horses? How on earth was Christina to live with herself, knowing she had instilled such fear in this vivacious and strong-willed young girl? That she had ruined something that had brought Sarah so much joy?

Her eyes began to burn, emotion and self-pity rising to leak out as tears. She did not want to be this person, someone who watched life instead of participated in it. Who stood at the side of the room instead of dancing, or who could not meet friends out for ice cream without panicking. She wished to be more like Sarah, carefree and adventurous, where she would look back on her life in forty years and feel good about the choices she had made . . . not look back and see only regrets and missed opportunities.

She took a step toward her room, ready to pull the covers over her head and spend the afternoon alone. *No, do something different.*

If she longed to be different then she could not keep doing the same thing, because that was no longer working.

Yes, different.

Spinning, she started for the workshop instead. She needed Oliver.

APOLLO JUMPED UP from the floor by Oliver's feet. Oliver's head lifted to see Christina come through the greenhouse door. Her face was pale, her mouth flat. Concerned, he put down his work and rose.

She bent to scratch Apollo behind the ears, not immediately speaking.

"Hello," he signed. "Is something the matter?"

She bit her lip, tears glistening in her gaze. Oliver immediately crossed to where she stood and engulfed her in his arms. He held her close and stroked her back. With her face pressed against his shirt, he had no idea if she was crying or speaking, but her shoulders shook slightly. He did not push her; she would tell him what had upset her in her own time.

Though he could not begin to guess at the cause. She'd been happy earlier when they surprised her with the archery set. What could have happened in such a short time to distress her like this?

When her breathing settled, he led her to a stool. Then he produced his linen handkerchief and let her clean up her face. He hated seeing her like this. It reminded him of the day she'd gone to see Van Peet. "What happened, sweetheart?"

She drew in a deep breath. "I . . ."

When she did not continue, he withdrew the pad and pencil from his pocket, placed the items in her hands.

Her anguished gaze met his as she returned

the writing instruments. "No, I prefer to tell you this time."

Dragging over another stool, he sat down across from her and waited. She sat up straighter and pushed her shoulders back. "Sarah has announced she no longer likes horses, that they are big and unpredictable."

He frowned. That seemed odd, considering Sarah's love of them the past ten years. "Was that not what you said that morning we went to the stables?"

"Yes, it is precisely what I said. Oliver, I do not want her to turn out like me. To be honest, I would much rather be like *her.*"

"What are you talking about? You are intelligent and strong, not to mention beautiful and kind. She would be lucky—"

"No, she would not be lucky. If she were like me she would not ride horses or climb rocks. She would be afraid and anxious. Timid and shy. The opposite of everything she is now."

"I wish you could see what I see," he signed and said. "You are not those things. You have lived your life by someone else's rules where your parents dictated your choices based on society's expectations. Yet you survived. You resisted in your own way, biding your time until fate brought you to me. You are a survivor—and now you may embrace whatever challenges life brings at you because you are not alone. We shall face whatever comes together."

"We shall?"

"I am not giving you up, Christina. Not after a year, not after twenty years. I am afraid you are stuck with me—that is, if you are—"

She launched herself at him, wrapping her arms around his neck. He guided her close and held her. Her reaction gave him hope she felt the same way and their marriage could last. He had not planned on a true marriage with her, but he could no longer imagine not having her in his life.

In a short time, she had become as necessary as air. He had not thought any woman would see beyond his bank account or his condition. Yet Christina had. She was not interested in money or the things she could buy with the Hawkes fortune. Nor was she fixated on her social status, pressuring him to escort her about town, a different party every night. No, she preferred to stay home, as he did.

It was so much more than that, however. She was a kind, giving person, even protecting her parents when they hardly deserved such generosity. Then she had befriended Sarah and helped entertain his sister. She was remarkable, always thinking of others more than herself.

He was dashed fortunate.

No matter how this marriage had started, the silly time limit he'd imposed, this was now forever. Fate had thrown this woman in his path and he had located the perfect other half of his soul. He just had not told her yet.

Perhaps today she needed to hear it.

Leaning back, he captured her face in his hands. "Christina, I love you. Whatever problems we have, we face them together. Do you understand?"

She stiffened but he only held on tighter. When another tear cascaded down her cheek, he brushed it away with his thumb. He'd never told a woman he loved her before. Were they supposed to cry?

She pointed her middle finger toward herself then crossed her arms to form an X in front of her chest. Then she pointed at him. Oliver's throat closed, warmth spreading around his heart. He'd never expected for her to say it back, let alone in his own language.

Bending, he pressed his mouth to hers, deepening the kiss until she clung to him. Her mouth was soft and lush, and he lost track of time. She fit him utterly and wholly, this complex woman he hadn't even known two months ago. Now he could not imagine his life without her.

When they broke apart, they were both breathing hard. He held her hand. "You are brave and wonderful. I will never give up on you—or on us."

Her gaze locked with his. "Do you mean it?"

"I always say precisely what I mean. I love you. That statement does not come with conditions or a time limit."

"Thank you, Oliver." Rising on her toes, she placed a kiss on his cheek. "Falling in your garden was the best thing that has ever happened to me."

"Me as well—not that I want you to do it ever again."

She smiled—and then her head swiveled toward the door. He glanced over and saw Gill there, the butler as distressed as Oliver had ever seen him. "What is it?"

"Come quickly," Gill signed. "Your cousin is here with some men."

Goddamn Milton. Would he never go away? "What men?"

"I do not know their names, but they arrived in an ambulance from the New York City Asylum for the Insane."

Chapter Eighteen

Asylum?

Christina's heart stopped as she looked at Oliver. Instead of laughing this off as some joke, his face paled.

That scared her like nothing else.

Without explanation he started for the door. She lunged for his arm, stopping him. "Wait, should you go? Perhaps you should . . . ?" Hide? Run? Whatever happened, she did not wish to lose him.

He gently removed her fingers. "It will be fine. I shall set them straight and send them on their way. Do not worry. Stay here."

Gill held open the door and Oliver quickly departed, the butler trailing him. Christina hurried after them. No matter what he had said, Oliver would not face this alone.

Though she was English, she had heard of what went on in New York's asylums. A female reporter, Nellie Bly, had famously written a story about the conditions at the Blackwell's Island women's asylum, which had been horrifying. The London newspapers had all carried the piece detailing the rotten food, mistreatment of the patients, and the cruel staff. It had turned her stomach to even read of it.

Why were they here? She could think of no good reason for Milton to bring men from the asylum into Oliver's home. Perhaps Milton's motives were not as nefarious as she feared . . . yet somehow she doubted it.

The group was in the entryway. Two men in gray suits flanked Milton, one of whom held restraints in his hands, and a policeman hovered in the background. She moved to Oliver's side, close enough that their shoulders nearly touched. He began signing angrily, with Gill translating. "What is the meaning of this, Milton?"

"That's him. You may take him now," Milton ordered the two men at his side.

"What are you talking about?" Gill kept his gaze trained on Oliver's hands. "What do you think you are doing, Milton?"

"I have a document here"—Milton shook a piece of paper in his fist—"declaring you legally insane. And it has been signed by a judge."

"That is ridiculous," Christina said.

Gill translated, "No judge would sign that without proof."

Milton lifted a shoulder. "Turns out my word was proof enough against a deaf and dumb recluse. I told them of your dangerous experiments, your hasty marriage to a woman you do not even know . . . and how I discouraged you from investing in a fraudulent alpaca farm. He agreed and now I have asked these fine gentlemen to escort you to your new facilities on Wards Island."

Next to her, Oliver stiffened. Anger and fear knotted in her stomach, but she was not about to let the others see it. *You are intelligent and strong,* Oliver had told her. She drew herself up. "This is preposterous."

A small figure emerged on Christina's other side. Sarah. "Christina, who are these men?"

She wrapped an arm around Oliver's sister. "No one to worry about, Sarah. They were just leaving."

"What are they saying about Oliver?" she whispered.

"A lot of nonsense." She squeezed the young girl tight. "Why don't you go back upstairs until they leave?"

"Hello, cousin Sarah," Milton said. "So nice to see you again. Too bad we are leaving now. Perhaps we will be able to catch up soon. Gentlemen, if you please." He swept his hand out toward Oliver.

Oliver began signing and Gill said, "Do not dare put your hands on me until my lawyer has had a chance to review that document."

Milton's upper lip curled into a sneer. "That is

not how it works, cousin. You no longer hold all the power. How does it feel to be at my mercy for once?"

"You have lost your mind," Oliver signed.

"No, according to the state of New York *you* have lost *your* mind." He nudged one of the hospital officials. "Let's go. We are wasting time."

The two men started forward, and Christina stepped in front of Oliver. "Do not touch my husband. Get out of this house."

Milton slapped the paper in his palm. "We may do this the easy way, where Oliver comes willingly, or we shall drag him out of here kicking and screaming like the lunatic he is. Makes no difference to me."

"Sir, come along peacefully," the police officer said. "We do not want anyone hurt."

The staff had gathered in the corridor, their wide gazes taking in the situation. Oliver glanced at his sister before locking eyes with Christina. She knew exactly what he was thinking, that he did not want his sister to see him dragged out of the house like an animal. "No," she whispered. "Please, Oliver. Fight this."

His bright green depths pleaded with her to understand. He leaned in to put his mouth near her ear. "Take care of her. And call Frank."

Frank Tripp, his solicitor. She nodded and hugged him. "Do not do this," she murmured into his shoulder, even though she knew he could not hear her. "Do not leave me."

He squeezed her hard, almost desperately, and said, "I shall be fine. Contact Frank and tell him what happened. He will have me home in no time."

Oh, God. How had this come to pass? She could not breathe at the thought of Oliver in an asylum. What would they do to him?

Much too soon, he released her and went to his sister, who was openly crying now. He started signing to the young girl, his face gentle and reassuring, and Christina's eyes stung with unshed tears. She rounded on his cousin. "Milton, do not proceed with this. It is not too late to do the right thing."

"The right thing?" Milton's brows shot up. "The right thing was for all this to be mine. My father deserved half of the Hawkes fortune; instead, he got nothing. So I've taken matters into my own hands and restitution shall be paid."

This was all about money? "You are about to ruin Oliver's life for a few hundred thousand dollars?"

Milton's eyes nearly popped out of his head. "A few hundred thousand? You really have no idea who you married, do you?"

"I know he is a good man who is of sound mind—sounder than *you*, apparently. You are perpetuating a grave injustice if you place Oliver into an asylum."

Oliver's cousin smiled, an evil twist of his lips that held no remorse whatsoever. "No, madam. I am righting the grave injustice done to my family years ago. Now, let's go already," he snapped.

Oliver met Christina's worried gaze and she saw the fear and uncertainty there. Rushing forward, she used her free hand to cup his jaw. *I love you*, she mouthed.

He closed his eyes and drew in a deep breath, his forehead touching hers. They stood there a second and then he straightened. Without another word, he took a step forward. The orderlies spun him around and affixed the manacles on his wrists. The group walked out of the house and down the steps, the policeman on their heels.

Heart in her throat, Christina watched as Oliver climbed into the back of the wagon and the heavy metal doors slammed shut behind him. Sarah threw herself against Christina's side, the young girl clinging to Christina through her sobs.

Milton remained, gloating in his cruelty. "I'd pack your bags, were I you, Mrs. Hawkes."

Her skin heated, anger licking her insides like white-hot flames. She had never hurt anyone in her entire life but oh, how she wanted to now. She wanted to strike him, to tear this man apart, and her muscles shook with the effort to restrain herself.

She lifted her chin. "However, you are not me, you miserable excuse for a human being. I shall fight you every single step of the way, no matter the cost. You have no idea what hell you have unleashed today. Now, get out of my husband's house."

HE KNEW NOT to struggle with the guards.

It would serve no purpose. Oliver's hopes now rested with Frank Tripp, who would certainly find a way to have that ridiculous judgment over-turned. In the meantime, however, he needed to endure whatever happened here. For Christina and Sarah. For himself.

He'd never forget the terrified look on Christina's face today, or the way his sister had sobbed at his departure. No matter what happened from here on out, he must bear it. Bear it, and then re-turn home to them.

After a short boat ride, he was loaded into an-other wagon and driven deeper onto Wards Island, a tiny block of land in the East River where the city shipped its undesirables. He hoped to God that conditions in asylums had improved since the newspaper articles had been printed.

When the wagon doors flew open, he stepped to the ground, ignoring the dour guards frown-ing at him. Above loomed a three-story Gothic structure constructed out of brick and stone, with a mansard roof on top. The building had one central part and two flanking sections ad-joining, almost like wings.

A guard grabbed Oliver's arm and roughly towed him toward the entry. Oliver did not resist.

His goal was to get before the doctors as quickly as possible, plead his case, and pray they saw reason. Surely they would evaluate him upon arrival to determine his level of mental acuity. Then they would understand this was all a mistake and let him go.

He hoped.

They led him into a narrow vestibule and the door shut behind him. His heart pounded a steady beat of terror against his ribs, a cold sensation sweeping through his veins. It took every bit of his control not to shove free of these men and run away. Only knowing it would not serve his purpose—a quick release—prevented him from fleeing. If he tried to escape, he would be caught and they would lock him up where Tripp would certainly never find him.

If they were talking to him, he had no idea. He kept his head down as two guards led him along the bare floors of a never-ending corridor. Most of the guards, he knew from what he'd read in the newspapers, were inmates of the nearby penitentiary. To say he feared mistreatment by their hand was an immense understatement.

They tossed him in the direction of a wooden bench. Oliver caught himself and sat, hands folded nonthreateningly in his lap. Glancing up, he saw a guard's mouth move. ". . . examination. Wait here."

He nodded, pressing his lips together to keep

from begging, shouting . . . demanding they release him.

Soon. He'd meet with the doctor and he would be released soon.

Several minutes passed, the guards watching over him as he waited. Movement from the corner of his eye startled him, and a man in a long white coat stepped through the now-open door. The doctor. Thank Christ.

Oliver rose and immediately the guards were there, each taking one of his arms. The doctor's mouth started moving but Oliver was unable to read his lips from this angle and the man quickly turned away. The guards shoved him forward, into the doctor's office, yet he somehow maintained his feet as he stumbled. Then he stood waiting in the middle of the room for the doctor to notice him.

The doctor was an older man, reed-thin. He had long whiskers along his chin and lip and he wore spectacles. There were rings under his eyes as if he'd been deprived of sleep for a few days, no hint of a smile on his face. If one hoped for a kindly, Henry Jacobs–type doctor, this man was not it.

Now behind his desk, the doctor lifted a stack of papers and gestured to the chair opposite. Oliver sat and began speaking, too scared to be shy about his voice. "Sir, I fear this is a misunderstanding. I am deaf, not insane."

The doctor lifted an eyebrow, his gaze landing directly on Oliver for the first time. "Determining an incoming patient's mental state is my job"—he checked his papers—"Mr. Hawkes."

"But this is a ploy by my cousin to have me committed. There is nothing wrong with me."

"And yet a judge and two doctors say otherwise." He dropped into his leather chair and picked up a pen. His mouth moved but his head was down, so Oliver could not read his lips.

"I cannot see your face. I have no idea what you are saying."

The doctor cocked his head, his expression skeptical. "Are you saying you are able to read lips? I have met several deaf people, Mr. Hawkes, and none could read lips as well as to follow a conversation."

"Nevertheless, I am able to do so."

Leaning forward, the doctor made notes on the papers. He began speaking again, his head bent where Oliver could not see, the mustache covering most of the man's lips.

"Again, if you are not looking at me, I cannot understand what you are saying."

The doctor folded his arms on the desk and gave Oliver a bland stare. "And so it is I who must accommodate you, Mr. Hawkes?" He shook his head as if the very idea was insulting. "I think you shall learn quickly that it is our patients who adapt while here."

Oliver kept quiet, merely staring at a doctor who obviously held little compassion for the people brought before his care.

"Now, what is your name?"

"Oliver Richard Hawkes."

"Where are you from?"

"New York City."

"How old are you?"

"Twenty-nine."

"What . . ." The doctor's head bent, obscuring Oliver's view.

"What was that last question?"

The doctor's head snapped up. "I do not care to repeat myself. What year is it currently?"

"Eighteen hundred and ninety."

"Do you know why you have been sent here?"

"Because my cousin is angling to steal my family's fortune."

"Says here that you . . ." He read off the paper, his lips not in Oliver's line of sight.

Heat suffused Oliver's entire body, an all-encompassing frustration that replaced his rationality. "I cannot hear you," he snapped, pounding a fist on the arm of the chair. "Either look at me when you are speaking or write it down for me."

The doctor's body stiffened and he sneered. "You must learn your place here." Addressing the guards, he said, "Show Mr. Hawkes our plunging bath. Make sure he understands—"

That was all Oliver could read before he was jerked to his feet and hauled away.

CHRISTINA PACED THE length of the entryway. She had not been able to eat, sleep, or rest since the moment Oliver was carted away by those men.

Once the wagon had departed this morning, she'd immediately contacted Frank Tripp and informed him of what happened. Now early evening, Frank had phoned thirty minutes ago to say he was on his way with news. She prayed this news was of the good variety. Hadn't Oliver suffered enough in his short life? Thank goodness Milton had not lingered to gloat. Christina very well may have punched him.

The bell jangled. She raced to the latch, beating the butler to the door, and ripped the heavy panel ajar. A grim-looking Frank Tripp waited on the stoop. "Good evening, Christina."

"Come in," she said and moved aside. "Let's go into the salon."

Frank did not even bother to remove his coat, just placed his bowler and cane onto the low table and followed her. When they entered the salon, Frank shrugged off his overcoat and tossed it on a chair. Gill followed, his hands clasped behind his back. "Would you care for a drink, sir?"

"Let's skip it until I am done. I wish I had good news," Frank said as he sat down, and Christina's heart sank. "I have seen the petition and, while it is a complete farce, they have bribed a judge to sign it. Your husband has made some powerful enemies, Christina. Apparently this judge is one of Van Peet's cronies."

"Van Peet?" Why would Van Peet have any interest in locking Oliver away?

"Yes. Oliver and Julius Hatcher were making moves to ruin Van Peet and the old man caught wind of the plan. Quite upset over it, too. Milton and his lawyer have used this to their advantage, finding a judge in Van Peet's pocket to get this judgment through."

"Dear Lord."

"Exactly." Frank crossed his legs. "Now, Oliver should have been evaluated by at least two qualified examiners before being shipped to Wards Island. Results of those evaluations have been falsified on the paperwork—"

"Then we may get him released," she said, a glimmer of hope sparking to life in her chest.

"In theory, yes. However, proving those evaluations were falsified may be difficult because the doctors were no doubt paid a handsome sum to lie. Getting them to admit the truth means they lose their medical licenses and their livelihoods. I think we'll have a better chance getting the judgment overturned. Within thirty days we are allowed to appeal it and obtain a rehearing. I have already filed the appeal on Oliver's behalf."

Christina covered her mouth with her hand, stomach twisting with horror. "Are you saying Oliver might possibly remain there for a month?"

"I am doing everything in my power to prevent that," Frank said, holding up a hand as if he were swearing in court. "I will push for a hearing to take place as quickly as possible, I promise."

She swallowed, clenching her hands together. This was awful. Just positively awful. Part of her wanted to go to Wards Island herself and demand they let Oliver go. Bang on the door, tear the building apart until she found him and could bring him back here. "What is involved in the rehearing?"

"We hope a judge will review the paperwork and let me plead Oliver's case. If not, they may summon a jury to decide whether Oliver is sane."

"And juries are notoriously unpredictable," Christina said.

Frank nodded once. "Unfortunately, yes. I should also warn you that your marriage is a part of all this. Milton claims Oliver did not possess the mental capacity to agree to a marriage and you took advantage of him, therefore the marriage should be annulled. If that happens and Oliver remains committed, Milton would be appointed guardian of the Hawkes fortune."

Annulled? Oh, good heavens. A lump formed in her throat. This was all much worse than she had feared. "Am I allowed to see him?"

"He is denied visitors, except his lawyer."

Her breath shuddered as she exhaled. It was the answer she'd expected but that did not make it easier to hear. "So when will you go?"

"First thing in the morning." His gaze softened with remorse and apology. "I would bring you if I could, Christina. I know it hardly eases your mind, but if there's any message you'd like me to pass along . . . ?"

There was so much she needed to say to Oliver, like how much she loved him. How fervently she missed him. That she would never give up. "Yes, please. Tell him we shall not rest until he is released."

Chapter Nineteen

The asylum was a hundred times worse than he'd feared.

What little food they were given was mostly rotten. There were no blankets or fires, the hospital clothing threadbare. During the day, many patients sat listless and vacant-eyed, either heavily drugged or too far withdrawn into their own minds to be talkative. At night he was grateful for a lack of hearing because he could feel the constant vibration in the walls and floors, the screams and cries of the men trapped inside this horrible place.

Thoughts of the plunging bath still haunted him. In the asylum basement sat a deep pool carved into the rock that filled with water straight from the river. During the summer it was used for bathing, but in the winter they used the pool for punishment. Oliver had been repeatedly dunked into the freezing water, held under the surface in a silent nightmare until he thought he'd truly go mad. He had never been so damn cold in his life, the kind of chill that settled into one's bones for days.

After that, he'd been dragged, naked, to a room only wide enough for a bed. A guard had punched him in the face twice, thrown him on the mattress, and left. It had taken forever for the tremors and chills to subside. When he could finally stand without toppling over, he found the door locked from the outside.

Eventually a guard returned with clothing and told him to get dressed. He had been allowed to roam free for a short period after dinner, until all the patients were sent back to their rooms. Sleep had proven impossible, the fear of not being able to hear an attacker keeping him awake until dawn.

After an inedible breakfast he was taken to an outdoor courtyard full of other patients and large rocks. They handed him a pickax and told him to break the rocks into smaller pieces. He had no idea why or what the rocks would be used for. No one spoke and he asked no questions, having learned his lesson earlier with the plunging bath. The guards carried billy clubs and they were eager to use them. Several men had been beaten for trying to take a short water break.

Oliver kept his head down and kept swinging the pickax. When a hand grabbed his shoulder, he flinched and twisted away. A guard stood directly behind him.

"You Hawkes?"

Bracing himself, Oliver gave a short nod. The guard jerked his thumb over his shoulder. ". . . a visitor."

He had a visitor. Thank Christ. It had to be Frank, and he prayed his lawyer had good news.

He hurried inside and was led down a series of dingy corridors. At the end, the guard turned a key in a heavy metal door and swung it wide enough for Oliver to squeeze through. In the room beyond were a few empty tables and long benches. Frank Tripp rose, his concerned gaze raking Oliver from head to toe. "Jesus," the attorney said.

Closing the distance between them, Oliver struck out his hand. "Tell me you have good news," he said, using his voice.

Frank pulled both hands away, holding them up, and nodded at something over Oliver's shoulder. Oliver glanced behind him and saw a guard stationed there. He looked at Frank for explanation. "They do not want us touching, not even to shake hands. Have a seat."

Sighing heavily, Oliver dropped onto the bench across from Frank. "You look like shit," Frank said as he sat. "May I assume that black eye is courtesy of the guards?"

"There was a communication issue upon my arrival yesterday."

"Christ, Oliver, I am sorry about all of this. I am doing my best to get the judgment over-turned." He told Oliver what Milton had done, the judge in Van Peet's pocket, and the falsified statements from the two doctors. With growing dread, Oliver processed the news about the annulment and the rehearing.

Fucking hell. It would take a goddamn miracle to get him out of this place.

Leaning on the wooden table, he rubbed his forehead with his fingers. Thirty days. He could be stuck here for a month. He thought of the food and the cold. The rocks. The lack of sleep. How in the world would he survive it?

Frank rapped on the table to get his attention. "Christina said to tell you that we would not rest until you are released. And we won't. I swear it."

A small smile twisted his lips at the thought of his wife. He missed her like nothing else. "How is she holding up?"

"Worried but determined. A backbone of pure steel, your wife. She is no weeping wallflower."

No, definitely not. Christina was the strongest woman Oliver had ever met. No matter what happened to him, he knew she would fight Milton with every breath she took. "And my sister?"

"I did not see her but I will ask during the next visit."

"When do you think you shall have a new judge?"

"I hope today. I sent the request to someone I

have known for years. He is a good man. Cannot be bribed."

"You have no doubt tried, I assume."

Frank's mouth hitched. "I never stop fighting for my clients, Oliver. You know that. No matter what it takes."

"And as one of your clients, I am damn glad of it."

Frank's gaze shot over Oliver's head and then he nodded once. "He says we are out of time." They both came to their feet. "I will be back, Oliver, I swear. Even if I do not have news, I shall come to check on you."

"That is not necessary. Check on Christina instead. There is nothing you can do for me here."

"Christ, I wish you were wrong about that. Stay sharp. Stay safe. I will do everything in my power to get you out as soon as possible."

A beefy hand wrapped around Oliver's bicep and tugged him away. He had one last glimpse of Frank before the asylum swallowed him back up.

"YOU ARE QUITE fortunate your father and I are still in town." The countess sniffed and raised her chin. "We were told in no uncertain terms to return to London."

Christina gritted her teeth and kept her stare fixed at the carriage window. It turned out her parents had not left New York because they remained unsatisfied with the allowance Oliver

had offered them. Today, she planned to use the
earl and countess's petulant resistance to her—
and hopefully Oliver's—advantage. "I am very
grateful for your help this afternoon." So grateful she had agreed to double the allowance origi-
nally proposed.

"For the record," Frank Tripp said, "I am against
this."

Christina, her parents, and Oliver's lawyer
were in a carriage on the way to City Hall. Frank
had repeatedly voiced his objections to this outing but Christina did not care. She would try
anything—including enlisting the help of her
parents—to get Oliver out of that hellhole.

Three days had dragged past. Three days since
he had been taken, imprisoned, and subjected to
God knew what. Frank would not provide details other than to say Oliver was in good spirits
and coping well. What on earth did such a statement even mean?

Christina had tried to keep busy with Sarah as
a way of distracting herself, but Oliver was never
far from the forefront of her mind. Everything reminded her of him. The house, the gardens, the
bed . . . Traces of him were everywhere and she
could hardly breathe for all her worry.

Today, she had decided to do something. Against
Frank's advice, she had asked her parents for a
favor. She insisted they use their titles as a way of
gaining an audience with the mayor of New York.
The earl and countess had agreed—for a price—

and cabled Mayor Grant once an amount had been settled upon. The mayor had granted them a small patch of time, one Christina planned to use to gain Oliver's release.

"Hardly surprising you object," the countess said to Frank. "You have been poisoning your client's mind about us since the wedding."

Frank sighed and rubbed his eyes. "How is it that two people are so completely opposite?" he muttered to Christina. "Are you certain she is your mother?"

The earl chuckled until the countess elbowed him in the ribs. "I am her mother and you would do well to remember that. Need I remind you who arranged for today's meeting?"

"I am capable of arranging a face-to-face with Mayor Grant, my lady. This is not London. We do not need to request an audience at court—"

"Enough," Christina said. "Frank, I hope that my parents' titles will be enough to convince Grant to help us."

"Grant values the almighty dollar, not viscounts and dukes—"

"My husband is an *earl*," the countess put in. "His title can be traced back to Edward II."

Frank rolled his eyes. "A hot corn girl working in the Bowery is worth more than you two."

"I have no idea what that means," the countess said to the earl. "Is he insulting us?"

"Never mind him." The earl pointed at the window. "We have arrived."

The earl descended first then helped his wife. Christina moved to leave but Frank stopped her. "Do not expect too much from Grant," he warned. "He is young and corrupt, which is to say he is unpredictable. Understand?"

She nodded once. "I have to try, Frank."

"I know, but if this fails we will come up with something else. Do not worry. We shall not give up."

Indeed, they would not. She refused to rest until Oliver was released. "Thank you."

Once inside City Hall they crossed under the huge rotunda toward the mayor's office. An assistant showed them to an outer room where they were told to wait. Christina sat on the sofa next to her mother, while the two men took the armchairs. "It all looks so new," her mother whispered. "Is it not terribly quaint?"

"Mother, please." The last thing they needed was for someone to overhear and become offended. "Remember our purpose."

"Of course, of course. You mustn't worry, Christina. It will give you wrinkles."

Wrinkles? Her husband had been committed to an asylum and her mother honestly thought Christina cared about wrinkles? Before she could respond, the door opened. A man about Oliver's age entered, a full beard covering his face. Goodness, he was young for a mayor. Everyone stood and Frank conducted the introductions.

"I am told you are to be called Lord and Lady

Pennington," the mayor said as they all sat. "Is that correct?"

"There's no need for such formality," the countess said. "'My lord' or 'my lady' will suffice."

Christina tightened her hands into fists, willing herself patience through these inanities that had nothing to do with Oliver.

The mayor crossed his legs. "This is a first for me, meeting an earl. Though we had a viceroy last year. I hope you are enjoying our wonderful city."

"We are most definitely enjoying New York." Her father's posture was perfect, every inch the English, albeit poor, aristocrat. "The reason for our visit today, however, pertains to my son-in-law, Mr. Oliver Hawkes. We are in need of your assistance."

"Is that so?"

"Mr. Mayor," Frank said, "Mr. Hawkes has been wrongfully incarcerated at Wards Island. Some papers have been falsified at the behest of his cousin and—"

"I am going to stop you right there, Frank. You should know that my hands are tied on this matter."

"What does that mean, your hands are tied?"

"It means I am not going to be able to help Mr. Hawkes."

Christina's jaw fell open. She and Frank exchanged a look while the countess asked, "Well, why not?"

Grant stroked his beard. "Your son-in-law made some powerful enemies. Those enemies happen to be friends of my friends. Do you understand?"

"No, I cannot say I do," the earl said, looking at his wife. "Have you an idea?"

The countess shook her head and Frank leaned in to explain. "Mr. Grant is backed by Tammany Hall. Think of them as the Whigs. Van Peet is a Whig, a powerful one. So the mayor cannot help us, the opposition, without angering Van Peet and all the Whigs."

Christina closed her eyes, the sound of her breathing loud in her own ears. Blasted Van Peet. Would she never be free of that man? Poor Oliver. If not for her, he never would've been committed to that horrible place.

"Come on, Grant," Frank snapped. "A man has been wrongfully committed. One letter from you could release him. Tonight."

"Tripp, you know how this works. I am up for reelection this year. Van Peet has threatened to pull the support for my campaign if I help you."

"And how, exactly, did Van Peet learn that you were meeting with us?"

The mayor at least had the grace to appear abashed. "There is not much that happens in these walls without Tammany's knowledge. Have you tried the courts? I am assuming you are Hawkes's attorney."

"We are trying the courts," Frank confirmed. "But your help would expedite the process considerably."

"Undoubtedly, but there is nothing I can do." The mayor turned to Christina. "Mrs. Hawkes, for what it is worth I am sorry. I hope you are successful in gaining your husband's release."

"Thank you," she said. Failure tasted bitter on her tongue. A few moments ago, she had been so hopeful. Now they had to start over, find another route to obtain Oliver's freedom. Furious at the injustice and corruption preventing Oliver's release, she snapped, "And for what it is worth, Mayor Grant, I will do everything in my power to see you do not gain reelection."

Frank made a choking noise then quickly stood, signaling an end to the meeting. Everyone followed suit. The mayor frowned as they exchanged terse good-byes and left.

"I am sorry, Christina," Frank said as they walked along the corridor. "I did not have high hopes for Grant, but even this failed to meet my low expectations. I had no idea Van Peet got to him first."

"It is not your fault." She took a steadying breath. "We cannot give up. There is a way to get him out. We must keep trying, Frank."

"And we shall. I promise you, Christina. We will get him out."

She had to remain positive and believe that

justice would prevail. However, it was beginning to seem that, for many, justice was hard to come by in New York City.

OLIVER WINCED AS he exhaled, his eyes focused on the dingy white ceiling. Every breath was excruciating. He had no memory of how he'd come to be injured or arriving at the medical ward, but something terrible had clearly happened. Now strapped to a bed, he was held down with leather restraints, his left eye nearly swollen shut. Both sets of ribs were on fire and his head throbbed like a drummer had taken up residence in there.

He had not felt this miserable in a long time, not since the bout of scarlet fever that stole his hearing.

The last thing he recalled was walking back from dinner last night. He had been alone, his head down, anxious to reach the sanctuary of his room. At night, once it grew dark, he needed to be in a familiar space with his back against the wall. A place where no one could sneak up on him. For some reason, the guards were enjoying scaring Oliver whenever possible. It had become a cruel game to catch the deaf man unawares and watch him jump.

Needless to say, Oliver was not amused.

Had they tried to scare him last night? He searched the muddled reaches of his sore mind. Damn it. Too much fog surrounded the memory. Obviously, someone had beaten him, and the other patients were unlikely suspects. Hardly any of the men confined here were violent; most were confused and gentle. Oliver could not see any of them pummeling him to this degree.

Had to have been the guards. But why? He had given them no cause.

Despair ballooned to replace the hope he had carried. Would he ever be released? If not, how would he possibly survive this place?

He must have dozed because a hand on his shoulder jarred him awake. Frank's pale face appeared above him. "My God, what have they done to you?" the lawyer said.

"I think I lost." Oliver attempted a smile but it hurt too much.

"Are you all right?" Frank's gaze swept down the length of Oliver's bed. "Have they strapped you down?" He lifted the blankets and saw Oliver's bound hands. Then he started shouting at the hospital staff. Oliver could not see what Frank was saying, but the attorney's face turned an alarming shade of purple, his shoulders heaving with effort.

A nurse rushed over. Frank gestured to Oliver and then pointed directly at the nurse. She attempted to calm Frank down by putting her palms up, but he kept going. Oliver closed his eyes and let himself drift. He was tired. The asylum had a way of stripping one's ability to cope. If it were possible, he would sleep all day and night instead of breaking rocks and trying to stay safe.

Jostling near his hands startled him back to consciousness. His lids flew open. Frank's face hovered above him. "They are removing the straps."

Relief flooded Oliver. He hated being tied down. After a few minutes, his hands were freed. He moved them tentatively, testing how badly his arms and shoulders hurt. Oh, yes. They fucking hurt.

Turning his head, he found Frank. "Thank you. Whatever you said must have scared them."

"I threatened to have a host of newspaper reporters here within the hour if you were not released."

"Was that an idle threat?"

"Hell no. I had drinks with Pulitzer last night. He owes me, seeing as how I got him out of a jam recently."

Oliver did not dare ask what that jam entailed. First, he was too tired. Second, knowing Frank, it could have been a whole host of things, not all of them legal.

"So who did this to you?" Frank asked. "If it is the guards I need to know."

"Why?"

"Because I shall take everyone in this damn place to court if they are attacking prisoners without just cause."

Gritting his teeth, Oliver rode out the wave of pain that rolled through him. When he could speak, he asked, "How do you know I did not give them cause?"

"I know you. There is no chance you provoked the guards."

Oliver tried once more to recall what happened. Unfortunately the events had not yet crystallized in his mind. "I cannot remember."

"Truly?"

"Yes. It is a blur."

Frank's mouth pulled into a frown. "If the memory returns let me know. We have no reason to believe this treatment will cease unless we go after those responsible."

Could Oliver survive another attack like this? Christ, he already felt so . . . dehumanized. Unimportant. After only a few days it was clear he did not matter to the staff. They thought him crazy, another lunatic undeserving of mercy or kindness. The patients were treated little better than animals. It embarrassed him to grasp for food or huddle with the other patients to stay warm, but he had no choice. Survival had become paramount. "How is the rehearing coming?"

"Slowly. However, this incident means you are in danger, so it is imperative the rehearing take place immediately. I plan to leave here and go straight to the judge."

"Will that work?"

"It must. We need to get you out of here, Oliver."

He wanted that . . . God, how he wanted that. He longed to ask about Christina and how she was faring, but everything hurt. And he was so tired.

Increasingly, he felt like a failure. He had allowed Milton to maneuver him into this horrible
fate, hadn't even protested when they carted him
away. And once here, he had not struggled or
staged a coup. Instead, he had turned meek and
cowardly, a person he hardly recognized.

This was all his fault. He had not fought for
anything, not since he lost his hearing. He walked
away from society because they had treated him
like an eccentric pet, and the few friends from
school had drifted away as he grew increasingly
reclusive. He'd hardly noticed, in fact. It was easier to be alone. He was convinced he did not need
anyone else, that he was better off on his own.

And now he truly was on his own, locked
away in a madhouse. If only he had tried harder,
forced society to accept him—even stayed in
touch with one or two of his classmates—he
would not be in this mess. Someone would have
risen to his defense.

No one would have believed him insane.

If Frank did manage to gain his release, Oliver
would appreciate every moment of freedom
from now on. He would not let anything stop
him from taking Christina where she wanted
to go. Shopping, theater, teaching her to ride . . .
whatever his wife desired. No longer would he
close himself off from the rest of the world.

However, if Frank's efforts at a rehearing
failed . . . He closed his eyes. Being locked away,
knowing all he was missing, would drive him

truly mad. Christina would live in that giant house, alone, known by all as the woman who'd married the lunatic. A fresh wave of pain went through him, centered in his chest. How could he ruin her life like that?

She was young. There was so much left of her life, now free from her parents and wealthy beyond her imagination. Why should she remain shackled to him, forced to hear of his slow descent into true madness during his incarceration? Better to allow her to move on with her future, alone.

Yes, that was the right thing to do.

He opened his eyes and stared up at Frank. "Draw up divorce papers."

Frank's jaw dropped. "Divorce papers? Have you lost your—?" He bit off what he was going to say, obviously realizing where they were.

"If the rehearing fails, I want her free to live her life. To move wherever she desires. She may have all the money she needs. Better her than Milton."

"Just give her a ridiculous amount of money and set her free. Is that your plan?"

"Yes."

Frank slapped his palm against his thigh in frustration. "That is the stupidest thing I have ever heard. It is clear the two of you are crazy—I mean wild about each other."

"I will not saddle her with a husband locked away in an asylum. Draw up the damn papers,

Frank." He paused, struggling to breathe through the pain in his sides. "Present them to her . . . when the rehearing fails."

"You mean if the rehearing fails. Have a little faith in me, Oliver."

"I am trying."

Regret and unhappiness lined Frank's face. "Do not upset yourself. I will draft the papers and have them ready. I doubt she will sign, however."

"When I am locked away in here for good she will change her mind."

Chapter Twenty

Frank Tripp arrived as Christina was breakfasting. His grim expression caused her to instantly push away her eggs and toast.

"Please, sit down," she said. "Have some coffee before you deliver your bad news."

Frank selected a chair, placed his satchel on the floor, and poured himself a cup of coffee. He dragged a hand through his neatly combed hair. "Thank you. I have had quite a morning."

"You saw Oliver?"

"Briefly, yes." Frank took a sip of his coffee then shook his head. "He asked me not to tell you, but I think you should hear it. There was an altercation last night."

Christina's spine went straight as a pin, her heart lodged in her throat. "An altercation?"

"I could not receive a straight answer on what happened. The administration claims Oliver argued with another patient and fisticuffs broke out."

"However . . . ?"

Frank rubbed his forehead as if trying to carefully select his words, and she knew then that Oliver's condition was bad. "He is in the medical ward. His face . . . Well, it does not look to be the work of one patient. He cannot recall what happened but I think he was beaten by the guards."

"Oh, my goodness." All the breath left her chest in a rush and she sagged in her chair like a rag doll. Poor Oliver. How dare they hit him? Her eyes stung, tears gathering like a storm. "Is he all right?"

"He will be fine. Some cuts and bruising, sore ribs, and he is concussed." She gasped and Frank reached to grab her hand. "I raised hell, Christina. Threatened them with every law I know as well as the newspapers. After leaving Wards I went to see the judge who is reviewing Oliver's case and pressed for an answer. I have a resolution, though it might not exactly be what we were hoping for."

"They are . . . Please tell me they are not leaving him in that place." Her insides froze at the possibility. Concussed? Cuts and bruising? God above, they must release him now.

"The judge has agreed to a rehearing. He plans to call in some experts, however, to view these experiments Oliver's been working on. Oliver will also be evaluated by two doctors and I insisted they possess experience with deaf patients."

"Thank heavens." She could sense from his expression there was more. "What are you not telling me?"

He sighed heavily. "The judge refuses to allow Oliver to demonstrate the invention. In fact, Oliver won't be permitted to leave Wards at all. His evaluation will take place in another part of the asylum."

"Then how will we know the examination is fair?"

"I have insisted on being present. That is not much comfort, I realize, but it is the best we can do at the moment."

"May I come?"

"Yes. In fact, you shall demonstrate the invention on his behalf."

"Me? Demonstrate Oliver's invention?" The idea filled her with dread, her stomach churning at the idea of speaking in front of a room full of people, especially with Oliver's life hanging in the balance. If she failed, he could be locked away forever.

No, she could absolutely not do it.

"I am the least qualified person to demonstrate the device—"

"That is not what Oliver tells me," Frank said. "Have you watched him operate it?"

"Yes, but no doubt others have as well. Besides, I am a woman."

Frank shrugged by way of answer, so she closed her eyes and struggled to remain calm as the walls began to close in on her. She could not take this on. How could she possibly stand in front of a room of experts and speak on Oliver's behalf? Her lungs pressed in on themselves, the air turning thick as molasses.

"Breathe, Christina," Frank said. "You shall be fine. We will work on what to say together. Then you'll go into the demonstration feeling confident. I do it all the time before a trial."

She started shaking her head before he stopped speaking. "I cannot. You must find someone else. Gill, perhaps. Or I could show you—"

"I am there as his lawyer. You must be there as well, speaking on his behalf. It cannot just be me coming to his defense. The more people who can stand up against Milton the better. I need you, Christina. Oliver needs you."

She dug her nails into her palms. They needed her—Oliver needed her. Hadn't she hated feeling helpless over his plight? Hadn't she been anxious to do something else to free him? Her meeting with the mayor had failed. *Well, this is your second opportunity. Do not waste it.*

Yes, but why must she be called on for *this* particular service?

She was entirely ill suited to give a presentation. She disliked standing in a room full of strangers, let alone having to speak in front of them . . . And with her husband's fate resting on her performance? It was too much. She put a hand to her stomach and tried to draw in air.

"I will help you prepare," Frank said again, his voice gentle. "You are able to do this. I believe in you."

Tears sprang to her eyes, the fear and frustration bubbling over until she could not contain it. "Do I have a choice? Is there anyone else? Gill? Or Dr. Jacobs, perhaps?"

"I am confident in your ability, not to mention that the presence of his wife will allay many of the rumors and fears over your marriage. We refute another of Milton's claims with you being there, speaking on Oliver's behalf."

She let out a shaky breath. How could she refuse? Oliver was stuck in the asylum, suffering from a concussion and God knew what else. He must get released soon, before he endured any more violence. There was no time for her silly fears; she had to be strong for Oliver. He needed her.

There was no other choice. She would have to give the best dashed demonstration those men had ever seen . . . and then Oliver would come home.

"As terrifying as I find the idea, I cannot refuse."

"Excellent. We shall start preparing after breakfast. However, there is one more unpleasant item of business I need to discuss with you." He rubbed his eyes tiredly then folded his hands on the table. "Oliver has asked me to draw up divorce papers."

She inhaled sharply, her body growing cold. "Divorce? He wishes to divorce me?"

"I told him not to do it. He is . . . There is no good way to say this. He is losing hope, Christina. If the rehearing fails, he believes you are better off on your own."

She stared at the table as the linen tablecloth swam before her eyes. Divorce. Hadn't he said he wanted a real marriage? That she was stuck with him forever? God above, she had actually believed him.

What a fool she was. Oliver wanted to divorce her, to get rid of her. Mercy, this *hurt*. It felt as if a band were pulling tight around her chest, squeezing the life out of her.

"This has nothing to do with you or how he feels about you, Christina. He loves you. This is about the rehearing and his attempt to protect you. He believes you will be happier if you are free of this union, should he not gain release from Wards."

That sounded like something Oliver would believe. Her husband had a big heart but he was not always right. "That is ridiculous."

"Yes, it is. I tried to reason with him but he was adamant. Be strong, Christina," Frank said. "Oliver might believe he knows what is best for you, but we will prove him wrong. We mustn't let him give up just yet."

She blew out a long breath and tried to sift through the thoughts swirling through her brain. What did *she* want? She wanted to stay married to Oliver. She loved him and, asylum or not, she would stick by his side. He did not get to decide for both of them.

Besides, he would soon be released from Wards. She would not rest, would never give up, until he was freed. "Tell him I refuse to sign anything until he comes home and asks me for a divorce himself."

THE ASYLUM'S THEATER held far more people than Christina had imagined. As the crowd found their seats, her hands would not cease trembling.

She stood off to the side of the large space with Frank, watching as the legal experts and onlookers settled in chairs. Why were there so many people here? Three long rows of chairs were full of attendees, with even more men standing in the back. She had never addressed such a large crowd, let alone one so intimidating. All those intelligent eyes staring at her . . . The urge to run and hide lodged in her throat and dried out her mouth.

What if she failed?

The judge waited in the middle of the room as the crowd assembled. Christina had met him briefly and he had been kind. She sensed he sympathized with their case but was determined to fairly evaluate the facts. While she understood that, Oliver was quite clearly sane and did not deserve the horrors happening somewhere inside these walls. It was torture to wait on the slow wheels of justice.

Eight days since Oliver had been taken. One hundred and ninety-two hours inside this hellish place. Today must go well. She let out a shaky breath.

"I will be in the front row," Frank said quietly. "Keep your eyes on me, if it helps, and just pretend you and I are the only two people in the room."

"All right," she forced out, her voice husky and rough.

"You will be fine. We have practiced this."

"Why are there so many men here? I expected only the judge and two or three experts."

"Word went around, apparently. It is not every day that a deaf recluse's electric hearing device is demonstrated in public. In fact, I recognize some of the men in the second row as from Edison's laboratory."

The butterflies in her stomach jumped, threatening to burst free. These men were not all onlookers; some were *scientists*.

"Ignore them. They do not matter," Frank said. "The only people in the room right now are the three men in the front row. Those are the ones deciding Oliver's fate."

Deciding Oliver's fate. Oh, heavens. She pressed a hand to her abdomen and fought the nausea in her belly.

Before she could again plead with Frank to take her place, the judge stepped forward. "Good afternoon. Thank you for coming. As you are aware, we are attempting today to fulfill an order by my court, which is to determine a man's mental faculties. To that end we are now to witness a demonstration of what the accuser has referred to as a 'dangerous and nonsensical' experiment. It is our responsibility to determine whether that claim holds merit. Mrs. Oliver Hawkes shall lead this demonstration." The judge turned to face her, sweeping his arm toward the cloth-covered box in the center of the room. "Mrs. Hawkes, if you please."

Drawing in a deep breath for courage, she stepped forward. The judge took his seat in front, Frank giving her a bold wink as he settled as well.

You can do this, she told herself. *Just as you practiced.*

"I am Mrs. Oliver Hawkes. My husband is a kind and intelligent man—"

"And crazy as a loon," she heard someone mutter.

"That is enough," the judge snapped and shot to his feet. "There will be no talking from any members of the crowd or I shall clear the room. Your presence here is tolerated only through my benevolence over a request from the scientific community. Do not give me cause to regret it."

Silence descended and the judge gestured at Christina. "Forgive me, Mrs. Hawkes. Proceed, please."

Fingers shaking, she whipped off the cloth

covering Oliver's invention. "Here we have the hearing device, comprised of a battery—"

"Speak up!" a voice in the back shouted.

Frank gave her a reassuring nod. Clearing her throat, she started again. "Here we have the hearing device, comprised of a battery, an earpiece, and a microphone." She paused and pointed to the microphone. "This is a carbon microphone, which has two metal plates inside separated by granules of carbon. When we add current from the battery, sound waves will strike the plates, vibrating them, and pressure builds in the granules to create resistance. This modulation of the current reproduces the sound waves in these wires."

She took a breath. "At the end of the wires is a speaker one holds up to his or her ear."

The men from Edison's laboratory began to murmur amongst themselves. The judge turned around and must have given them a quelling glance because they quickly fell silent. When the room quieted, the judge asked Christina, "Yes, but does it work, Mrs. Hawkes?"

"Yes, it does." Not only had Oliver shown her how it operated, she and Frank had also tested it together. "Would you care to listen?"

"I hardly see how that would be a fair test." The judge rose and went over to an older woman in the front row. He helped her to her feet and then led her closer, until she stood next to Christina. "I have asked my neighbor's aunt to come here for the purpose of a demonstration," the judge said. "This is Mrs. Peterson and she has lost nearly all of the hearing in both ears. Perhaps you'd be so kind as to demonstrate the device on her."

Christina had no choice. Besides, who better to demonstrate with than precisely the type of person who would benefit from such an invention? Frank dipped his chin as if he had read her mind and agreed with her. Heart pounding a riot in her chest, she met the judge's keen gaze. "Of course."

She faced the woman. "Mrs. Peterson, I shall repeat three numbers." The woman watched Christina's mouth carefully, as Oliver did, and Christina knew the woman was reading her lips. "If you are able to hear me then please call the numbers out. Do you understand?" The woman nodded and Christina moved a short distance away. She turned, giving Mrs. Peterson her back.

"Forty-five. Eighty-three. One hundred and two."

She spun toward Mrs. Peterson. "What three numbers did you hear?"

The older woman's face tightened, brows knitting as she concentrated. "Five. One. And . . . I don't know. I could not make out the last number."

Christina switched on the large battery and handed Mrs. Peterson the earpiece, instructing the woman to put it up to her ear. She presented her back once more, speaking near the microphone but not directly in it, and repeated the numbers. Mrs. Peterson gasped, her expression full of wonder. "I heard all of them. Forty-five. Eighty-three. And one hundred and two." She put a hand over her mouth, eyes glistening as if she might cry. "I have not heard that well in over twenty-three years. That is remarkable."

Christina swelled with pride for Oliver and his invention. He would have been so pleased to see Mrs. Peterson's reaction.

The judge thanked Mrs. Peterson and then addressed Christina. "I see that the hearing device works, yet I understand your husband has not applied for a patent, nor has he tried to sell the device. Why?"

"He believes it is too expensive. In its current form, the device would cost around four hundred dollars." A murmur went through the crowd at the large figure but she ignored it, keeping her focus only on the judge. "He has been trying to make a smaller, more portable battery for the last year. He hopes to bring the cost down and to ensure the device is easier to use in everyday life."

The judge stroked his chin and concentrated on the device, while conversation broke out in earnest throughout the room. Now feeling awkward, Christina had no idea what to do with herself. She edged toward the side of the room, not sitting in case there were more questions, but ready to have the device replace her as the center of attention.

"Making a battery!" a loud voice scoffed in the rear. A man stood—and she inhaled sharply. *Milton.* He was actually here. She could not believe the worm had the gall to attend today's demonstration. He sneered at the crowd. "Oliver Hawkes is no scientist or engineer. He never even graduated from a college and now resides in an asylum. And you want us to believe he has been able to produce this invention just like *that*?" He snapped his fingers.

The roots of her hair tingled with fury, anger washing over her like a giant wave. She could not believe he dared to influence the proceedings like this. Was this legal? "He has been working on this for years," she shouted at him, raw emotion making her words sharp as knives. "He is intelligent and decent, someone interested in helping others. He wants to aid those with diminished hearing to better communicate. What have you ever done in your miserable life but live off his money and cause trouble?"

Her tirade did not gain her shock or censure from the crowd; rather, all heads swung toward Milton. A flush spread over his skin and he shook a fist at her. "How dare you speak of things you do not understand, you harpy? You are just as mad as your husband!"

"That is enough," the judge said. "Mr. Hawkes, you were specifically prohibited from attending today. But seeing as how you did, let me be the first one to share the news. Based on the successful demonstration of this device, I have made my decision: Oliver Hawkes is not insane. I hereby order him to be released."

Applause and chatter overtook the room, including Milton shouting from somewhere in the back, but Christina paid no attention. She sagged against the wall in relief, her knees nearly buckling. They had done it. Oliver would come home. Frank hurried toward the judge, papers and pen in hand. Oliver's attorney had been ready with release papers all along.

When Frank finished with the judge, he came straight to her. "You were wonderful. I could not have done it better myself."

"Thank you, but I never could have managed this without your help and encouragement."

"You deserve the credit, Christina. I am quite grateful—and I know Oliver will feel the same."

Her cheeks grew hot under his praise but she did not argue. Perhaps he was right. Perhaps she was stronger than she'd thought. "Let's go fetch my husband."

OLIVER STARED AT the suit of clothes on his bed. What did this mean? Dare he hope?

He turned to ask but the guards had already left, so he began to dress slowly, his injured body still recovering from the attack four days ago. It felt strange to put on real clothes instead of the coarse outfit he had been issued at the asylum.

As he finished buttoning his vest, the doctor

strolled into the room. Oliver tensed. This was the same man who'd ordered the plunging bath, the one who had not bothered to assess Oliver before committing him. Oliver shrugged into his coat and said nothing.

"Mr. Hawkes, you are looking well." The doctor ensured that Oliver could see his mouth clearly as he spoke. "I wished to have a word, if you do not mind."

Had he a choice? Within these walls, the doctor held all the power. No way would Oliver risk another trip to the cold bath or a beating. He gave one short nod.

The doctor clasped his hands behind his back, all smiles. "We see quite a number of patients admitted here and we do our best during the screening process. It is not a perfect system, however. I do hope you understand."

Oliver did not understand. How could a doctor—someone sworn to heal his fellow man—condemn a patient to such a horrific fate without a proper evaluation? "Why are you telling me this?"

"I am pleased to say we have reevaluated the merits of your case and you are being released today."

The relief nearly knocked Oliver over. He bent at the waist and braced his hands on his knees, taking deep breaths despite his aching ribs. Oh, *thank Christ*. He was *leaving*.

When he straightened, he saw the doctor was

speaking. ". . . attorney is here, ready to take you home when you have collected yourself."

"I am ready." Oliver did not wish to spend one second longer here than absolutely necessary.

"Excellent. Shall we?" The doctor gestured to the door and the two started the trek down the long corridor.

It was bizarre to wear his clothes again and navigate the building on his own, without looking over his shoulder for a guard or another inmate. Part of him worried this was some kind of prank, that the guards would snatch him at the last minute and drag him back inside. His muscles remained ready, on edge, as he followed the doctor through the building.

When they rounded the last corner, Frank Tripp came into view, the lawyer pacing the length of the main entrance hall. At Oliver's approach, Frank visibly relaxed. "Oliver, thank God."

The attorney strode right up to Oliver and did not hesitate before embracing him. Oliver's ribs protested but he remained silent. "Good to see you, my friend," Frank said when he stepped back.

"You, too. Shall we go?" The outer door was right there, the dying afternoon light a gray cloud through the glass. Still, the outside world had never looked so good to Oliver. The sooner they left, the better.

Frank started for the door, but the doctor put a

palm up to stop Oliver's escape. "I wish you well, Mr. Hawkes." The doctor held out his hand. Desperate to get it over with, Oliver quickly shook the man's hand.

The doctor studied Oliver's face. "I trust we shall have no issues once you leave us?"

The other man's motives were as obvious as daylight. He was worried Oliver would raise a ruckus about the treatment patients endured inside the facility. Oliver hadn't a clue what he would do yet about that, but he knew better than to promise anything. "Good-bye, Doctor."

Frank led the way outside where two broughams waited at the curb. Oliver could barely restrain himself from running toward the vehicles. Part of him was still worried this opportunity would be stripped away and he'd be sent back inside. Only once they were far from here would he actually believe he'd been granted his freedom.

Movement out of the corner of his eye caught his attention. The door to the first brougham opened. Christina emerged, her foot on the top step as her gaze swept the length of him, and everything else ground to a halt. He became aware of every breath, every blink. The whisper of the cold breeze over his skin. Dash it, she was just as perfect as he remembered, and heat washed over him as he drank in the sight of her. She was his refuge, his light, and he needed to touch her, now.

He started toward her, not even bothering to look back at Frank. "Oliver," her lips formed, relief and happiness in her eyes. He felt like falling at her feet in gratitude; perhaps he would once they were safely away from Wards Island.

Frank clapped him on the shoulder, gaining his attention. "That carriage is for you and your wife. I shall take this one. Enjoy your freedom, Oliver."

Anxious to get to Christina, Oliver shook Frank's hand. "Thank you for everything. I owe you."

"You are welcome. And do not worry—I will bill you. Go, be with your wife."

Wife. He never thought he would see her again. Spinning, he hurried to the other carriage and gingerly climbed inside. When he shut the door, Christina launched herself at him. He caught her before she crashed into him, his body aching. The carriage began moving as he took his wife's face in his hands. "God, I have missed you."

She pressed forward and joined her mouth to his. He needed a proper bath and to clean his teeth. A decent night's sleep and a nourishing meal. None of that mattered right now, however, not when he had Christina in his arms for the first time in over a week. He kissed her hard, his mouth greedy, a starving man who had gone months without food.

The wheels bumped and shook, but neither of them noticed. As he often did with Christina,

Oliver felt as though he were falling, his brain dizzy with want of this woman. He was not even worried about doing anything more than this; he simply needed the connection to her. She was the air he'd been missing for eight days.

Moisture gathered in his eyes, the terror finally subsiding to allow relief and happiness in, and he broke off to rest his forehead against hers. "I never thought I would see you again."

She angled away so he could see her mouth, her fingertips lightly sweeping the bruises on his face. "Are you all right? I have been so worried about you, and then Frank said you had been attacked—"

Damn Frank for worrying her. "I am fine. A bit sore but healing quickly."

"Will you tell me what happened to you in there?"

God, no. He did not wish to relive it and the truth would only upset her. However, if he decided to speak about his experience in the hopes of helping others, she would hear the details then. He would need to tell her privately, prepare her. "Yes, but not now. I would rather forget it for a little while. How is Sarah?"

"Missing her brother. I tried to distract her from your absence as much as possible. She is getting quite proficient at archery."

He picked up her hand and kissed the back of it. "Thank you for that. I am very grateful to have you in my life."

"I am happy to hear it, considering you were planning to divorce me."

Ah, yes. That. "Only if committed for life. You deserve better than a husband locked away in a madhouse."

Her frown deepened. "I would prefer if you allowed me to decide my future and what I deserve. You told me you loved me, yet you tried to cast me aside the second circumstances grew difficult."

"I do love you, which is why I would never force you to remain married to a lunatic."

Her palm cradled his jaw. "You are not a lunatic. You are strong and intelligent, the best man I have ever encountered."

His heart swelled with a rush of emotion so swift that it stole his breath. "I only want the best for you, even if that means letting you go. But I never wanted to let you go, Christina. I do not want to spend one moment apart for the rest of our lives if I am able to help it."

"Nor do I, but you do not get to decide alone," she said. "My parents did as much to me for years, Oliver. I never had a say in my own fate. In order for this to work between us you must allow me to participate in the decisions affecting my life."

The words were a lance through his chest. How had he forgotten this? Of course she should have input into decisions affecting her, affecting *them*. She had been drowning for years under her parents' care because she hadn't been allowed to voice her thoughts and opinions. Had been made to feel as if she did not matter. Now he had done the exact same thing—twice. "I apologize. I should have known better and talked to you instead. Forgive me?"

Her lips curled. "Forgiven, as long as you never do it again."

"I swear I will consult you on everything from now on, including what I promised myself if I was released."

"And what was that?"

"The only way Milton succeeded in having me committed was because I had hidden away from the world for so long. You helped me see how isolated I had been, how cynical I had grown. I do not want to be that man any longer. I want to show you the city and take you to the ocean." He kissed her lips swiftly then broke apart. "Shopping and walks in the park. I want to do everything with you."

She squeezed his hand, her smile full of affection. "I would like that, Oliver."

His lungs filled with happiness. As much as he longed to kiss her, however, he had to know what happened. "Was there a rehearing?"

She blinked a few times. "No one told you? Not Frank or the hospital staff?"

"No. They said I could leave and I did not exactly stand around to chat."

"The judge insisted on a demonstration of your hearing device to ascertain whether it worked—"

"Of course it works."

"Yes, we know that. However, the judge wanted the device demonstrated so there could be no doubt as to your mental faculties. A room full of people today saw your device applied . . . and it succeeded with flying colors."

He could not complain—the demonstration had gained his release, after all—but he would have loved to have been there and seen the demonstration. "A room full of people? Who was there, exactly?"

"The judge, Frank, and myself. Also, the judge's neighbor who has hearing loss was there as the test subject. The rest were onlookers and busybodies. Milton attended and the judge scolded him for it."

"Good." His cousin deserved a hell of a lot more, which Oliver would see to tomorrow. "Who were these onlookers and busybodies?"

"Men from Edison's lab, Frank said. Not certain who else."

Disappointment sank in his stomach. Dash it. No use worrying about a patent now. Edison's men would take his ideas and run with them. But he shouldn't complain. As long as the hearing impaired received the invention, who cared who was responsible? "And who performed this demonstration?"

She bit her lip and looked at her feet. He could not see her lips. "Deaf, remember? Who performed the demonstration?"

She lifted her head and her expression turned sheepish. "I did."

"Good." He leaned in to kiss her, but her hand braced his shoulder, stopping him.

"Wait," she said. "Are you not even a bit surprised that I was able to do it?"

"Am I surprised you secured my freedom with an undoubtedly brilliant application of my invention?" When she nodded, he dragged the back of his knuckles along her cheek. "Absolutely not. I am quite certain you impressed the hell out of every single man in the room."

"How could you possibly be so certain?"

"Because I know you are stronger than you believe. You merely need the opportunities to prove it to yourself. Now, kiss me. I have eight days to catch up on."

She angled away and placed a finger to his lips. "Wait a moment. Are you certain you feel better? I do not wish to hurt you."

He leaned in to rub his nose alongside hers, nuzzling her. "Not kissing you is killing me at the moment. Please, rescue me, dear wife."

And so they rescued each other all the way home.

One year later . . .

Christina accepted a glass of champagne from her husband, admiring the way his green eyes sparkled in the gaslight. Intermission had started at the Metropolitan Opera House's Friday evening performance of *Faust*. Oliver had taken a box this season in the fancy "Diamond Horseshoe" row, right between J. P. Morgan and one of the Vanderbilts. Christina had come to love the opera and the two of them used the box often, more so when Sarah visited from school. The box allowed her to feel part of the audience while providing a private space in the back to escape for a moment or two.

However, she was growing more comfortable with crowds, especially with Oliver by her side. True to his promise when released from the asylum, he had escorted her on adventures around the city. Now that her parents had returned to London, she was enjoying the discovery of who she was as Christina Hawkes.

At least Milton no longer plagued them. Oliver's cousin had left New York right after Oliver's release, choosing to disappear instead of face bribery charges. Oliver had hired a Pinkerton to find his cousin with no success thus far. At least wherever Milton had gone, he no longer had access to any of the Hawkes fortune.

She settled on the sofa in the small salon at the back of the box. She placed her glass on the table and signed, "You appear happy tonight."

Oliver, along with Dr. Jacobs, had been teaching Christina sign language. She now tried to communicate exclusively with him by signing but there were times when she needed to ask for help.

The side of his mouth hitched as he lowered himself in the chair across from her. "I just had a very interesting conversation," he signed. "An associate of Mr. Bell approached me in the smoking room. He would like me to come work in Washington, D.C., at Bell's new Volta Bureau."

She blinked. Oliver spoke when he signed to her so she was able to understand all these words easily. Still, she was confused. "Who is Mr. Bell? And what is a Volta Bureau?"

He patiently waited for her to finger spell the names. "Alexander Graham Bell, the inventor.

He did some work at a Boston school for deaf children. His bureau researches ways to improve the life of the deaf."

"You mentioned wanting to help deaf children, now that the hearing aid project has been sold."

He took a sip from his glass and then placed it on the table. "Bell believes the deaf should speak, not sign. We had quite a lively debate over it a few years back at a lecture."

"I thought some deaf people find speaking difficult."

"They do, which I explained to Bell. He still maintains the deaf must assimilate by speaking."

"Oh, dear."

His brow furrowed. "I hate the idea of deaf children growing up and being told there is only one right way to communicate. More teaching of sign language is not a bad thing. It should be encouraged."

"So what will you do?"

He stroked his jaw. She sipped her champagne and waited for him to sort his thoughts. Oliver was much more willing to hear outside opinions since his release, no longer always convinced he was right. They had grown closer, with him listening and taking her desires into consideration. She was happier than she had ever dreamed.

Society had been surprisingly welcoming to them. Everyone treated Oliver with respect, perhaps because his invention had made quite a stir—not to mention his trip to the asylum. He had written up the entire ordeal for a newspaper, which had been the talk of New York for several months as reforms were pushed through the state legislature. Christina liked to tease him that he was now a bona fide celebrity.

Moreover, the society women who had been mean to her before were cordial, if not downright friendly, now that she had married a famous millionaire. Though she tried to remain polite to everyone, her true friends were Patricia, Anne, and Kathleen. The four of them had grown quite close.

"I have an idea," Oliver signed, "but I want to know what you think." She nodded, and he continued. "What would you say to moving out and using the house as a school for deaf children?"

Her mouth fell open. She had not expected him to suggest moving. "That was your childhood home. What about your parents, your memories? Sarah?"

He lifted a shoulder. "My parents would have loved the idea of turning the house into a school. And I shall always have my memories. Moving will not take them away."

"Where would we live?"

"Wherever you want. We may move to London, if you wish to be closer to your—"

"Be serious, Oliver," she signed, fighting a smile at his teasing. "Would we stay in New York?"

"If you like. Are there any other cities where you wish to live instead?"

They had not spent much time outside New York, except for Newport. The seaside town in Rhode Island was the stuff of fantasy, with big houses right on the water. Sunshine and fresh air. She loved walking by the surf whenever they visited. "What about Newport?"

"I had a feeling that would be your answer. Shall I build you a big gorgeous cottage right on the water?"

"Are you able to do that?" The Cliff Walk was already crowded with existing properties. Where could they build?

"Not me personally," he signed. "Though I am quite handy with a hammer, I would prefer to hire a team to oversee it."

She rolled her eyes. "You know that is not what I meant," she signed. "Newport is crowded. Could we find property near the water?"

"My dear, anything is possible if one has enough money."

"What about Sarah?" Christina had come to adore Oliver's sister. She did not wish to make a decision like this without considering the young girl.

"Newport is closer to her school. We would probably see more of her there than here in the city. I am happy to discuss it with her if it makes you feel better."

"Yes, it would. But moving there sounds lovely."

"Then I will do so tomorrow." His gaze turned

speculative. "How invested are you in staying for tonight's performance?"

"Why? Are you not enjoying it?"

"I am. However, I am able to think of several things I might enjoy far more than the opera."

His gaze turned heated and a tingle spread throughout her limbs. Still, she could not resist teasing him. She bit her lip and signed, "Such as?"

"Come home with me and I will happily demonstrate them."

"All of them?"

He gave her a brisk nod. "Every last one."

Excitement fluttered in her chest. "And what if I wish to demonstrate as well?"

"Then I shall fall at your feet in gratitude. What do you say? Shall we leave early?"

She rose and started for the door, pausing to sign, "I thought you would never ask."

Author's Note

The Gilded Age was a fascinating period in the Deaf community. Whether to teach manual (sign) language or oral language was debated at the time, with most experts and deaf educators (including Alexander Graham Bell) insisting only oralism be taught in schools. American Sign Language did not gain a strong foothold until the late 1950s.

Also, technological advances of the day allowed inventors to begin working on electronic devices to assist those with hearing loss. It should be noted that Miller Reese Hutchison (not Oliver) is credited with inventing the first working electronic hearing aid in 1898.

For Oliver's dry-cell battery, I used details from the work of German scientist Dr. Carl Gassner, who is credited with the invention in 1888.

For the asylum, Nellie Bly's *Ten Days in a Mad-*

House was an invaluable resource. This was an account of the reporter's time spent as a patient in the Women's Lunatic Asylum on Blackwell's Island in 1887.

All errors are my own.

Acknowledgments

This book was made better through the work of so many. First, I must thank my mother-in-law, Cindy, for her invaluable input on Oliver's character. An ASL interpreter and the child of two Deaf parents, she was instrumental in teaching me about Deaf culture. Also thanks to my husband, who patiently answered many questions about his grandparents.

Thank you to Elliott Dunstan and Jen Welsh for their tremendous input and guidance on both Oliver and the story. You have both taught me so much.

My gratitude to Ainsley Wynter, Eliza Knight, Sarah Webber, Anne Kenny, Sonali Dev, Lin Gavin, and Jenni Villegas Wilson for helping with plot points and character development. Ladies, you rock. Also thanks to my critique peeps, Michele Mannon, Diana Quincy, and JB Schroeder. Your input was spot-on, as usual.

Many thanks to editor extraordinaire Tessa

Woodward for helping me streamline this baby. Maybe I'll use some of those other forty plot points in future novels. ☺ Thanks to everyone at Avon Books—most especially Elle Keck, Pamela Jaffee, Caroline Perny, Angela Craft, Kayleigh Webb, and Guido Caroti—for all their work on my books and being lovers of all things romance.

A huge shout-out to the Gilded Lilies on Facebook. You are all amazing! Thanks for sharing my enthusiasm for this time period.

As always, thank you to my family for all their love and support. It means the world.

Be sure to check out the rest of
Joanna Shupe's thrilling Four Hundred
series and explore Gilded Age New York!

A Daring Arrangement

Lady Honora Parker must get engaged as soon
as possible, and only a particular type of man
will do. Nora seeks a mate so abhorrent, so completely unacceptable, that her father will reject
the match—leaving her free to marry the artist
she loves. Who then is the most appalling man in
Manhattan? The wealthy, devilishly handsome
financier Julius Hatcher, of course . . .

Julius is intrigued by Nora's ruse and decides
to play along. But to Nora's horror, Julius trans-
forms himself into the perfect fiancé, charming
the very people she hoped he would offend. It
seems Julius has a secret plan all his own—one
that will solve a dark mystery from his past, and
perhaps turn him into the kind of man Nora
could truly love.

A Scandalous Deal

They call her Lady Unlucky . . .
With three dead fiancés, Lady Eva Hyde has positively no luck when it comes to love. She sets sail for New York City, determined that nothing will deter her dream of becoming an architect, certainly not an unexpected passionate shipboard encounter with a mysterious stranger. But Eva's misfortune strikes once more when she discovers the stranger who swept her off her feet is none other than her new employer.

Or is it Lady Irresistible?
Phillip Mansfield reluctantly agrees to let the fiery Lady Eva oversee his luxury hotel project while vowing to keep their relationship strictly professional. Yet Eva is more capable—and more alluring—than Phillip first thought, and he cannot keep from drawing up a plan of his own to seduce her.

When a series of onsite "accidents" make it clear someone wants Lady Unlucky to earn her nickname, Phillip discovers he's willing to do anything to protect her—even if it requires a scandalous deal . . .

31901063737383